Ch

and the

"Thanks to Micha
Charlotte Markham a
intelligent, and comp

—Jonat
au

"In *Charlotte Markham an*
Boccacino has delivered a
welcome contribution to t
rolling back to Brontë and d
trait of a woman enveloped i
in atmosphere and carried by
of most debut novels, this is no

—Christopher Rans
author of *The*

"With *Charlotte Markham and t*
Boccacino has created a new visio
one moment stunningly beautiful an
next, darkly sinister and without pity.
Michael Boccacino is a writer to watch

—Susie Moloney, author of *The Dw*

CHARLOTTE MARKHAM *and the* HOUSE *of* DARKLING

CHARLOTTE MARKHAM *and the* HOUSE *of* DARKLING

MICHAEL BOCCACINO

wm

WILLIAM MORROW

An Imprint of HarperCollins*Publishers*

This book is a work of fiction. The characters, incidents, and dialogue are drawn from the author's imagination and are not to be construed as real. Any resemblance to actual events or persons, living or dead, is entirely coincidental.

P.S.™ is a registered trademark of HarperCollins Publishers.

CHARLOTTE MARKHAM AND THE HOUSE OF DARKLING. Copyright © 2012 by Michael Boccacino. All rights reserved. Printed in the United States of America. No part of this book may be used or reproduced in any manner whatsoever without written permission except in the case of brief quotations embodied in critical articles and reviews. For information address HarperCollins Publishers, 10 East 53rd Street, New York, NY 10022.

Designed by Diahann Sturge

ISBN 978-1-62090-324-7

For my mother

CHARLOTTE MARKHAM *and the* HOUSE *of* DARKLING

PART I
The Other Side

CHAPTER I

The Unraveling of Nanny Prum

Every night I dreamt of the dead. In dreams those who have been lost can be found, gliding on fragments of memory through the dark veil of sleep to ensnare themselves within the remains of the day, to pretend for a moment like a lifetime that they might still be alive and well, waiting by the bedside when the dream is done. They never were, but I could not stop myself from wishing for the possibility that everything I remembered was a mistake, a nightmare taken too literally by the imagination. But morning always came, and with it the startling realization that the dead continued to be so, and that I remained alone.

That night the pleasant rest of black, unthinking oblivion gave way to a dimly lit ballroom without any ceiling or walls, a place lost in the bleak abyss of time. Crystal chandeliers hung above the marble flooring untethered to any surface, threatening to crash down upon the guests, who were dressed in moldering finery that would have been out of fashion decades before. The dance began with a slow, melodious waltz that felt akin to a waking sleep, and I let it wash over me, swaying with the rhythm until someone from behind took me into his arms. I did not need to see his face; I knew who it was. My late husband, Jonathan, turned with me across the ballroom, faster and faster, never reaching any wall or barrier, never colliding with another couple, until he dipped me deeply. My mother and father were next to us, warm and whole, younger than I ever remembered them being. This was the dance of the dead.

The music stopped. My husband let go of me and bowed before retreating into the dark place beyond the ballroom. The room began to fill with people I did not recognize—leering strangers with faces that were really masks, ready to slip at any moment. My parents disappeared into the crowd. I tried to find them, but the crowd was too large and the music began again, this time an eerie, cruel sound, a broken music box filled with regret. A man appeared before me dressed all in black, his features cloaked in shadow. As he took my hand I knew with a certainty that only dreams can provide that he was not a stranger; we had met before. His hands were cold and his lips, though I could not see them, were smiling. The other dancers spun around us until they blurred together. He pulled me close against his body, into the darkness that surrounded him until I was falling, the chandeliers trailing away as I spun through the void, screaming into nothingness.

I woke upon the realization that the screams were not my own. A woman was shrieking in the night. At first I was deeply annoyed, for anyone blessed with the company of another could at least have the decency to keep their nocturnal enjoyments to themselves. But then I wondered at the length of the cry, and the tone. Whatever was happening didn't sound very pleasurable, and if it was meant to be, then both parties involved had failed. There was something primal and finite in it, and when it stopped it did not begin again. The sound had come from outside my window, and for a moment I thought to tell my father, but then I remembered that he was dead and my heart fell as I lost him all over again. The feeling passed quickly, as it was something I was accustomed to; the same thing happened at the end of every dream.

I shook my head, refusing to dwell on it. A woman was in trouble, and there were not many who lived within the confines of the estate that I would not count as my friends. I threw off the blankets and ran to the wardrobe, pulling out my warm dressing gown. Winter was coming, and the house was growing colder every evening. I pulled my hair over one shoulder, like my mother used to, thinking how much it was like hers—soft and pale gold in the moonlight, lacking only her distinctive scent of lilac and jasmine. I observed myself quickly in the mirror. Every photograph of my mother had been lost in a fire years before, and when in need of comfort or strength I could sometimes find traces of her in my own features. Though I was taller than she had been, I had the same short, pointed nose and lips that were always slightly parted, as if I had something to say (which I often did), and hazel eyes like my father's. I slid the robe over my white cotton nightgown, the one Jonathan had loved so much, and left my room.

Everton was a large country house, and while it had once been very fine, it had fallen into a comfortable state of disrepair well before my arrival nine months earlier. The burgundy carpets in the hallway were worn and fraying at the edges; the gaslights, turned down to candle flames with just enough light to cast rich black shadows along the walls, were tarnished; the floral pattern of the wallpaper cracked and withered on the vines as it peeled away from the walls. This condition was not for lack of trying.

Mrs. Norman, the housekeeper, seemed to hire new maids daily in her futile efforts to bring the house back to its former glory, but it was no use. The manor continued to crumble away. Just the week before, the cook claimed to have seen mice scurrying about her kitchen. The other servants had started to whisper that the spirit of the house, if there ever were such a thing, had died with its mistress the year before.

For my part I did not mind the imperfections of the place. There was a warmth to it, a kind of intimacy that only comes with age, like the creases around the mouth that appear after years of excessive smiling, or a favorite blanket worn down from friendly use. It was certainly less intimidating than the cold, austere manors found in the larger towns and cities. Everton was happily flawed, like any person of true merit. It was a house of character, and I sustained that thought as I padded down the dark hallway.

The children had their nanny in a room connected to the nursery, but all the same I felt responsible as their governess to look in on them. Nanny Prum was known to drink after putting the children to bed. She was a very silly drunk, tripping over carpets and talking to birdcages as if they were party guests in a very high-pitched voice that was not at all like the deep baritone she usually employed while sober. Because of her predilections she slept very deeply, and a random sound in the night was unlikely to disturb her whereas it could very well tip the younger of the two boys into a web of nightmares that the both of us would then have to spend the remainder of the evening cooing and coddling away.

The door opened as I approached it, and a small head with wild blond hair emerged from the gloom, peering in my direction with round green eyes.

"Charlotte?"

"Go back to sleep, James." I took him gently by the hand and led him back into the room, but not before he stuck out his bottom lip with indignation.

"But I heard a noise and Nanny isn't in her room and I'm scared," he said in a single breath. I sat him down on his bed and smoothed out his hair, brushing it away from his face as his older brother, Paul, growled dangerously from beneath a mound of covers at the other end of the room, apparently as resolute in not being disturbed by the nocturnal rustlings of the house as his five-year-old brother was in taking part in them. James had left Nanny Prum's door half open.

"Are you sure she's not there?" I asked him in a voice just above a whisper. The little boy nodded carefully, wide-eyed and eager to be of help in the strange business of adults that only takes place when children are asleep in bed. I lifted him so that he straddled my waist and entered the nanny's room.

The bed was indeed empty, and I began to worry. Nanny Prum was not the sort of person to leave the children unattended, and she was certainly not the type to wander the grounds of the estate at night, even while intoxicated. She was a woman of some physical substance, and there were few people in the village who were not intimidated by her girth.

I tucked James back into bed and stroked his forehead until he fell asleep again. Paul continued undeterred from his slumber, and I sat in Nanny's rocking chair curled into a blanket like an old maid, which was how I felt—full of maternal feeling for the children and anxiety at the absence of my friend and confidant. Only a year before I would have been lying next to my husband in bed, the mistress of my own estate. How odd are the places one finds oneself as time passes. It's best not to look back, but how can one resist? I slept very briefly, the specters of the past only just uncoiling from my subconscious like a blot of ink unspooling itself in a pool of water, before the door to the nursery was opened by one of the maids.

"Mrs. Markham?" she whispered in surprise. I put a finger to my lips and met her by the door, careful not to wake the children. She appeared very frightened, and I placed my hand over hers. She was shaking.

"What is it, Ellen?"

The maid closed her eyes and grasped the silver cross that hung around her neck with callused fingers. She was a stout, rotund woman, never one to talk out of turn and hardly ever intimidated by anything, but all decorum seemed to have left her as she took my hand and kissed it. Her lips were as rough as her hands looked.

"Oh, thank the Lord, Charlotte! When I went to your room and found it empty, I was certain that . . ." She stopped herself and sighed. "You're needed in the kitchen."

"At this hour?"

"It's a dreadful thing, too dreadful to mention so close to the ears of the children, be they sleeping or awake. I'll keep watch over them while you're gone."

She patted my hand but would tell me no more than she already had, so I left the boys in her care. The house was still dark, but now there were footsteps in addition to my own, and voices. In another room, a woman who was not Nanny Prum spoke quickly in a trembling voice. I crept along the hallway, down the grand staircase, through the dining room, and into the kitchen, where a small group of people had gathered over a pale figure collapsed on the cool stone floor. It was Susannah

Larken, the apprentice seamstress from the village, wife of the local barkeep, and my friend.

Her head was in the large lap of Mrs. Mulbus, the cook, who knelt on the ground and stroked the side of the poor girl's face, which was now nearly as red as her hair. Mrs. Norman, the housekeeper, and Fredricks, the butler, stood anxiously beside them.

I bent down and took her hand. The wild look in Susannah's eyes abated slightly, and her breathing returned to normal.

"Oh, Charlotte, it was dreadful!" She blinked away tears and began to sob.

Mrs. Norman, a severe, controlling woman with a hook nose and an anxious, birdlike disposition, continued speaking where my friend could not. "There's been a murder," she said with a hungry, ghoulish enthusiasm.

I wanted to slap the housekeeper's face for her repulsive insensitivity, but I restrained myself as Susannah sat up and continued her story.

"I was taking Mr. Wallace home from the pub. He'd had a bit too much to drink, and Lionel was busy behind the bar. Mrs. Wallace couldn't be bothered to collect him. You know how that woman is."

I nodded in agreement. Mildred Wallace was the village busybody, eager to know everyone else's business so that she might forget her own. For years her husband had been the most loyal customer of the Larken brothers' pub, the Crooked Stool, but she continued to deny it, telling anyone who would listen how much her dear Edgar loved his nighttime strolls about the village.

Susannah curled her lip into a sneer. "Wouldn't lift a finger to help a soul, not even her own husband. I took him home to his cottage and went back by the path along the lake. That's when I heard the scream, that terrible sound, and I saw them at the edge of the forest behind Everton. There was a man standing over a woman on the ground, a man dressed all in black." Suddenly I remembered the man from my dream. My mouth went dry and a chill prickled across the surface of my skin. I brushed the thought aside as mere coincidence and begged her to go on.

"Lionel had given me the club, just in case I had any trouble." She fingered the wooden bat at her side, a small, heavy thing with just enough force to knock some sense into a drunken attacker, but perhaps not enough to ward off someone with murder on his mind.

"I ran over to help her, but there was nothing to be done . . ." Her voice gave out, and she closed her eyes as if to stop herself from seeing it all again. I squeezed her hand, and brought it to my cheek.

"Who was it, Susannah?"

She took a deep breath and opened her eyes.

"It was Nanny Prum . . . all in pieces. Like she'd come apart from the inside."

I looked up at the others, but none of them could meet my gaze. They were all lost in shock. Even Mrs. Norman's unpleasant interest in the matter had soured. For myself I could not believe that something so horrific could possibly have happened in a village as quiet as Blackfield, at a house as great and noble as Everton. I believed Susannah and everything she said, but just as I did when I woke from my nightmares, wishing them real and everyone I ever loved still alive and well, I hoped that there had been a misunderstanding, some mistake, perhaps a play of shadows and moonlight over the ground that had made the situation more grotesque than it actually was.

"The constable . . ." I spoke up weakly but felt as if I might be sick, for when I said it aloud I knew that there could have been no mistake. Susannah, having worked for many years in a dress shop and in a pub, had an eye for detail no matter how small. Something unspeakable had happened to Nanny Prum in the woods. Who would tell the children?

Fredricks spoke up in a wavering, nervous voice that was not much different from the one he normally used. "Mr. Darrow and Roland have already gone to fetch him."

"He saved my life . . ." Susannah's eyes began to glaze over again with a look lost in terror and madness. Her nails dug into the flesh of my hand. "When I ran to help her, the man in black tried to come toward me. He smelled dreadful, like the very depths of Hell. It was so strong it burned my throat. I nearly fainted, but then Roland was there and the man fled into the woods. He saved my life." She started to sob again, but then caught herself. "Someone must tell Lionel."

"Of course." I looked to Fredricks, and he left to fetch Susannah's husband, who was probably still closing down the pub. Mrs. Mulbus made a pot of tea while we waited for the constable to arrive. He was not much help when he did.

"Looks like wild animals to me" was the first thing he said after he swept into the kitchen with Roland, the groundskeeper of the estate, whose burly appearance belied a gentle, soft-spoken disposition. He nodded to me as he leaned against the wall, recovering from what I could only imagine to be an extended state of exhaustion and shock. Constable Brickner, a portly, balding man with a weak chin and a mustache too large for his face, was not a popular man. Whatever the crime, he didn't inspect it so much as pass judgment on it, disregarding facts and eyewitness accounts in favor of his own infallible opinion. Luckily, his opinion was easily swayed by whomever he last spoke with, and all anyone had to do to win an argument was to be the last one to speak to him before the case was closed.

Behind him, the door stood open, the dark of the forest beyond fractured in the moonlight until Mr. Darrow, the master of the house, stepped forward to follow the constable inside, his skin pale and radiant against the shadows, his dark blond hair tangled and windswept, his cheeks mottled from the cold. He looked at me directly as he crossed the threshold into the kitchen, and in his eyes I saw that it was as bad as anything I could imagine. We were the closest to Nanny Prum, and for a moment it was just the two of us in the kitchen, framed in that moment of time by the beginnings of grief and an almost conversational familiarity with death.

"But there was a man, I saw him!" Susannah was feeling much better now and sitting at the cutting table, eating from a plate of biscuits that Mrs. Mulbus was nearly forcing into her mouth with meaty fingers.

Brickner stroked his mustache and squinted. "Surely no man could do *that*." He did not elaborate, but the emphasis on the word was enough for me to envision what was left of my friend on the floor of the forest. Nanny Prum had been a force of nature in her own right, and whatever happened to her, it would have taken an enormous amount of strength in addition to the obvious brutality.

"Perhaps he found the body before you did and ran off for fear of being mistaken for a killer." Constable Brickner picked up two biscuits, and then another, eating each in a single bite.

Eventually Susannah pushed the plate toward him, but Mrs. Mulbus took it away with a look of disgust before he could finish them all off.

"He came toward me when I tried to go to her. He was going to attack me." Susannah's voice began to rise, but Brickner shook his head with blustering confidence.

"No man in town could do such a thing. Must have been an animal. I'm sure of it."

Susannah stood from her chair, but Lionel came in at that moment with Fredricks and instead of launching herself at the constable, as she appeared ready to do, she collapsed into the arms of her husband. He took her home, a sobbing mess of nerves, while Mr. Darrow joined Roland and Brickner in collecting the remains of Nanny Prum. Mrs. Mulbus cleaned the kitchen after everyone had left, while Mrs. Norman and I went back to our rooms.

"Someone will have to tell the children," said the housekeeper.

I wondered if she was assigning me the task or asking to do it herself, so all I gave her was a weary nod of the head. I did not look forward to the days ahead. The children had already seen too much death in recent years with the passing of their mother, the late Mrs. Darrow, the year before, and the loss of another woman from their lives was bound to do untold damage to the boys' already broken hearts.

"Tomorrow," I said quietly. When I relieved Ellen of her watch over the children, they were, fortunately, fast asleep. I returned to my room and slipped out of my winter robe, back beneath the covers of the bed, already chilled from my absence. But I could not sleep. I rarely dreamt of the same thing twice, but that night I could not repel the fear that if I closed my eyes I would find myself once more in the infinite and mysterious ballroom, my lost loved ones now accompanied by the large, imposing figure of Nanny Prum, dancing amid a room full of strangers led by the man in black, further and further into the darkness.

I rose from my bed and paused at the door to my room, fingertips grazing the doorknob with trepidation, knowing full well what would happen if I left my chamber and wandered the dim corridors of Everton until I found refuge in the place I went when the nightmares became too much to bear.

I opened the door and stepped into the hallway. The air was cool inside the house, but the carpet was soft and warm against the soles of my feet. I ventured up the stairwell of the east wing and came to a set of double doors I had discovered on a similar evening months earlier, just after my arrival at Everton.

The loss of Jonathan had felt especially fresh that night, but I refused to cry alone in my room. I needed to separate myself from the sorrow, to put it somewhere and lock it away for safekeeping, where it would be waiting for me to take it out again on other lonely nights, so that I might explore it in the darkness that lay beyond midnight.

The space behind the double doors might have once been a music room, but the instruments had been covered in sheets and stacked against the walls for storage. The only piece of furniture that remained was a simple divan. I had found Mr. Darrow standing before the window gazing pensively into the night. I tried to turn back, but he had already noticed my presence and beckoned for me to join him.

"This was her favorite room. She played music, you know . . . the harp, piano, violin . . . They said she was a prodigy when she was young."

"Jonathan liked the accordion. It was utterly ridiculous, but he always made me laugh with the dance he did as he played." I smiled at the memory and noticed that Mr. Darrow was staring at me with a curious look, as if he were searching for something in my eyes. I turned away.

"There are times I'm in town, or in the city, when I see a woman from behind. I know it can't be her, but her hair may be just right, and her dress so familiar that I want to take her into my arms before she can turn around and break the illusion. Am I insane?"

"Grief makes us all mad. I often imagine that I'm able to speak with him one last time."

"What do you say?"

My throat tightened, but still I smiled, a portrait of Victorian composure despite the maelstrom of pain and regret that spun so quickly in my chest I felt as if it would tear my flesh away in strips from the inside out, until nothing would be left and everything I felt erupted out of me to devour the world.

"So many things. What would you say to your wife?"

"I would tell her about the boys, as best I could. She loved them so. I'm afraid I've been rather distant with them. I would ask for her forgiveness on that point as well."

"She would forgive you."

"You're a kind soul, Mrs. Markham."

"We're only as kind as people perceive us to be." I almost finished by calling him Jonathan, but caught myself before the word could form on my lips. Instead it stayed with me, calming the whirl of emotion that had built inside, and even though I kept the name in the silence that settled over us as we sat down beside one another on the divan, I knew that I had given it to him already. From that night on, we became nocturnal confidants, meeting in the sanctuary of the music room whenever fate and mourning compelled us to happen upon one another and remember aloud our lost loved ones as the sky beyond the windowpane turned with the stars into morning. At times our sessions together would only end when the sun threatened to appear over the horizon; at others they would continue on until a lull in the conversation became punctuated by a prolonged stare, or an accidental touch of one hand against the other charged the space between us with something unspoken and unacknowledged. We filled the music room with many things, but always left them there when we were done.

It was with great relief and little surprise that I found Mr. Darrow on the divan the night of Nanny Prum's murder, and together we sat in the darkness to wordlessly become reacquainted with the third member of our party: death.

CHAPTER 2

An Inconvenient Holiday

The funeral was held at St. Michael's Church, a little toy parish on top of a hill overlooking the quaint village graveyard overrun with wildflowers and ivy. The vicar, Mr. Scott, a middle-aged bachelor with hair so fine and delicate it seemed to float over his head like a halo, gave an unusually somber sermon, only sporadically interrupted by Mr. Wallace's drunken outbursts. The poor man hadn't stopped drinking since he'd heard what almost happened to Susannah after she took him home from the pub the week before. His wife, Mildred, stood stiffly beside him clutching his arm, trying not to grunt as she struggled to keep him standing through the service. The two of them swayed back and forth, nearly making the rest of the mourners seasick. In a way, I felt that Nanny Prum would have approved of the spectacle.

I stood with the Darrow family at the front of the church, before the colossal casket that Mr. Darrow had purchased. Nanny Prum had no family, or at least none that she ever spoke of, and so Mr. Darrow had spared no expense with the costs of the funeral. She had been a large woman in life, and the size of her coffin only highlighted the strangeness of her demise. Stranger still were the boys themselves. James held my hand and fidgeted in his seat, unable to stay interested in even something as extreme as the murder of his nanny. He did not cry, whereas his older brother, Paul, wept so profusely that the entire front of his shirt grew damp with tears. I tried to comfort him—to take his hand, to kiss his forehead, as I had seen Nanny Prum do so many times before—but he refused to be touched, preferring instead to be alone in his grief.

Mr. Darrow sat on the other side of the children with a glazed expression, his bright blue eyes lost in some distant memory. I had come into his employment only three months after the death of his wife, but I imagined her funeral must have looked very similar to Nanny Prum's: the same people, the same graveyard, even the same time of year. Death, it seemed, was another season, an inconvenient holiday put aside like any unpleasant responsibility, only to reappear once it's been forgotten, a reminder that time has passed, life has changed, and that nothing ever stays the same.

The next day Mrs. Norman and I put away Nanny Prum's things. Constable Brickner and his men had already been through her room looking for clues, despite his insistence against the evidence that the attack had been perpetrated by some wild animal. They were careless and cavalier in their search efforts, leaving the dresser drawers overturned on the bed and her belongings scattered across the floor.

There was very little clothing, only a couple of severe, high-collared black cotton dresses and a soft velvet maroon gown that she wore for special occasions. There were also books: a King James Bible, a volume of fairy tales, and a novel of some romantic melodrama told in three parts. I found a small wooden chest next to her bed filled with scraps of paper, pieces of jewelry, and faded pictures. I supposed it was a memory box, and I imagined her going through it each night before bed, thinking of all the children she had ever raised, gone off into the world, grown and with families and memories of their own. Perhaps she consoled herself by thinking that they thought of her every now and then when they remembered their youth, and that they might have smiled when they did.

"I warned her this would happen." Mrs. Norman stood in the shadow of the wardrobe, sliding dresses from their hangers and folding them in a sharp, mechanical fashion with her thin, bird-like fingers. She did not turn in my direction as she spoke. The wardrobe was now empty, and the contents of the room were slowly being siphoned away.

"What did you tell her?"

The housekeeper went still for a moment, and then craned her neck toward the entrance of the room, listening to the ambient sounds that filled the house: women gossiping and snickering beneath their breath, heavy footsteps on creaking floorboards, a distant cough, metal scraping against wood . . . She added to them as she crept to the door and closed it with a soft click. Mrs. Norman took my arm and sat us on the bed, where she brought her face close to mine and began speaking with quiet urgency.

"That she was in terrible danger." A wave of dread went through me, and as she continued I could only think of the man in black standing over Nanny Prum's body, poised to lash out at Susannah. "Someone must watch over this family, now that dear Mrs. Darrow has left us, God rest her soul, and I do what I can in my way. I clean up afternoon tea, every afternoon tea, and one can't help it if one sees something in the leaves." She pursed her lips, and appeared for a moment wearier than I had ever seen her before. "Someone must watch over them, and warn them when necessary of the things that are coming. There is evil here. I did my part, I warned Nanny Prum, but she failed to heed my advice."

This was the longest conversation I'd had with the housekeeper in my nine months at Everton, and while her words were jarring, she spoke with a conviction that I could not ignore. "What did you tell her, Mrs. Norman?"

"There was a man in her life. Who, I'm not sure. But he meant her harm, and from what Susannah Larken saw, he meant her a great deal more than that."

"Have you told anyone else?"

"What would be the point? Most people no longer believe." Mrs. Norman suddenly took my hand and looked into my eyes. "Do you believe, Charlotte?"

I thought of my childhood in India, of the holy men and mystics, and of my mother gasping for air in her sickbed. I had been alone with her when she finally died, my father shouting at the doctor just outside the door. I never told him about the man in black who suddenly appeared next to her bedside. The room was dimly lit, so I could not make out his features, but when he moved in to touch my mother's body, I launched myself at him, kicking and biting with all my might. In the instant I reached him he was gone. My father reentered the room with the doctor a moment later and lost himself in his grief. There had been no time for the man to escape unnoticed and so I said nothing, thinking it all a dream until years later when my father and I were dining in the conservatory of our estate.

One moment he was smoking his pipe, gesticulating wildly at the azaleas as he explained his feelings about a certain political party, a wreath of smoke around his head, and the next he was grabbing his chest and slumping to the tiled floor. I cradled him in my lap and refused to cry before the doctor could arrive. When the bell rang, my father's manservant left us to answer the door, but I could sense we were not truly alone. The man in black stood by my side, wiping a bead of sweat from my father's brow. I knew then that he had died in my arms.

"Who are you?" I shouted at the stranger. He placed a gloved hand beneath my face and tilted it to meet his own. Even at such a close proximity his features were occluded by a perpetual shroud of gloom. I shrank back in horror and clung tightly to my father, but the man stepped away from us, the plant life in his immediate vicinity shriveling to brown decay and dust.

When I was married I told Jonathan about what I had experienced with my mother and father. At first I wasn't sure he had believed me, but then he wrapped his arms around my waist and whispered in my ear: "I believe that the world is far more complicated than we could ever possibly understand. Perhaps you saw a hint of something that most people aren't meant to see. Death comes to us all, my love."

And so it did. The fire came for my husband only a few months later, and as he lay dying on the charred remains of our estate, I was met by the man in black for a third time. I was too weak to attack him or to even shout after him as he closed Jonathan's eyes with his gloved fingers. But I did ask him a question: "Do you cause this, or are you simply a vulture come to pick at the bones of my life?"

He tilted his head to the side, but whether or not it was some kind of response, I never knew. In the morning they found me still clutching my husband's body, the trees and grass around us suddenly withered and dead, though the fire had never made it to the forest.

With each passing year I became more convinced that it was as Jonathan had said; for whatever reason, Death made himself known to me as he took the souls of my loved ones to the Other Side. I said none of this to Mrs. Norman. Instead I met her gaze and replied: "I believe that the world is far more complicated than we could ever possibly understand."

"So you'll believe me if I tell you that you're in danger?"

"What sort of danger?"

"The same as Nanny Prum. A man waits for you. He watches you."

My face suddenly grew very hot, though I could not decide if it was due to panic or anger. Susannah had seen a man dressed all in black. If it was the same one that I had encountered, then was I being stalked by Death? And if so, then who might he take next? I was nearly shaking.

"How do I stop him?"

"Be careful. Be watchful." She lifted the trunk from the bed and took it out of the room, providing a knowing look in my direction, and then said nothing more on the matter. We put everything else away, into boxes and cloth sacks, and left them in the hallway. Roland would load Nanny Prum's belongings into the wagon and take them to the church. There would be a bazaar at the start of winter, and the people of Blackfield would pick through Nanny Prum's things, dispersing her memories like seeds on the wind.

In the days that followed the funeral, I moved into the room connected to the nursery and filled the empty spaces with pieces of myself. I couldn't help but wonder, in the morbid way of all people who have lost more than once, what would be made of my things if I were to die before my time. There was the wedding ring I placed in a drawer of the table next to my bed, unable to wear it any longer, the weight of the thing too great a burden to bear; a lock of my mother's hair, bound in a thin blue ribbon, her scent intact, that I used for a place holder in the book upon my nightstand; my father's pipe, with a crack in its bowl, a dried husk of Sunday afternoons in his study, on his lap, reciting poetry, now with my mother's jewelry in a small box in the wardrobe. This was where I kept my memories, ensconced in little tokens that would be meaningless to anyone else. I wondered how people would remember me, what might cause them to stop, many years later, and pause for a moment to recall a woman named Charlotte.

To remember Nanny Prum I kept an ivory brooch that she used to wear about her throat, engraved with the image of a woman. Perhaps it was her mother or her grandmother? I never asked. Perhaps she had bought it secondhand at a bazaar, or took it to remember a lost friend as I did. It was elegant in a simple way, and it reminded me of the time we first met, during my first day at Everton.

Jonathan had not been the only one to perish in the fire. Six members of the household staff had died as well, leaving families with no means to support themselves. Against the wishes of our lawyer, Mr. Croydon, I used what wealth I had at my disposal to provide them with an element of comfort, though it could never have replaced the loved ones they had lost. I could not have lived with myself otherwise, and the thought of making a new home for myself, orphaned, widowed, and alone, was too much to bear. I still had my father's military pension. It was not enough to continue the kind of life I had been accustomed to, and so Mr. Croydon begrudgingly agreed to find me some kind of employment as a governess, where I could insert myself into someone else's life and family, if only for a little while.

Within a matter of weeks I found myself wandering the hallways of Everton, admiring a painting of a bleak, gray landscape, the signature of the work an enigmatic "L. Darrow," when a hefty woman in heavily starched black skirts and the aforementioned brooch waddled down the corridor to meet me.

"Mrs. Markham!" Her voice barreled off the walls in a loud, rolling crescendo. She approached me with open arms, and her thin, wide lips stretched into an effortless smile rounded off by apple-colored cheeks. The woman would have been plain if her sense of cheerfulness hadn't been so infectious. I found myself laughing as the stranger embraced me with thick, fleshy arms.

"Wonderful to meet you, my dear! I'm Nanny Prum." She released me from her grip and I quickly tried to catch my breath.

"The pleasure's all mine."

The woman cackled and slapped me on the back with a hand like a round steak. She took my arm and led me down the hallway.

"I expect we'll be like sisters, or at the very least a pair of silly aunties to little James and Paul! Such good boys, sweeter children I've never known. Very different temperaments, mind you, but sweet just the same. I wouldn't go so far as to call them angels, because they are children, after all, but their hearts are in the right place. Although I suppose you're more concerned with their minds, hmm?"

"Their well-being is my primary concern."

Nanny Prum nodded in approval and led us up the grand staircase, careful to avoid the holes in the red fabric that covered the stairs, and the cracks that had started to appear in the wood.

"So you've met Mr. Darrow?"

"Yes, he seems to be a fine sort of gentleman."

"To be sure, very fine and rather strapping if you ask me. But then his late wife, the boys' mother, was also very beautiful. Such a pair they made! So sad that she was taken from this world so young. But it is not for us to dwell on such things. We must help the children *forget*."

"I'm not sure I would say *forget*, exactly . . ."

In hindsight, it was the first and only disagreement we ever had, and one, I'm sorry to say, that I would win. I would not let the children forget their late mother, or their nanny.

We turned the corner at a painting of a nocturnal landscape with a castle looming in the distance. Nanny Prum pointed to it as we passed.

"Mrs. Darrow enjoyed the fine arts: painting, singing, sculpting, that sort of thing. Although I daresay she had a rather morbid aesthetic." She stopped at the end of the hallway and entered the nursery.

The children were waiting for us. Paul was nearly thirteen at the time, thin and pale with dark hair like his mother, whose portrait hung in Mr. Darrow's study, and intense blue eyes. His brother, James, was four; a sandy blond–haired little boy who wore a light, playful expression on his round, dimpled face. He held a small bouquet of wildflowers, and bowed politely while his older brother leaned against the wall.

"We are very pleased to meet you." said James.

"And I must say I'm very pleased to meet the both of you! I knew there was already one gentleman at Everton, but I had no idea I'd have the pleasure of acquainting myself with two more. And what lovely flowers!" I clasped my hands together in approval and smiled as I was expected to do, even though I had no idea what I would do with them. Flowers always made me nervous, especially when given as gifts. One is expected to keep them alive, to help them flourish for a short while, and if they do not, well, then what does that say about a person? Too much can be inferred from such a failure: *Is she simply incapable of keeping anything alive? Dear me, I do hope she does a better job with the Darrow children!* And so on and so forth. "I haven't smelled anything so wonderful since I was a little girl in India."

James immediately perked up. "You lived in India?"

"Yes, for many years. My father was stationed there when I was about your age."

"Did you get to see a cobra?"

"Within striking distance! But thankfully it was under the spell of a snake charmer at the time, so it was probably much less of an adventure than you'd like to think. But I did see many wonderful things, and if you're at all interested I'm sure we could devote a small portion of our class time to the discussion of the Far East."

"Please, ma'am!"

Paul appeared to be uncomfortable during this entire exchange. He looked around as if he couldn't wait to leave.

"I do apologize, Paul. Sometimes I forget that not everyone is interested in hearing my stories."

"Oh, it's not that, ma'am. It's just that we're late, you see."

"Late?"

Nanny Prum pushed me aside and took the boy by the arm. "Not now, Paul dear. We can do that some other time."

But I continued to press the issue. "On the contrary, I have no intention of disrupting anyone's daily routine, especially if they have an appointment elsewhere."

"It can wait."

"Really, I would feel just dreadful if I imposed on anyone my first day here."

Nanny Prum sighed, shrugged her large shoulders, and released the boy. "If you insist. I'll help the boys with their coats."

I assisted Nanny Prum with this endeavor and followed them out of the house into the sunlight. She and I walked beside one another as the boys trailed ahead of us, Paul with his hands in his pockets, quiet and distant, and James, skipping along singing some nonsensical song at the top of his lungs. We followed the path down to the entry gate and turned onto the road that led to the village of Blackfield below, situated comfortably at the base of the hill that provided Everton with a justified air of importance.

The village was full of thatched buildings and cobblestone streets. It was a small, wholesome sort of place despite having two pubs. Nearly all the people of Blackfield found this to be a sign of progress and perhaps evidence that the village was slowly becoming a town, except for Mildred Wallace, who complained bitterly to anyone who would listen that one pub was sinful, but two was simply decadent. After a while it was left to poor Mr. Wallace to listen to her ravings, as the rest of the villagers would turn around corners or move indoors as soon as they saw Mildred coming. It went without saying that this had something to do with Mr. Wallace's frequent patronage of both establishments.

We continued down the road until the buildings were overtaken by farmland and rolling hills. St. Michael's stood on its little hill at the edge of the town, a small country church with stone walls and a quaint, well-kept vicarage. A graveyard sat between them, and as we neared it Paul hastened his pace. He was through the gates and winding around the tombstones before I realized what we had come to do. James caught up to his brother and they knelt before a sizable headstone that bore their mother's name. The earth was still settling where she had been buried. Nanny Prum held me back as the boys chattered with enthusiasm at the plot of dirt that held their late mother; she spoke to me in a soft whisper as different from her normal voice as was possible while the children updated their mother on everything that had transpired since their previous visit.

"They come every day, the poor dears. I'm not sure that James even understands what's happened to her. He didn't cry at the funeral. But Paul . . . it cut him deeply." Even as she spoke it was apparent that Paul was taking the most time talking to his mother, and James became distracted by a pair of butterflies. To Nanny Prum's horror, he chased after them, hopping from one grave plot to another. She shouted after him. "James Michael Darrow, stop that at once!"

Paul ignored his brother and continued his conversation with his mother, but he was surprised when I joined him before the tombstone.

"Please don't stop on my account," I said to him. The sun was heavy in the sky.

The boy squinted at me, and then looked on as his nanny chased after his brother, the hem of her skirts in her hands as she tried to avoid offending the dead. "She thinks it's strange."

"It's difficult for people who have never lost someone close to them to understand what it's like."

Paul looked back at the tombstone and traced the inscription of his mother's name with his fingers. "I was the only one who wasn't there when she died." He looked up at me, a question in his expression.

"Why was that?" I asked.

"I couldn't bear to see her like that. I tried, I truly did. I held her hand and I kissed her cheek, but then she would begin to wail. It wasn't even her anymore. It was as if something had taken her place, this thing that lived inside her skin, not even human, only just alive. I didn't want her to see me cry, so I kept away. I'm a coward."

"You are no such thing," I said, placing my hand tentatively on his shoulder. "She knew how you felt, I'm sure of it."

"I dream about her almost every night," he sighed.

I thought of my own dreams. I looked forward to them more than most things in life, and even when they turned into nightmares, I still found a sense of relief in seeing my mother dance or hearing Jonathan laugh. They became real in a way that memory could not make them.

"That must be wonderful."

"Sometimes. But when I wake up I have to remember that she's gone."

James shrieked in the distance. Nanny Prum had lifted him by the waist and held him under her arm. The little boy was screaming so ferociously that the vicar stepped out of his cottage to see if someone was being murdered in the graveyard.

"Is everything all right?" Mr. Scott was a few years younger than my father would have been had he survived, and his hair billowed over his head, threatening to blow away completely as he looked frantically for the source of the screaming.

Nanny Prum waddled over to him, full of cheerful exuberance. "Yes, Vicar, quite all right! Little James must learn to respect the dead."

Paul and I left the grave and joined the others before the cottage. Nanny Prum set James back onto the ground and straightened her dress, even though it was so heavily starched that it was impossible for it to wrinkle. She introduced me to the vicar, and he inquired about my family before becoming embarrassed by the question when he learned that I had none.

We continued our daily trips to the graveyard, despite Nanny Prum's apprehensions about appearing to be too morbid, and every day Mr. Scott made a point of it to greet us before we left. It was something the boys and I would continue to do even after she died.

Nanny Prum's tombstone was not so very far from Mrs. Darrow's grave, and while the boys had considerably less to say to their late nanny than they did to their late mother, they did keep her updated on the happenings at Everton. Paul even began to bring her bits of gossip he had overheard from Ellen and the other servants, and while I scolded him for eavesdropping, I did not dissuade him from continuing to bring her news she might have enjoyed while she was alive.

James frequently grew tired of the game before it was time to turn back, and so he would go through the graveyard familiarizing himself with its other residents, having grown out of the habit of skipping from grave to grave thanks to the persistent conviction of Nanny Prum's large, heavy hand against his bottom.

Paul always seemed less morose on the walks back to Everton. We had a specific route that we followed through Blackfield, starting with Mr. Ingrams at the blacksmith shop, who pulled and twisted burning metal in a shower of sparks like it was taffy, then to Mr. Wallace, who was the local clockmaker in addition to his duties as the village drunk. None of the clocks kept the same time, and so every moment in the shop was punctuated with the clanging of chimes or the cooing of a cuckoo, but the boys didn't mind. James relished the noise, and Paul watched with genuine interest when Mr. Wallace opened the clocks to show him the interlocking cogs and springs. He even smiled.

After the clock shop it was impossible to avoid Mrs. Totter's bakery. She always kept the door open, even on the coldest days of the year, and the scents of freshly baked cakes and chocolate croissants and mincemeat pies all tangled together, snaking through the streets of Blackfield, a crisp, golden brown siren's call promising a warm, full stomach. I only let the boys purchase one item a week, usually a cookie the size of a dinner plate, but for the most part our trips to Mrs. Totter's were largely exercises in excruciation.

Mrs. Willoughby's dress shop was next, since that was where Susannah worked as an apprentice seamstress, and the week after Nanny Prum's funeral we found her alone in the front of the shop, pushing over a dressing mannequin out of frustration. She jumped when she saw us in the doorway, and then blushed furiously at her own display, her emotions laid bare with the mannequin rolling about on the floor.

"Hello," she said in a surprised, falsely tranquil voice, brushing away a strand of red hair that had fallen into her eyes. She bent down to pick up the dummy. "How was the church?"

I frowned at her while her back was turned, but quickly removed the expression from my face. This was how the people of Blackfield referred to our daily visits to the graveyard. Most of them couldn't bear to name it for what it was, except for Susannah, who normally had no qualms about describing things exactly as they were.

"It was fine." I smiled, not judging her for attacking the lowly mannequin, who, for all I knew, might have had it coming after a day of uncooperative participation in the fine art of dressmaking. "And how are you?"

The question uncorked the remaining emotions that Susannah had thus far been successful in containing. She gripped the mannequin so tightly that I could have sworn she bent its metal frame. She sat down with a beleaguered sigh. "Dreadful, Charlotte, just dreadful!"

I sat down beside her, amid the reams of fabric, which Paul examined thoughtfully with his hands, listening but not really listening, lost in his own morose thoughts, while James pulled needles of all shapes and sizes from their pincushions and stuck them into chairs and tabletops with a violence unique to little boys, absolutely determined to not be bored by the dull conversation of adults.

Susannah went on. "Brickner came by the shop, to tell me, to *tell me,* that I was mistaken in what I saw—the hysterical ravings of a frightened woman. Can you imagine?" She was waving her hands as she spoke, before catching herself, and stopping. "Well, I suppose you can. But I wasn't hysterical, not then anyway, not that night. I know what I saw. Wild animal indeed!" Susannah sat back, deflated, and looked at me with searching eyes, waiting for me to say something.

"It goes without saying that I believe you, and so does half the village for that matter."

She seemed genuinely relieved by this, and whatever was taken from her by Constable Brickner's lazy certainty was replaced with newfound confidence, stronger than before, like mended bone.

"Then why doesn't Brickner?" she asked.

"Simple people like simple explanations," I said before I could stop myself. Paul stifled a small laugh.

Susannah smiled briefly, and then became dark and serious once more. "It's not for myself that I want to be believed, you know. I don't need justice served, but she most certainly does." She nodded curtly and looked past the boys at some distant memory of Nanny Prum, who some months before perhaps sat in that very same spot, having a very similar conversation about something moderately less sensational than murder.

"I would think," I said carefully, trying not to get her hopes too high, "that Mr. Darrow would be of a similar mind."

"Could he be convinced to speak with Constable Brickner?"

"I don't know about convincing, really, but it could certainly be suggested, yes."

Susannah leapt up from her chair and threw her arms around my neck. "Oh thank you, Charlotte!"

"No need to thank me yet. Wait until I've at least done something mildly useful!" I hugged her back and extricated myself from her embrace, rising to leave with the children before she found it necessary to inflict upon me the same force of emotion that she showed to the poor dressing mannequin, who now appeared fatally dented along one side. Paul helped me pull James away from the cutting shears before he could do any damage to them. The three of us continued on our way through Blackfield, rising with the incline of the path to the steep hill that held Everton, hidden behind a line of trees dusted with autumn.

When we arrived back at the manor, I sent the boys inside and wandered through the wood at the back of the estate until I found the flattened patch of earth where Nanny Prum had met her end. Even with the onset of fall, it was impossible to deny the peculiar ring of dead grass and brittle, shriveled plant life that encircled the place where she had died, the center of it still stained with flakes of dried blood as dark as the shadows that cloaked the man in black's smiling, hidden lips.

CHAPTER 3

The Mistress of Everton

Mr. Darrow was not the sort of tragic figure to stay forever locked away in his study, which was itself one of the last bastions of Everton's former glory, with waxed oak-paneled walls, a tidy, ash-free hearth, and antiquities that had been collected from around the world by the master of the house and his late wife, whose adventures had been chronicled on the marble globe that stood at the center of the room, their travels marked by glittering jeweled pinpoints of color. No one ever saw Mr. Darrow tend to the cleaning of his study, but as he did not allow anyone else to do it for him, everyone supposed that that was what he did when he was alone, perhaps beating the curtains with sullen determination as he stared longingly at the portrait of his late wife that hung above his desk.

But he was not always in his study. There were a number of occasions where I went to the door, in need of additional pocket money for school supplies, or to seek his permission for a day trip to a particular castle or battlefield, and I would find the room empty. No one knew where he went, and no one could say that they saw him depart. He did not like to leave Everton, and so I imagined him haunting the shadows of the hallways or drifting into unused rooms, resting on a chair that had long ago been covered over in cloth sheets, or pausing before a clock to wonder if it had stopped with the death of his wife.

He did not usually dine with us, and so the children and I were visibly surprised when two weeks after Nanny Prum's funeral he sat down at the head of the table in the dining room, looking rather dour until Fredricks, the butler, who either was very drunk or had completely forgotten how to use his own hands, lost hold of the soup kettle and tipped it down the front of his uniform. After establishing that the liquid was not so hot as to be scalding, everyone laughed together, and even Mr. Darrow seemed to enjoy himself for a brief moment, but then he looked at the other end of the table, where the late Mrs. Darrow would have sat, and he retreated into his comfortable melancholy. I do not know why he chose that night to join us. Perhaps the reality of Nanny Prum's death had sunk in and he needed the company, or perhaps he was reminded of his children's existence and sought to comfort them with his distant, sad presence.

Soon after dessert, the grandfather clock began to chime. I took the boys upstairs to change for bed, saying good night to Mr. Darrow and leaving him alone at the table to finish off the contents of a wine bottle. I worried about his state of mind, but I was too busy adjusting to my new responsibilities with the children to think too intently on it.

In the days that followed Nanny Prum's death, it had quickly been decided that the most practical thing would be for me to take on her duties. I already spent a great deal of time with the boys as their tutor, and if I were able to control their lives beyond the schoolroom it would make life that much easier for everyone else. I would have been remiss to turn down such an offer, especially since it was accompanied by a nanny's salary in addition to my own. I understood the value of such an opportunity and was eager to please the apparent generosity of Mr. Darrow.

It was not so awkward a transition as might be imagined. As governess I had still been expected to deal with the well-being of the children at every occurrence of illness or injury, and I easily transitioned from in-class paper cuts and bleeding nostrils to bed-wetting and bad dreams.

That night after Mr. Darrow's surprising appearance at dinner, I tucked James into bed and read him a story while Paul perused some obscure volume of poetry, his back toward me. He was very much like his father, especially in the eyes—very blue, large, and thoughtful. I wondered what Mrs. Darrow had been like, if she had been as erratic and adventurous as James, or something else altogether. When James fell asleep, or at least pretended to in order to get me out of the room, I left them alone. I did not have to go far.

The nanny's room had two windows that overlooked the forest behind the house, and while the grounds of Everton seemed to respond to Roland's care better than the house itself did to Mrs. Norman's, the wood still had a wild look about it, especially at night, when the depths of the forest were hidden even from the light of the moon.

I changed into my nightgown and slid into bed, trying not to think of anything. Not of Nanny Prum and the dead circle of undergrowth that marked her demise behind the house, or of poor Mr. Darrow, probably still drinking himself into oblivion. But then the very act of not thinking about something is rather self-defeating, since one must think about the things one wants to avoid before nothing can be thought of. With that last tangled thought, my attention drifted inadvertently to Mr. Darrow.

It did not escape me that my new position had effectively made me into a mother of two. I was, for all intents and purposes, their guardian. I saw to it that the boys were fed, bathed, schooled, and looked after. I was the closest thing to a mistress of Everton since Mrs. Darrow's passing. I cannot deny that this pleased me, or that I did not spend those last moments before sleep thinking about my time with Mr. Darrow in the music room, hands beside one another, almost touching, and what would happen should one of us decide to cross that fraction of space . . .

I drifted off and dreamt of my childhood in India, of temples and jungles and crumbling, many-armed statues, tigers and cobras and monkeys, and of our home in the colonial residency of Lucknow. It was a familiar scene, the same one that ended every dream about my youth: my mother's room, with the lights dimmed as she lay in bed with cholera, her body slowly drying out and withering into the shape of a child, gasping desperately for air, each moment a struggle until death. My father was nowhere to be found, and the servants avoided coming into the room. This part of the dream always ended the same way, would only end if I crawled into the bed to be with her, over sheets and pillows and shawls, unable to find her until at last I reached the center of the bed and realized that I must enact her death, live through it in order to wake. I would feel someone standing over the bed and observing me writhing in the damp sheets, a man dressed all in black. I struggled to see his face, but it was dark, and despite the fact that it was a dream, I could not will the face into existence. It was as if it were separate from my mind and from the dream of India. I tried to sit up from the bed, but instead sank down deeper into the mattress. However, unlike in the other occurrences of the dream, this time the figure whispered to me:

"Children need their mothers."

It was a woman's voice, and as she retreated to the other side of the room I died on the bed, choking for air with long, unbearable pauses between each breath until I was back at Everton, gasping as sweat trickled down my chest and face. I threw the blankets off the bed so as not to get them damp, and was about to change when there was a knock on the door to the nursery.

"Charlotte?"

James opened it without waiting for me to respond. He had been crying, his face as wet with tears as mine was from perspiration. Both of the boys seemed to have unique problems with nightmares. Being the more courageous of the two, James often dreamt himself into outlandish adventures featuring ghouls, mummies, and spider women, just to name a few from his well-populated menagerie of monsters. Occasionally, the capacity of his imagination to invent horrors would outpace his actual ability to tolerate them, and he would wake up in the middle of the night absolutely convinced that the spider on the windowsill was an agent of the malevolent Spider Queen, intent upon making him pay for the theft of her enchanted silver webbing.

Paul was another matter altogether. Quite often he would already be awake when I entered their room to take care of his brother, angry that he had been aroused from a most wonderful nightmare, as he was that night when I took James back to his bed.

"I was at a ball," he said as James nestled his head against my chest. "And Mother was there. She was young and beautiful. I tried to move across the dance floor to speak to her, but it was too crowded. Every person in the ballroom was dancing with something inhuman, and Mother took the hand of a creature who only pretended to look like a man. She waved to me from across the room, and I was about to go save her, but then James started screaming about the stupid Spider Queen." He shot his brother a spiteful look.

"She's not stupid!" James lunged out of the bed, his tear-streaked face furrowed in rage, but because he was in my arms and only five years old, I was able to hold him back without much effort.

"It's nothing to me if you want to kill one another," I told them. "I imagine that it would be much easier to care for one child as opposed to two. But I daresay your father would be furious with whichever one of you murders the other. If violence and murder are the methods you choose to use when dealing with family, then we can only surmise the tactics you might use when dealing with your peers would be that much worse. We would be forced to lock you away in the attic for the good of the village. I don't believe that such an existence would be a very pleasant one, but then it's not up to me to make your decisions for you."

The boys had no idea which one of them I was talking to, and as they tried to sort out what I had said, their anger abated. I tucked them into bed so tightly that it was difficult for them to move about, even Paul, who was completely horrified that I had the gall to treat him like his younger brother. Rather than struggle against it, they both gave in to the hour of the night and fell asleep. I watched them for a while to make sure there was no relapse of flared tempers, and when I was satisfied that they were truly asleep, I retired to my room. By then the notion of sleep had left me completely, so I changed into a fresh nightgown, combed my hair, read for a bit, and finally decided to make myself a cup of tea.

I always preferred Everton at night. It was not a noisy house, the sort of place that creaked or groaned a whole symphony of innocuous sounds that, when taken together, could twist a shadow into something tangible and dangerous. It was simply dark and quiet without any pretense, with the kind of rich, musty smell that only comes with age.

Mr. Darrow was still in the dining room. He was startled when he saw me, but not drunk. The wine bottle was gone and had been replaced by a full afternoon tea spread, despite the fact that it was well past two in the morning. There was a large pot of black tea, still steaming, the usual cream and sugar, as well as tea sandwiches, scones with clotted cream, and a chocolate tea cake that sat on his plate, conspicuously untouched. He invited me to join him, and though there were many chairs to choose from, I sat down beside him rather impulsively and felt my face flush. He was a very handsome man, and the dining room was not the private refuge of the music room.

"Good evening, Mr. Darrow."

"Trouble sleeping?"

"James had a nightmare." He looked concerned, and half rose from his chair, but I touched his arm and he sat once more, his eyes lingering where I had touched him. He gaped for a moment until I reassured him. "It's all right. He's asleep again."

Mr. Darrow regained his composure. "And now you're not."

"An occupational hazard, I'm afraid. May I?" I reached for a teacup, but he grabbed it before I could and filled it with the black, aromatic contents of the teapot.

"Darjeeling."

"Wonderful."

"Scone?"

"Please. Mrs. Mulbus has truly outdone herself, considering the hour."

"You underestimate my cowardice, Mrs. Markham. I would never approach dear Mrs. Mulbus's door at this time of night demanding food and drink. There is a specter of death that seems to hover over Everton, and I do not wish to tempt it." There was a weariness in his gaze, his blue eyes peering over the lip of his cup, framed by strands of his dark blond hair, fixated once more on the other end of the table, as empty and silent as the rest of the house. But then he smiled and reached for a scone. "Besides, I'm not completely incapable."

"Of course not."

"I mean, why must one wait until the afternoon to have afternoon tea? That part of the day is so busy that one can rarely enjoy it."

"I quite agree."

"But I must say that it is nice to have your company outside of the music room."

I tipped my cup toward him, and he returned the gesture. We sipped our tea in silence.

"You know, Mr. Darrow"—I finished my cup and set it in the saucer, carefully choosing my words—"if you require company during the daylight hours, I'm sure I could make the children available."

He nodded thoughtfully and refilled my cup. "Yes, what must you think of me? Locked away in my study or wandering the halls of the house. I only seem to reclaim some semblance of my old life after everyone's gone to sleep. I'm afraid I've become something of a ghoul. It's rather pathetic."

"That's not how I meant it."

"But it is. Lily's been dead for . . . God, has it nearly been a year? And now Nanny Prum. How did you recover from the loss of your husband?"

"I'm not sure one ever does. It still hurts for me to think of him. I miss him so." I relaxed as I said aloud what I always felt: his absence. I could tell that I was beaming as I thought of him. I dabbed my lips with a napkin. "But there is something fortifying about the pain. It reminds me of how much I loved him, and my love is equal to the pain. It protects me, and it grows stronger the more I think of him. I'm sure that someday it will be the same for you and Mrs. Darrow."

"Perhaps, but then again . . ." His brow contracted into an expression of anxiety as he finished eating a cucumber sandwich. "Mrs. Norman will be up soon, and I like to avoid her when possible." He smiled weakly at me and stood from the table.

"Mr. Darrow, before you go. About Nanny Prum."

"Yes?"

"Well, it's Susannah Larken. She's one of the most honest, reliable people that I know, and—"

"I believe her."

"You do?"

"Every word that she said. I've been meaning to speak to Brickner about the way he's handling the investigation, or lack thereof, but I've been preoccupied."

"I'd be very grateful."

"In that case, I'll be sure to pay him a visit tomorrow. You can count on it."

He nodded to me, and together we moved the plates and scraps of food back into the kitchen, leaving them in the sink for Jenny, the scullery maid, to take care of the next day. With that done, we awkwardly parted ways, and I found that I had to restrain myself from looking back at him as he left for his chambers. I hated myself for my slavish devotion to propriety, but what else did I have to be devoted to?

I went to my room next to the nursery. I felt relieved at the thought of allaying Susannah's concerns, and at the possibility of finding whoever had killed Nanny Prum. Sleep came, but not without a struggle to quiet my mind.

I dreamt of Heatherdale, my family's estate, where Jonathan and I lived for three glorious years. The dream was a recurring one, but as with the others, it was always different. I found it strange that this time I was detached from the scene, watching myself sleep in bed with my husband, his strong arms around my waist. I felt larger than myself, my body not a body at all, wrapped between the bones of the house, shifting them dangerously out of place. There was also a great heat radiating from my skin, curling the wallpaper to black char, eating away at the wooden beams that supported the house, and it caused me to expand with reckless abandon. I cackled, and sparks erupted from my throat in a plume of black smoke.

Jonathan woke gasping for air. He shook the other Charlotte awake, and together they ran through the house. But it was too late. I was all around them, singeing their skin and hair, choking them quickly back to sleep. Jonathan noticed a curtain that I had not yet touched, one of the only things that had not been burned. He wrapped it around his wife's body and picked her up in his arms, even as she struggled and screamed for him to stop, and plunged them both into the flames.

I tried to stop him. I tore at his skin until it blistered and cracked, at his hair until it burned down to the scalp, but still he ran through the remains of the manor, not stopping until he was outside, collapsing into a ruined heap while his wife cried over him, begging him to wake up as the man in black observed the scene in silence, the light from the flames extending his shadow over the dying underbrush.

CHAPTER 4

A Lesson in Dreaming

The next morning, after taking breakfast downstairs with the children—Mr. Darrow was good as his word and had already left to meet with Constable Brickner—I marched the boys up to the schoolroom to begin their daily lessons.

During the first few weeks after my arrival, Mrs. Norman and I scoured the empty rooms of the manor, lifting the covers off of antiquated pieces of furniture in search of practical desks, and kicking up small clouds of dust as we traveled through parlors, bedrooms, and servants' quarters that hadn't been used in generations. We eventually discovered a small attic at the top of the east wing of the house.

It was large enough that it had a proper staircase rather than one that had to be pulled down from the ceiling, and very little was actually stored up there. The ceiling was low, and both sides of the room slanted at an angle, reaching up to a point like a church steeple. It felt very much like a small country schoolhouse, with windows on each end of the wide room, and I knew when we found it that it was just what we needed.

Having discovered a desk in an unused study (presumably belonging to Mr. Darrow's father or grandfather), I had Fredricks and Roland carry it up into the attic. It was not an easy task, but then, as I reminded them, neither was the education of children. The desk was placed at the front of the room for my own use, before a blackboard Nanny Prum had kept in the nursery. Two low tables were found for the boys, and they were placed far enough apart as to avoid easy physical confrontation. The back of the schoolroom contained many of the items that had been found there upon its discovery. I arranged some old end tables, rusted gaslights, and empty picture frames into a sort of artists' corner, stocked with supplies I had brought to the house myself. An intellectual education was of course deeply important, but I felt that an aesthetic curriculum was equally worthwhile, especially in light of the late Mrs. Darrow's rather prolific creative accomplishments.

Each day I began the boys' lessons with arithmetic. Mornings were best suited to intense study, as it loosened the mind for the interpretation of literature later on in the day. Whenever I felt that I was losing their attention or interest, I would quickly end whatever it was they were doing and challenge them to tackle some artistic accomplishment.

That afternoon, in the difficult time before lunch when children begin to think with their stomachs even though the next mealtime is at least an hour away, I was still fixated on the problem of dreams. The boys looked tired, and I myself hadn't been able to sleep very well after the nightmares of the past few evenings. It was silly that we should all suffer so much from self-inflicted trauma. I once read that dreams were the products of unacknowledged emotion and feeling, and that setting them down with either words or images often lessened their power. To understand fear was to control it.

Paul yawned. James followed suit, and I was obliged to set down the book of poems they were reading through and send them to the back of the schoolroom.

"That's quite enough of that. I have a new task for you."

James yawned again. "But it's nearly time for lunch!" He clutched his stomach as if he would waste away to nothing before the end of the hour.

I ignored him. "You are to describe your dreams from last night with either drawings or prose."

Both of the boys grabbed the colored pencils on the table and ignored the mention of prose, despite the fact that this was my favorite medium. I frowned but said nothing, remembering that their late mother had created the majority of the artwork that decorated the walls of Everton.

Paul began scribbling furiously without hesitation. He paused every few minutes to look out the window, and continued drawing, in fine detail, a meticulous landscape of Everton from a bird's-eye view. James had more trouble deciding what to draw. He had many dreams every night, and so choosing the most exciting and violent one to illustrate was no small task. Eventually he settled on what he knew best and began sketching the hulking black thorax of the Spider Queen.

When the boys had finished, I led them back to their desks and asked them to present their artwork. James, who always demanded to go first and threatened to throw a magnificent tantrum if he didn't get his way, had found no purchase with me by using this tactic, despite a glorious performance involving impressive physicality with thrown chairs, toppled tables, and broken vases, during which I clapped and cheered him on as if I had paid for the privilege of his outburst, and eventually he relented to alternating turns with his brother. Nevertheless, it was his turn to present first. He stood from his chair and moved to the front of the room beside the desk.

"I drew the Spider Queen." The paper contained a black blob of a body with eight spindly appendages, but the face of the creature was very much like that of a young woman, with curly silver hair and pretty features. "She lives in a cave beneath my bed and eats up the goblins whenever they try to steal my breath. Sometimes she has me over for tea, and sometimes we're friends, but other times she sends her children after me because I've stolen some of her treasures." He stopped and clutched his stomach again in an effort to remind me of his delicate and very hungry condition, but I did not let him return to his seat.

"But why would you steal from her? It sounds as if she's doing you a favor by gobbling up the goblins."

James looked at me as if I were quite slow. "To buy back Mother's soul from the Goblin King."

My heart sank, and for a moment I did not know how to respond. What was there to say? It was a beautiful, sad sentiment, but I quickly recovered. "Why would he have your mother's soul? She went to Heaven."

The boy thought about this and shrugged his shoulders. "I dunno. It was just a dream I had." I nodded to him that he could return to his chair.

Paul stood up and took his place before the blackboard. He held up his re-creation of Everton, which now resembled something like a treasure map.

"Last night I dreamt that I went to Mother's house."

I took a deep breath and wrung my fingers together. This was not going at all the way I had expected. But then, what did I expect? The boys had lost their mother. Of course they were dreaming of her. I *knew* that they were dreaming of her. I had lost my mother nearly fifteen years before and *still* dreamt of her. It was not something that ever truly went away. The three of us would perhaps always be bound by our grief, never truly finished with the long nightmare of loss. But if that were true then we were also bound together searching in our dreaming for new memories of the mothers we lost. Children need their parents in whatever form they're available, and I shivered for a moment as I thought back to one of my dreams the night before.

Children need their mothers.

Paul continued to explain his drawing.

"She came for me in the night and led me through a wood." He pointed to his illustration of the old-growth forest behind the house. "The wood turned into an orchard, and there was a great house. Mother said we couldn't go inside just yet, that we had to do it in person. She's waiting for us."

The specificity of his dream was unnerving. I folded my hands on the desk and peered carefully at the young man. "Why would she do that?"

He looked down at the ground, his large blue eyes fixated on nothing particular but still lost in thought. He spoke without looking up. "She misses us."

With those three words he nearly reduced me to tears. I felt the years of built-up sorrow at the loss of my own mother materialize as a tightening in my chest and the prickling sensation behind the eyes that heralded the impending arrival of tears.

"Paul"—my voice almost broke—"your mother is gone."

He finally looked up, his face creased in a pleasant, knowing expression that should have been impossible for someone who had just turned thirteen. "I know. But every now and then, when we're in the village, and I see the back of a lady with long black hair, I always hope that it's her; that everything I remember is wrong. That she didn't die. It was all just a misunderstanding."

It was almost identical to what his father had told me that first night in the music room. We stared at each other in silence for what felt like a long while, until James grew tired of not being the center of attention and spoke up.

"Can we go?"

"Lunch isn't for twenty more minutes," I reminded him.

"Not to eat; into the woods." He pointed at his brother's map.

"Whatever for?"

The boy shrugged, and his older brother spoke up. "Aren't some dreams true?"

While I wanted the boys to find solace in the idea that their dreams were not real, I hadn't anticipated them finding so much relief in the notion that they were. If I took them into the woods, they would find nothing there and be forced to face the fact that their mother was truly gone. If I did not, then it was likely they would find some way to use the map when I wasn't looking, and the last thing I wanted was for the boys to go off into the wilderness on their own, especially in light of the fact that whoever had killed Nanny Prum was still at large. There was only one option: I would take them, show them the reality of death, and deal with the consequences as they came.

"I suppose we *could* take our lunch outside this afternoon; I do enjoy picnics."

At the mention of a meal James clutched his stomach again and did his best to look pathetic. Paul looked over his handmade map with a frown, but said nothing.

"Does that sound like something you'd both enjoy?"

The older boy folded the map carefully and placed it in his pocket. "Yes, thank you." He smiled placidly. I was beginning to notice that he was unreadable when he wanted to be. It was an unnatural quality in one his age, and I made a note to watch him more carefully.

"Can we go now?" James whined, taking my hand before I could respond and leading me down to the parlor, where I had them wait as I negotiated our picnic with Mrs. Mulbus. Luckily, Jenny was in the village running an errand, and so the usual shouting and arguing that accompanied a visit to the kitchen was replaced with complaints from Mrs. Mulbus about the scullery maid's tardiness and general laziness. As I provided a sympathetic ear to the cook's woes, she had no trouble procuring a basket full of finger sandwiches, slices of roast chicken, bread, cheese, pork pies, and fruit for our afternoon adventure. She even supplied a sturdy blanket for the occasion.

After I'd collected the boys, we set out from the back of the house and found a patch of grass at the edge of the forest still awash in sunlight. It was unseasonably warm despite the impending arrival of winter. I spread the picnic blanket over the ground and laid out the contents of the basket. As we filled our stomachs, the shadows of the tree branches marked the length of the meal like a sundial, and when we finished, I fell back into the tall grass. The children danced around me in circles like giants among the dying wildflowers, happy and full, finally collapsing into a breathless, red-faced heap of tousled hair and grass-stained shins.

"We all fall down!" James giggled into the hem of my dress as Paul tugged at his leg in an effort to twist it off. The little boy squealed, and I sat up with a dramatic sigh.

"Paul, must you do that to your brother's leg?"

"It wouldn't come off when I pulled."

"I imagine it might be difficult to continue the day's activities if you have to carry your brother's leg around."

"Maybe, but he won't give me back my map."

"James?"

"But I want to look at it!"

"It seems to me that I've done a very poor job of teaching you the importance of sharing, and it may be time for a precocious little song."

James scrambled up and serenaded me with a series of high-pitched screams, a sound that, despite the ringing it left in my ears, spoke of the intimacy and affection that had quickly formed between us in the weeks since the loss of Nanny Prum. Paul put his hands over his ears and attempted to trip his brother.

"Yes, you should run! You've heard me sing! But by now you must also be aware that I happen to find threats and subterfuge a much more effective means of communicating with inscrutably dense children."

James stopped running and turned to squint back at me. "What's *dense*?"

I leapt from the ground and snatched the paper from the young boy's hands. I was so quick he barely had time to register what had happened before I handed the homemade map over to his brother.

"Paul, what does *dense* mean?"

"That we still have a lot to learn about the world."

"That will do for now, I suppose." I kissed James on the head and lifted him into the air, placing his legs so they straddled my waist. He scowled but put his arm around my neck anyway.

"Now, where does it say to go next?"

Paul held the map close to his face. It was eerily accurate as he compared it to the landscape, looking across the field toward the overgrown forest up ahead.

"Over there, into the woods."

"Off we go then." I set James back on the ground next to his brother and gathered up the remains of the picnic into the basket. As we marched away from the field, the sun slid behind the twisting, knotted tree branches and the ground swelled with half-buried roots and rocks, both big enough to trip over and small enough to get trapped at the bottom of a shoe.

"Paul, how much farther?" I asked, becoming a bit nervous as the shadows grew longer.

"It was just ahead in my dream."

I said nothing for a moment, prepared to let reality speak for itself as it tore away the curtain of hope to reveal the cruel actuality of death, which had been unable to grab hold of the children, even though James, at least, had been at their mother's side when she had passed on—a prime example of the power of the heart to overwhelm the mind. "And what do you expect to do if there isn't anything there?" I said after a while.

"I'll keep dreaming." Paul said this matter-of-factly, without turning away from the task at hand, stepping over underbrush, moss-covered boulders, and rotted logs with complete determination. I held James's hand and continued my minor lecture as we walked.

"Dreams are my favorite things in the world. Sometimes they even come true, but sometimes we must learn when to wake up."

Paul ignored me and pointed excitedly at something up ahead. "There!"

The path ended at a small fallow creek, but began again on the other side to disappear around a dark, massive cage of roots at the base of an ancient oak tree. Whatever lay beyond the magnificent tree was obscured in a thick, roiling patch of fog. James wrenched himself free from my hand and leapt over the creek, bounding into the mist before I was able to stop him.

"James!"

I quickly hoisted my dress up to my waist and jumped over the brook, glancing back at Paul to wave him on. Together we chased his brother into the mist.

The air around us grew heavy with a dampness that remained even as the fog subsided, and we found ourselves in the middle of a vast orchard. While it had been daylight mere moments before, the moon now hung low in the sky, larger than I had ever seen. It was so vast and oppressive I felt that if I were to reach toward the sky I might be able to push the orb back where it belonged, high above on the black velvet mantle of the night.

"It's nighttime here." Paul was behind me, hugging himself against the cool air.

"Perhaps I misjudged the time . . ." I said with uncertainty as I took his hand very tightly into my own and began to march between the rows of squat orchard trees. "We must find your brother."

Paul was silent as he walked, his knuckles white as he peered between the trees at the shadows that stretched out to us when we passed, sensing us with hungry anticipation.

"Is this the place you dreamt of?"

Paul shivered against the chill in the air, observed the heavy moon in the sky, and shook his head slowly. "No. There was an orchard, but it was different."

Normally, I would have been very interested in such a sudden change of landscape—and apparently, time—but I was anxious to find James. My heart began to pulse in my ears, throbbing so intensely that my body seemed to reverberate with each beat. I refused to panic. Instead, I felt a heightened awareness of the atmosphere around me, of the curling fog behind a distant tree, of the rustle of branches around us, the movement of the shadows in our direction as we passed, of the very alien nature of the place that Paul's map had led us to.

"James!" My voice did not echo through the air, nor could we hear the sounds of our footsteps on the hard, cold earth. Still, I continued to call out until I was hoarse. Paul dragged behind me, gasping every time he looked back to where we had come from, seeing nothing but a gloom as opaque and tangible as the fog that had heralded our arrival to this strange, dark land. It was building around and behind us, pushing us toward a destination neither of us wanted to think about.

"Charlotte . . ."

"We'll leave as soon as we find your brother."

I stopped at what appeared to be the main thoroughfare and peered in both directions, trying to decide which way James might have gone. Behind me, Paul pressed himself against the nearest tree, as if to block the creeping darkness from his line of vision. Thin branches and twigs cracked and broke around his body, and his head grazed the bottom of a low-hanging piece of fruit with enough force to knock it free. It dropped down into his hands.

It was about the same size and shape as a grapefruit, but before he could get a good look at it, he glanced up at me, clearly frightened, sensing that something was wrong. The fruit quivered, and with a wet, tearing sound it began to unroll from the inside out, the air laced with the scent of peaches as the thing in his hands untwisted its arms and legs from the pulpy interior of its body and wrenched its head free from its shell. A baby's face blinked at us with pale blue eyes as Paul dropped it onto the ground with a look of utter terror, backing away, his gaze transfixed on the thing as it fell onto its back, protected by what was formerly the leathery skin of the fruit.

It smiled at him with thin, sharp teeth.

Paul let out a manic, consuming scream that frittered away the last remaining edges of his youthful courage and curiosity and exploded into his legs. He ran past me, past the trees, never looking directly at them, at the fruit, perhaps afraid that it might look back; his voice never breaking through the air as he shrieked, never echoing, but rather circling back in on him like a vulture, an eater of dead things, pecking away his every last hope, every rational thought, every instinct but the one that told him to run for as long as it took to escape.

I trailed behind him, struggling to follow his voice, which was quickly muffled by the rows of trees, but as he was running in a straight line I was able to catch up to him when he stopped, panting and heaving at the edge of the orchard before a great house as grand as anything either of us had ever seen before.

The doors of the house stood open, and silhouetted against the light that streamed over the threshold as vibrantly as the darkness churned in the orchard was a woman, tall and regal, even at a distance. James was at her side, clinging to her waist as she descended the steps leading up to the house with slow deliberation, almost gliding to the ground, a beautiful phantom with a small, worried smile as she approached Paul and gently touched his face. He collapsed against her and sobbed so loudly into her shoulder that I was unable to dispute the name that he immediately and distinctly gave her:

"Mother!"

CHAPTER 5

Bargains with the Dead

For a moment, I could only stand at the foot of the great house in an attempt to catch my breath, my mind reeling, searching for some way to escape with the children. Lily Darrow was dead. There had been witnesses and a funeral and a painting commissioned to hang over the desk in her husband's study, a portrait of a raven-haired creature with glittering eyes like cracked jade and a playful expression of mock superiority, which he stared at for hours on end when he didn't think the servants were watching. And yet . . . the likeness was so startling that I had to shake myself of the very notion that the woman before us could possibly be the late Mrs. Darrow.

They had *mourned* her. What kind of wife and mother would allow her family to feel the things that her death had inflicted upon them if she were not well and truly dead? It was unfathomable. This was some act of trickery, a cruel impostor toying with the emotions of children. I would not stand for it.

Paul sobbed into the woman's shoulder, crying and apologizing—"I'm sorry I wasn't there, I'm so sorry"—as she stroked his head and cooed away his sorrows. I stepped forward, stopping as I happened upon the crinkled hand-drawn map of the forest left behind on the ground of the orchard, a thing crafted from the scraps of dreams. How could anyone have influenced the boy to lead us into the woods? Was such a thing even possible? There were so many questions, all of them overshadowed by the one thought I could not ignore:

"No one ever comes back," I said.

James pulled his face away from the skirts of the mystery woman, and looked her over carefully before returning my pleading gaze with a confused expression. In his eyes I could see that there was no doubt the woman he clung to was his mother.

Paul didn't bother to remove his head from the other woman's shoulder. He had awoken from his nightmare and it had all been some terrible misunderstanding. Everything he hoped for had come true.

"But she has. She's alive again."

The woman ran her fingers through Paul's hair and raised his chin so she could look into his eyes. "No, my love, I am not."

His face fell, and he slowly backed away from her, dragging his brother with him. I quickly grabbed them both by the shoulders a little more roughly than I meant to and held them tightly before they could run off.

The great house before us was more appealing than the dark, oppressive gloom of the orchard, with the shadows that twitched and snaked about the ground, but I would not hesitate to escape the way we had come. I considered the woman who purported to be Mrs. Darrow. To anyone who might ask, I would deny that I had any belief in ghosts, but then what of the man in black? A mysterious shade prone to the company of corpses was just as unlikely as the resurrection of a young mother taken before her time. Was she a liar, a ghost, or something else altogether?

My heart continued on its perilous drop deep into the nether reaches of my chest, and I realized with no small amount of revulsion that I might soon begin to panic in the way I had witnessed other women do, as I was perhaps expected to do. But I refused to faint or swoon; the fearful emptiness I felt inside instead began to swell, blood raging in my ears, until it changed into something solid and substantial. Nothing would happen to the children—I would not allow it. It was a very odd sensation, unlike anything I had ever experienced. We were in danger, true danger, and it thrilled me to know that I was equal to the challenge presented.

Perhaps the woman saw this fearlessness in my gaze, which I imagine had become rather hard and fiery, for it was then that she sighed, her comfortable, dignified composure falling away. She folded her hands before her like the woman from the portrait in Mr. Darrow's study and began to look a bit desperate.

"Please, I've come back to you." She took a step forward, and the boys huddled against me. The woman stopped again and smiled faintly. "I suppose I should have expected as much. I've been gone from you both for so long."

"And Father." Paul had let go of me, but did not move toward the other woman. He spoke with a slight edge in his voice.

At the mention of Mr. Darrow, the woman quickly looked back at the house and then returned her gaze to Paul. "Please don't be angry with me. I never wanted to leave you, which is why I've come back. I would have returned to Everton, but there were rules I had to agree to."

"Come home with us." James stepped away from me to join his brother's side.

The woman shook her head. "This is my home now, and you're welcome here anytime you'd like." She motioned to the massive house.

The boys looked at one another, and then to me, but I remained unconvinced.

"Do forgive me for being skeptical," I said, trying to contain the smoking flesh and boiling blood surging beneath the confines of my skin. "But how can we be sure that you are really Mrs. Darrow, and not some impostor intent on doing us harm?"

"I can see that my husband chose well." She paused at this, making an implication that was not lost on me. "If that were my intention, why would I be reasoning with you to believe my story? Wouldn't I have done something by now to prove your point?"

"I do not pretend to understand the whims of the dead."

"A wise decision. So you believe me then?"

I shot her a steely glare and changed the subject. "This place is hardly fit for children."

"How can you be sure? You have not yet been inside. The House of Darkling can be whatever you choose to make of it." She had begun to regain her confidence, much to my dismay, and her lips formed into a tight smile at her own cleverness. I would have none of it. I turned with the children pressed against me and began to trot briskly back into the orchard. The woman called after us, desperate once more, which was the only way I would deal with her. Desperate people are more likely to make mistakes.

"Please! You must give me the chance to prove myself! Ask me anything. Something that only Lily Darrow would know."

I stopped at the edge of the orchard and turned around slowly, searching my mind for every scrap of information I had ever learned about my employer's late wife.

Paul spoke up before I could. "What was the name of the lullaby you used to sing to us?"

The woman smiled and closed her eyes for a moment, as if listening for the music on the soft wind that began to blow through the orchard trees, the fruit on their branches swaying in the breeze. "'Every Night at Everton.' We made it up together, and it was different every night depending on what had happened during the day."

This was enough proof for both of the children. They returned to their mother's side and hugged her tightly, immediately sorry that they had ever doubted her intentions. I, on the other hand, was dubious even as the thrill of danger dissipated into caution. When a person died, they did not come back to their children, but if this had somehow been reversed for Mrs. Darrow—and I was not convinced that it had, nor that this was not some elaborate ruse to take advantage of the children of a wealthy widower—then why had none of my loved ones been able to do the same? It was for this reason and this reason alone that I followed them into the great house with unease, remembering those that I had lost and hoping against hope that if what the woman said were true, then perhaps the place contained more than one departed soul.

The parlor was small and intimate, the walls lined with square wooden panels and elaborate tapestries depicting the room itself filled with a strange pantheon of creatures, perhaps from some obscure mythology or religion with which I was unfamiliar. As I stared at the fabric, examining the intricate patterns and threading, I realized with some bewilderment that the shapes were changing, reknitting themselves from left to right in an impossible act of defiance of the rules of scientific propriety, recasting the occupants of the room until I recognized myself and the children as carefully constructed embroideries. I reached out to pull aside the tapestry, but I stopped myself before I could uncover the mechanism enabling its manipulation. Against my better judgment I preferred to believe, if only for a little while longer, that the house and the alleged Mrs. Darrow were part of something extraordinary.

A squat, muted chandelier hung low from the ceiling, casting the room in dim amber light. I sat on the edge of a thick leather armchair, determined not to sink back so far as to be rendered incapacitated should the strange situation spiral any further out of my control, even as I promised myself that it would not. To my bewilderment the cushions expanded as if the chair were fighting against me so that I might be more comfortable. Was it possible for furniture to become offended? I firmly kicked the leg behind my right foot, and the chair regained its former shape.

Before sitting down, Mrs. Darrow gently touched three of the wooden panels along the wall, each of them clicking open to reveal the different components of a full afternoon tea spread. She removed cups and a steaming pot from the first, a pedestal of finger sandwiches and scones from the second, and a chocolate tea cake from the last. I fought to ignore a pang of sympathy as I realized that the cake was the same as Mr. Darrow had provided during our midnight tea. She left it on a plate to the side of the table, as conspicuously untouched as her husband's had been. I imagined the two of them sitting alone in two different houses, Mr. Darrow at Everton and Mrs. Darrow at the place called Darkling, staring at the empty chairs that surrounded them, silence shrieking, with tea cakes perched on lone plates like ceremonial offerings to memories not quite dead.

I eyed the boys carefully as they sat beside the woman who claimed to be their mother, sprawled on a plush divan before the large stone fireplace at the front of the room. The flames contorted into various shapes, casting shadows of flickering animals and their masters along the back wall. The children marveled at the trick for a long while, slowly drifting off to sleep as the alleged Mrs. Darrow watched me back, her eyes gleaming in the firelight, as dangerous and silver-green as a cat's.

"Your tea will cool," she said. Both boys were nearly asleep in her lap; even Paul, who was too old for that sort of thing.

I looked at the saucer and brought the cup to my lips, careful to seal them to the rim so as not to allow any of the liquid into my mouth. I was already at a disadvantage if the woman meant us any harm, a fact I firmly kept at the forefront of my mind, and sitting in the parlor of a woman who claimed to be dead, in a strange land with shadows that crawled and pieces of fruit that walked, the least I could do was avoid a potentially poisoned cup of tea.

I brought the cup away from my mouth and placed it back onto the saucer sitting primly in my lap. The other woman turned away from me and gazed into the fire.

"Is my husband well?" The tone of her voice was emotionless and elusive. It reminded me of Paul's.

I considered the question before I answered. A vague, bland answer might lead to an informal inquisition, but a detailed one might hint at a relationship that was more involved than was true.

"I've been with the Darrow family for nine months, and in that time I've come to know Mr. Darrow as two very different people. The first man smiles when someone says something clever and eats as voraciously as the groundskeeper. But then there are times when he sees something either in the house or in the boys that makes him grow very distant. He is my employer, and so I don't pretend to know him as one might know a friend, but whenever he is overcome by such an episode, I've begun to suspect that he's thinking of what he has lost, and there is a sadness in his distance that leads me to believe that he may forever remain two people: one struggling to enjoy life, and the other trapped in sorrow."

The woman did not look away from the fireplace. Her chest rose and fell in an uncomfortable quiet broken only by the ambient sounds of the room—the embers in the fire crackling; the grandfather clock chiming; something shuffling across the floor in one of the upper chambers of the great house. I brought the cup to my lips again, pretended to drink, and set it back onto the saucer.

"You are very thorough, Mrs. Markham."

I placed the saucer on the table between us and stood to circle the room. I spotted a bookcase filled with obscure texts whose titles seemed to be in a language I had never seen before. I fingered the spines lovingly and turned back to Mrs. Darrow. "The one detail I find myself most curious about at present is the fact that I'm having a conversation with the alleged late wife of my current employer."

The woman smiled, and the stoic decorum that had framed her every action since we entered the house partially melted away. She lifted herself gingerly out from beneath the children and stood before the fireplace.

"You are right to be suspicious of me."

"The children believe you. Who am I to disagree with them? But by all accounts Mrs. Darrow died."

"So I did."

"I have lost many people from my life—my mother to cholera, my father to a heart attack, and my husband to a fire—and when they died, they did not come back." The end of the last word sharpened in the air for a pregnant moment until I began again. "While I do not doubt the power of a mother's love for her children, I will not believe that the love of my family was somehow inferior to yours." I said this evenly, without hope of masking the jealous curiosity that had replaced my confidence, but I was determined nevertheless to have a cordial, honest discussion. "In order for this conversation to continue, I feel that I must ask—why you?"

The woman did not appear to be surprised at the directness of my question; in fact she seemed relieved. The alleged Mrs. Darrow spoke facing the fireplace, a silhouette before the flames.

"When I first took ill, I told anyone who would listen that I would conquer my sickness, that I would not accept anything less than a full recovery; that God was testing me. I followed the doctor's instructions: I continued with my social engagements, I ate healthily, exercised regularly, and yet each day I grew more weary.

"Food began to make me queasy, and I lost the ability to stand under my own volition. I became confined to my bed and slowly wasted away until the skin hung from my bones, loose and pallid. People came to my bedside and whispered words of solace and comfort, but that was of little consolation after I went blind, and even less when I lost my hearing.

"You would think that a person in such a state would be adrift in the darkness, but I could still feel; I could still smell. I knew when my family was nearby; when Henry kissed my forehead or pushed a strand of hair from my face, when James took my hand into his to keep me company, just as I knew that Paul could not bring himself to see me bedridden. I knew that I would die and that they would miss me, though death was a thing I craved more and more each day.

"The very act of breathing slowly drove me to the brink of insanity. Even in my delirium I found it ironic how a thing that gives one life could become the most unbearable part of living. The moments between each breath grew further and further apart, a series of contractions as I delivered my own end, until finally, I stopped.

"I realized I had died when I opened my eyes and could see again. A man stood before me, as unremarkable and ordinary a person as I have ever encountered. He wore a black suit and a bowler hat, and he held out his hand. He said nothing, but he did not have to. I knew who he was, and what he expected me to do. Free from illness, I felt revitalized, elated even, and yet something whispered to me: a voice in the place between life and death. It spoke to me, whereas Death did not; it told me I was special, and that exceptions could be made for any rule. It told me the story of my life, one that did not end with a woman in her sickbed.

"The forgettable man in the ordinary black suit grew fainter and fainter, retreating down a corridor made of light until he was gone altogether. The voice grew more substantial, until there was a hand, and it took me someplace else . . . to a place for the Things That Do Not Die."

I felt a chill run through my body. I was near a window, and the darkness outside seemed to press against it, flexing the glass with an ominous groan.

"And here you stand," I whispered.

"I do not know why it was different for me. Perhaps I was in the right place at the right time. Regardless of why the opportunity presented itself, I took it. Children need their mothers, little boys most of all."

I paused at that turn of phrase. The old nightmare of my mother's death returned, as did the voice of the mysterious woman from my dream, who, it was now so obvious, sounded very much like Mrs. Darrow. My heart fluttered with a mixture of anger and fear. I approached the divan with the sleeping children, clutching the lip of the seat.

"The children can't stay here. It isn't safe."

"Nothing on the estate would dare hurt the children."

"And their governess?"

Mrs. Darrow, for by that point I could no longer pretend to think of her as anything else, stepped closer and put her hand over my own. She was warm to the touch, more so than any living person I had ever encountered. With the children between us, I relaxed for a moment.

"I mean no one any harm," she said.

I looked her carefully in the eyes, their catlike quality replaced by something more somber and quiet. Suddenly her intrusion into my dream seemed more sad than threatening.

"I've dreamt of you. You tricked us into coming here."

"I did what I had to do in order to see my children."

"What is it that you want from them?"

"More time."

"To what end? You have passed on, and it can't be healthy for them to meet you somewhere in between."

"Is it any worse than allowing them to grow up without me? You must have seen what happens to some children who lose their parents."

A barrage of heartless, foulmouthed little boys passed before my mind's eye, hitting and shouting, stealing and spitting, raping scullery maids in the middle of the night.

"That can be avoided."

"Yes, it can. That's why I came here. They don't have to be without me. I don't have to be gone."

The woman moved her hand up, grasping my wrist. There was a desperation in her grip.

"You never were."

Mrs. Darrow dropped her hand away and turned back to the fireplace. The flames licked at the embers, which had stacked themselves into something like a house.

"I'd like them to visit Darkling, when they can. Time passes differently here, and it would be as if they'd never left Everton. My husband would never know."

"You don't wish to see him?"

"He can never know."

"He's lost without you." My throat tightened as I said the words.

"You must not tell him!" The woman's voice raised in pitch, waking the boys with a start.

"Mother?"

Mrs. Darrow was back at their sides before they could lift their heads, kissing their faces gently as she lifted them off the divan. I felt that I had touched upon something important, perhaps even powerful. She was afraid, and her feelings for her husband were clearly complicated. Suddenly the situation became very manageable. She was no different from any other person and could be manipulated if necessary. I was surprised at the callousness I had discovered within myself. It was not in my nature to have thoughts so overtly cunning, but then I had never been faced with such a dangerous situation. I wondered if the person one becomes when faced with such things is the person one truly is, or only a temporary mask worn to survive. Again, a shiver ran through me.

The woman looked from the boys to me, and then smiled sweetly at her children. "I'm afraid I'm very tired. Our visit must come to an end."

"But, Mother, we just got here!"

"Please don't leave us!"

Mrs. Darrow and I stared at each other during this exchange, and I searched myself deeply for a response I would not live to regret. There would be consequences from dabbling with the dead, this I felt most certain of all. But was there also not a wealth of things to learn? The veil of death had been lifted for this regal, beautiful woman, so stoic and frail, broken by the end of her own life in a way that perhaps even the children would be unable to fix. Were there others like her? I attempted to stifle the thought before it became fully formed, but it was too late. It blossomed in my mind, accompanied by images of Jonathan and my parents.

I could not ignore the strength of Mrs. Darrow to overturn the rules of existence, to find a way out of death, and to fight for her children. There was something powerful in such love, such conviction, such devotion, and at the same time such desperation, a weary stubbornness to deny what must occur. I could not refuse her or the children or my own curiosity, despite the danger I sensed in the agreement I was about to make.

"There will be other visits, and I imagine that we'll be seeing your mother again soon enough," I told the boys.

"She can't come home with us?" James stuck out his bottom lip. His eyes welled up with tears.

"Oh, my darling James, I wish that I could. But this is my home now."

"Can we bring Father next time?"

"I'm afraid you mustn't, Paul."

"Why not?"

"It's almost like a spell that's keeping me from leaving you forever, and if you tell your father, it will be broken. Do you understand?"

Both boys nodded and hugged their mother tightly around the neck. She kissed each of them roughly on the lips and turned them back over to my care.

"Mrs. Markham, it was truly a pleasure meeting you."

I took the hands of the children into my own and squeezed them, searching for further conviction.

"And you, Mrs. Darrow."

"Please, call me Lily."

The woman escorted us out of the parlor and into the main foyer of the House of Darkling. Many stories above, I saw someone leaning against the railing of the grand staircase, watching us and smoking casually in the dark. But before I could look more closely, the doors swung open and the damp, cool air of the orchard swept over us. Lily kissed me affectionately on the cheek, and ushered us out the door.

"Please come back as soon as you can," she said.

The boys waved at their mother as we set out for the main path between the trees. Something howled in the distance, the sound of it languishing in the chilled air. We continued into the gloom until we came to the familiar wall of mist, and passed through to return to sunshine and the world of the living.

* * *

That evening, I struggled to put the children to bed. James sang and squealed slowly toward exhaustion, jumping up and down on his bed and playing so loudly that I was finally forced to threaten him with an ancient form of Indian torture I had learned as a young girl in Asia. This prompted an inevitable inquiry into my life abroad, and soon the excitement the boys felt over their rediscovered mother was eclipsed by curiosity, and they were able to listen to my tales of the Far East as they drifted off to sleep.

I left the nursery dabbing the perspiration from my forehead with a handkerchief. I was about to return to the schoolroom to organize my lesson plan for the following day when I realized I was not alone in the hallway.

"Mrs. Markham."

I jumped and quickly laughed at myself. I had been so absorbed in the strange events of the day that I had not noticed Mr. Darrow standing behind me, the pale illumination from the gaslights suffused in his golden hair. He was a tall man, with a lithe frame and a distinguished, sharp face that was more beautiful than handsome, and the way his hair glowed in the darkness gave his appearance a quality that bordered on angelic.

"Mr. Darrow! I apologize, I didn't notice you."

"From the sounds of it, the boys had you on the run this evening." He smiled at me and pointed down the corridor. "Would you mind joining me in the study before turning in for the night?"

My stomach twisted into knots. Did he suspect that something was amiss? Or—I could not help but let my mind wander to the strange, romantic thoughts one cannot avoid while traveling through a dark, old house at night—perhaps he had something else in mind? Even in light of meeting his late wife, I could not deny that I found the second possibility rather exciting. Is that not the way most stories go? With the young governess falling in love with her handsome widowed employer and living happily ever after? We both deserved some happiness. Even the dead, it seemed, were entitled to get the things they wanted most.

"Not at all."

The gaslights flickered above us in their cracked glass husks, fighting against the darkness that attempted to envelop the house. I was unpleasantly reminded of the agreement I had made earlier in the day. I wrung the handkerchief in my hands.

"Are you all right?" Mr. Darrow paused at the door to his study and nearly touched my shoulder, but he seemed to catch himself and placed his hand against the door instead, pushing it open. I stood stupidly in the hallway, rousing myself from the day's events and wondering what his hand would have felt like against my skin.

"Yes, perfectly fine." I followed him inside.

He sat behind his spotlessly clean desk and folded his hands, framed beneath the portrait of his late wife. At the other side of the room, the door to the office stood open.

"The children seem very happy," he said.

"They have a wonderful home and a loving father. How could they not be?"

"You are doing wonders for them, and I want you to know that I intend to compensate you accordingly."

"Mr. Darrow, I can assure you that my current salary is more than generous."

"A fact of which I'm quite aware, but even so, I think you deserve a raise. It's been a difficult year for our family . . ." His voice cracked, and for a moment I was unsure if he would be able to continue. "You were right the other evening, I'm afraid I have been growing distant with the children."

It was true that since Nanny Prum's death, Mr. Darrow had been keeping even stranger hours than usual, having afternoon tea in the middle of the night, taking meals in his study, and on the rare occasions that he did join us he drank too much. He was in mourning again, not just for his late employee, but, I felt sure, for his wife. It was a pain I knew too well.

"With all due respect, you must not ignore the impact of your loss."

Mr. Darrow attempted to smile, but instead he looked faraway and sad. "Quite right. We used to spend every weekend together as a family, but ever since Lily . . . They remind me so much of her."

"Perhaps you could reclaim your time with them on the weekends? We could plan an outing by the lake."

"Perhaps." He sat back in his chair and sniffed the air. "Mrs. Markham, have you chosen a new perfume?"

I felt my chest tighten. I must have gotten too close to Mrs. Darrow during our visit to the House of Darkling.

"No, why do you ask?"

"It's nothing; I suppose I'm just tired. I don't mean to keep you."

He stood from his chair and leaned against the mantel behind his desk, averting his eyes from the portrait of his wife that hung above it, keeping them trained on the fireplace.

"The lake. Yes, that would be splendid."

"Good night, Mr. Darrow."

I crept out of the room and left him to his thoughts.

CHAPTER 6

A Question of Spirits

The next morning I woke before sunrise. I had decided in the middle of the night to run a very specific sort of errand to help alleviate some of my concerns about the promise I had made to the children the day before, and so I chose a long black dress from my wardrobe—the kind of severe uniform one would expect a typical governess to wear. I hardly thought of myself as ordinary, and while I much preferred to wear something lighter and more colorful, I had set my mind on this particular mission and knew that it would be best to dress for the occasion. I even wore the brooch I had found in Nanny Prum's room.

The house was dark and quiet except in the kitchen, where Mrs. Mulbus berated Jenny for failing to adequately clean the soup kettle.

"There's a ring of filth around the rim!" As she was a big woman, she lifted the heavy pot without any effort, flailing it in the air above Jenny's head.

"Yes, Mrs. Mulbus. Of course, Mrs. Mulbus."

"Don't get sharp with me, Jenny Saxon!"

"I wouldn't think of it, mum!" Without turning from the sink, Jenny performed a small curtsy.

Mrs. Mulbus slammed the pot down on the counter and clutched her chest. "You'll be the death of me, I swear it!"

"I shall make it my personal duty to put wildflowers on your grave every Sunday morning."

There was a sudden murderous look in Mrs. Mulbus's eyes, and as she motioned to grab for the heavy pan once more, I spoke up to make my presence known.

"Good morning, Mrs. Mulbus."

The cook turned away from Jenny, who had never turned away from the sink, halfheartedly scrubbing the dishes that always seemed to be there.

"Good morning to you, Mrs. Markham. I hope we didn't wake you?"

"Nonsense. I have an errand to run this morning."

"This early?"

"I'm afraid it must be done before the children wake."

"Of course. Might you want something to eat before you leave?"

The kitchen was small for such a large house, but it was filled with food. Baskets of fruit and freshly baked breads, smoked meats hanging above the butcher block, stacks of pungent cheeses, rows of spices from India and the Far East (bought by catalog in a very sweet effort to appease my palate), jars of jellies and preserves, and large glass containers filled with caramel toffees. I picked up an apple and tucked it away into the small basket I carried at my side. "A piece of fruit will do nicely."

The cook was visibly disappointed, and as I left the house through the back of the kitchen, I heard Mrs. Mulbus launching a new tirade at the scullery maid: "Spots! On the silver!"

I passed Roland as I crossed the grounds, and we smiled at one another as the shouting continued in the kitchen.

"Early morning for you, mum?"

"I should hope that I'm a little young to be called 'mum'!"

"Sorry, Mrs. Markham, just trying to be respectful is all."

"I can't imagine you being anything less." The young man had started at Everton a few weeks before my arrival. There wasn't much need for a gardener as the grounds were rather small, but Fredricks was getting older and someday soon would be unable to tend to his duties. When Roland wasn't outside, he followed the butler around attempting to understand the old man's mumbling and increasingly senile instructions. The week before last, Fredricks had asked him to bring Mr. Darrow a box of his favorite cigars, which was alarming since the only member of the Darrow family who had ever enjoyed smoking was Mr. Darrow's father, and he had been dead for over fifteen years.

"Roland, have you noticed anything strange around the grounds since the night Nanny Prum was attacked?"

"How do you mean?"

"I'm not sure exactly. Everything about what happened was so unusual . . . and with the murderer still at large, I worry for our safety."

"I walk the grounds with the rifle for a bit every night before I turn in, but no trouble yet. Not even that strange smell that was all over the place it happened. No, I think the bastard that did it is long gone. Pardon my language."

"If you see anything suspicious, do let me know. Even the smallest thing could be important."

"Of course. Miss."

"Now that's more like it."

Roland winked at me and tugged on his hat, about to set

off toward the caretaker's shed, but he stopped and nervously wrung his hands together like a schoolboy.

"And how is Mrs. Larken?"

"Susannah is coping as best she can. She's very grateful to you."

He blushed. "Good woman, there." He looked dazed for a moment, and then continued. "If you see her, tell her that I'm keeping an eye out, so she has no cause to be scared."

"I'm sure she'll be very pleased to hear that, Roland."

He nodded once more, and I descended the hill toward the village below. Blackfield was just beginning to come to life. Mr. Wallace was in his shop with key in hand, hurriedly winding each clock face to match up with its siblings, but he was too hungover and slow, and the clocks chimed at him sporadically out of spite. Mr. Rookway, the butcher, stood on a ladder behind his shop window hanging the day's offerings of plucked geese, sausage links, and cured beef. I stopped in the dress shop to see Susannah, but Mrs. Willoughby had her busily sorting through containers of buttons for a set with a mother-of-pearl finish she desperately wanted to use for Mrs. Reese's dinner gown but had apparently misplaced. I promised Susannah that I would come back after my errand and continued on my way to the church.

St. Michael's was a small country church with stone walls and a family of sparrows nesting within the steeple. The vicarage sat behind it, a modest little cottage with a half dozen birdhouses carefully placed in the surrounding trees. Mr. Scott had been trying for the last three weeks to convince the sparrows to move out of his church, but with little success. His sermons had taken on an air of hysteria as he struggled to shout over the annoying but otherwise lovely birdsongs while the faithful attempted to dodge being sanctified by any unwanted sacrament from above.

Despite all this, attendance at the Sunday morning service had never been higher.

The sun was just coming up. I shifted my basket to the other hand and rapped sharply on the door. There was a stumbling, a muffled curse, and the door wrenched open to reveal Mr. Scott.

"Mrs. Markham?" His hazel eyes were watery in the young sunlight.

"Good morning, Vicar. I hope I haven't disturbed you?"

His hair was mussed and his collar crooked. He fumbled with them as he replied. "Of course not! I always have time for the devoted." He motioned for me to enter the cottage.

It was as small on the inside as it appeared from the exterior, sparsely decorated with every surface covered in what appeared to be birdhouses in varying degrees of construction. Mr. Scott moved a birdhouse from one of the chairs and motioned for me to sit beside him. "Now, what seems to be the trouble?"

"What do you make of spirits?"

He looked disappointed. "I wouldn't know. I don't touch the stuff. Man of the cloth, you know."

"Not spirits, *spirits*. As in apparitions of the formerly living."

He paused and rubbed his chin. "Well, I can't say that *I've* ever seen one." He looked at me strangely, as if I'd suddenly grown a pair of horns.

I quickly elaborated. "Neither have I, of course. But I've been reading the children ghost stories, and James asked me if all spirits were evil. I didn't want to answer him until I'd consulted an expert."

"Expert?" Mr. Scott squinted for a moment, and then blushed. "Oh, you mean me? Mrs. Markham, you flatter me. I'm afraid I don't know any more about ghosts and spirits than you do."

"But surely the Bible says something on the subject?"

"Well"—he stood from his chair and paced the room—"I do recall a line from the Gospel of Luke. I believe it says that spirits are not permitted to return to the earth without a valid purpose, such as offering up a warning."

"So not all spirits have malicious intent?"

"It's hard to say. The Book of Job mentions that demons have no power that God himself does not allow. So I suppose that spirits must work along the same lines. They might wish a person harm, but only as a test of faith."

"I see. And how would one defend themselves from spirits or demons, if God had decided to test them?"

Mr. Scott opened his mouth to speak, but closed it again. He narrowed his eyes in amusement. "James was very specific with his questions. He sounds like a clever young man."

"He does have an excellent governess."

"So I see. Well, if one is being tested by God, then there really is no protection available, but none should be needed. God is a force for good in the world, and he loves each of his children. On the other hand, the demons and spirits you mentioned may be given their power by God, but are more frequently the tools of Lucifer in his quest to lure mankind into damnation. Such creatures use temptation and trickery over physical harm or injury. The best defense against such tactics is good judgment and honorable choices."

"I see." I looked around the room and noticed a small crucifix hanging above a doorway. "And what about holy relics? Crosses, holy water, that sort of thing?"

"It couldn't hurt, I suppose, but again, these are complex questions. What good would holy articles do against forces that have their power sanctioned by God, regardless of whether or not they're in the employ of the Devil?"

"Such are the mysteries of life, I suppose." I said this with sullen annoyance at the complexity of my situation.

"Indeed." The vicar nodded with heavy importance.

I stood and turned for the door.

"I do apologize, Vicar. I didn't mean to interrupt your morning routine. You've been most helpful."

"No trouble at all, always happy to assist. I suppose I'll see you on Sunday?"

"I certainly hope so," I said darkly under my breath, thinking of the agreement I had made with the late Mrs. Darrow. I left the vicarage and headed for the path back to the village.

In the dress shop, Susannah was stacking small paper button boxes, Mrs. Willoughby apparently having found the buttons with the pearl finish for Mrs. Reese's gown. Susannah flinched when I entered the shop, the little bell at the top of the door ringing shrilly to mark my arrival. She dropped the boxes she was holding, scattering lacquered buttons of various sizes across the floor with a small yelp. She closed her eyes and bent down to pick them up.

"Is everything all right?" I knelt down to help her, and soon we had the buttons all gathered up and stowed in boxes on the back shelf. I sat Susannah down in a chair behind the counter.

"No, everything is *not* all right. Mrs. Willoughby knew that I didn't want to be left alone, and she still went to prepare for tea with Cornelia Reese. I've been a bundle of nerves ever since."

"Whatever for? It's just after sunrise."

Susannah narrowed her eyes and lowered her voice in a conspiratorial tone. "There's a strangeness in Blackfield."

"That's no surprise, what with all the strange people." I smiled at her playfully, but she maintained her serious demeanor, so I quickly changed my expression to match her sense of gravity.

"Ever since that night in the woods, I've felt that there's someone watching me."

"You've seen someone?"

"That's just it, I'm not sure. I swear I've seen the same figure out of the corner of my eye when I'm walking through town, but it's always gone when I look at it directly.

"It's only natural to be nervous after what you've been through. Perhaps it's Roland? He seems a bit smitten with you."

"The groundskeeper? No, there are other things. When I'm alone, I can't seem to keep the lights lit, whether it be candle or gas. And I've been noticing a smell, the same one I noticed near Nanny Prum's body. I fear that someone may be following me."

"Have you told Lionel?"

"Of course. He's worried sick, the poor thing. He walks me to the shop every morning, and walks me home in the evenings. Won't let me work in the pub at all anymore."

"Perhaps we ought to tell someone?"

"Like who, Brickner? He barely believes me as it is." Even so, the constable had been proceeding with the investigation in the wake of his conversation with Mr. Darrow, though there was still very little evidence to go on and minimal progress had been made.

I sat with Susannah until Mrs. Willoughby returned from her tea with Cornelia Reese. Susannah gave her employer an icy reception, which melted into a heated discussion on who, exactly, was the owner of the dress shop. This then escalated into which of them was the better seamstress, until eventually each woman became so frustrated with the other that they broke down and began to sob in one another's arms, promising everlasting friendship and, on Mrs. Willoughby's part, a more careful consideration of her apprentice's nervous state of mind. I left them to their reconciliation and returned to Everton, where I spent most of my morning deflecting the boys' requests to visit their mother.

"But you promised!" James kicked at the leg of his desk.

I stood in front of the chalkboard, my skin powdered with flecks of white dust. I pointed at two sets of arithmetic problems written neatly on the board, one for each of the boys. "And you promised that you would finish your lessons for the day. I hardly think your mother would want to be visited by such lazy children." I again pointed forcefully at the board. "Now, would either of you care to solve your equation?"

James kicked the leg of his desk again, but raised his hand to attempt a solution. He was wrong, but it was a step in the right direction. By midafternoon the boys had calmed down and I noticed them looking out the window with wistful, silent agony. I steeled myself against their longing, and I would continue to do so until I was confident that I could protect them from whatever lay beyond the veil of mist in the old-growth forest.

When it was lunchtime, I took the boys to the dining room. Everton buzzed with the flurry of daily life. Fredricks left Mr. Darrow's study with an air of distinction, carrying the tray of an empty tea set with hands so tremulous that Roland walked carefully beside him, catching stray cups and saucers before they crashed to the floor. Meanwhile, Mrs. Norman circled around the nervous maids like a vulture, the young women frantically dusting and sweeping to avoid her wrath.

I was suddenly reminded of her warning about the mysterious man who was waiting for me and told the boys that I would meet them in the dining room. Paul and James were more than happy to be rid of me, as I had made it perfectly clear that for the time being I would not change my mind. I returned to the landing on the stairs where Mrs. Norman ran her finger along the railing, testing it for dust in the presence of a young maid named Catherine. It was clean, much to Mrs. Norman's dissatisfaction, and she dismissed the maid as I approached.

"Good afternoon, Mrs. Markham."

"Hello, Mrs. Norman. I was hoping you might be able to help me with something."

The older woman was immediately suspicious. "How might I be of service?" she asked with not a small hint of sarcasm.

"I was wondering if you might be able to tell me about spirits."

I could see immediately that it warmed Mrs. Norman's stony heart to know that when it came to the occult, people thought of her, but she maintained her haughty composure and raised a single eyebrow.

"There is much to say on the subject. What is it that you wish to know?"

"Are they predominantly good or evil?"

Mrs. Norman waved her hands impatiently. "You ask a question that has no answer. Are people predominantly good or evil? I should say that every man, woman, and child has a great capacity for both, but the discipline for only one or the other. I suppose it depends on whose spirit you are seeing."

"I'm asking more for the sake of curiosity than from experience. I can't say that I've been lucky enough to receive any visits from the Other Side."

She observed me carefully. "I see. In that case, it depends upon the relationship between the spirit and the person it's sought out. Spirits only return when they have unfinished business. I suppose the only way a person would be in danger is if they either caused the death of the person who became the spirit or meant to impede it on the completion of its otherworldly task."

I waited for Mrs. Norman to say more, but it seemed that she had finished doling out advice on the supernatural.

She raised her eyebrow again. "Is there anything else?"

"No, you've been most helpful. Thank you."

She seemed to falter for a moment. "The other afternoon in the nursery . . . the man who watches. Have you found him yet?"

I had been trying not to think about the housekeeper's warning. "No, I have not."

"Find him before he finds you." Mrs. Norman went up the stairs and left me alone on the landing. I felt very weary. I had been going round and round with my dilemma, trying to decide if such extraordinary events warranted disregard of the suspicion I felt deep in my heart. There was something wrong with Mrs. Darrow's proposal. There was something wrong with the mysterious house in which she lived. And yet, I could not shake the feeling that there would be something terribly wrong with me if I did not assist the boys in sharing a little more time with their late mother. Had I had such an opportunity with my mother, even at present, I would have risked life and limb for a moment's conversation. There is always so much left unsaid, even when one has the opportunity to say good-bye, and despite my apprehension, I continued to return to the same conclusion: I would take the boys to visit their mother. I would be guarded, and I would bring the appropriate articles of protection, even if I doubted their usefulness, and I would remain alert for the slightest sign of mischief. Heaven and Earth had been moved to accommodate Mrs. Darrow, and I could not find it in my heart to deny what was so obviously a mother's right to demand. As for the woman herself, I believed that she could be managed. She loved her family, and if she wished to have access to them, then she would do so on my terms.

I found the children in the dining room devouring plates of roasted pheasant and slabs of cheese on toast. For all my inner turmoil, I had lost my appetite and was anxious to continue with my plan before I lost my resolve.

"Would you care to take the remainder of your lessons outside?"

The boys looked up at me, their mouths full of food. Before they even swallowed they were dashing away from the table to grab their coats out of their room. I took a heavy shawl and placed it in my favorite basket.

As I took the children out the back of the house, we could hear Mrs. Mulbus still shrieking at Jenny. "How could you scrub the fine china?!"

Once outside, the boys took my hands and pulled me along toward the forest. I closed my eyes for a moment and let them lead the way as if I were caught on the sharp autumn wind.

The light dwindled as we entered the woods, and suddenly everything was silent except for the sound of our shoes crunching through the dried leaves and twigs that littered the ground. We came to the tall cage of roots at the base of the large oak tree, and were overcome by the thick, swirling mist that separated the living from the dead.

PART 2
The Human Fashion

CHAPTER 7

The House of Darkling

The light from the moon cast pale, sharp silhouettes that danced between the orchard trees. I wondered if there was such a thing as daytime there. The boys tried to race ahead, but I kept hold of their hands and struggled successfully against them. Despite the safety that had been assured to us by Lily Darrow, I did not trust anything about the place. If the former mistress of Everton was strong enough to turn back death, then I was obviously in no position to deny her something she had worked so hard to earn. It's not every day that the natural order of the universe becomes subverted, and if death could be turned back once, then perhaps it could be done again.

If the woman proved to be malicious in her intent, then I hoped that I would be able to deal with her when the time came. I had put on a silver cross necklace before we left Everton, but even as it pressed against my skin, it did little to soothe my apprehension as the gloom moved around us.

We walked along the path between the trees. Paul was careful not to stray far from us, and he avoided looking too closely at the bulbous pieces of fruit that twitched on the ends of the branches. Something moved up ahead, more solid than the ominous darkness that swirled languidly around us as we headed for the House of Darkling in the distance. It stepped into the center of the path and knelt down on one knee.

It was a child, a boy of about nine or ten, smartly dressed in a black waistcoat, the chain of a gold pocket watch hanging from his side. His face was long and thin, fixed with an expression of sly amusement, and yet there was something soft about his features. His face lacked any lines or creases; there was an indistinctness about him that was unsettling. I assumed it was just the light, but his skin had an orange pallor similar to the color of a peach. The boy rose from his bow and placed a finger before his lips, wordlessly silencing the children and me before leading us the rest of the way through the orchard.

The doors to the great house stood open much as before. Without the pressing anxiety that had accompanied my first visit I was better able to get a sense of the place. The entrance from the orchard was actually at the back of the house. The entryway sprawled out toward the massive oak doors at the front of the foyer, which were taller than half a dozen men standing head to toe, but the entrance was empty save for the grand staircase that spiraled away into the distance many floors above us, and the strange glittering tiles that covered the floor.

The tiles nearest to the walls were made of stone, and the band after that of rough marble, and then glazed ceramic. The tiles themselves were rather plain, but at the center of the display was a mosaic made from shards of metal and glass, the color of which shifted depending upon where one stood. As we walked over the various strata on the floor, the room changed. In the ring of stone the place was empty just as it had been before, but once we moved over the line of marble, the walls, which were tastefully paneled in wood, began to glow with an inner warmth revealing intricate etchings that seemed to tell a single story, the light burning through the designs, each panel a stained-glass window made from wood. The elegant crystal chandeliers that hung in empty space above the room began to bloom with liquid flame, light erupting out of them like stars to illuminate the corners of the space where gilded curios and antique end tables held glittering, unknowable things: strange pools of water that rippled in place but did not drip or cascade onto the floor; an iridescent apple with skin so glossy and sleek that the light it invited made it appear translucent; a portrait of a crying old woman whose tears smeared the paint; a pair of shears so sharp they seemed to cut the very light that touched their edges. But these baubles were nothing compared to the transformation that occurred at the center of the room in the mosaic. The floor was blazing with a radiant fire, pulsing in time to the silent song of the universe, throbbing with life and energy, searing not the eyes but something secret in the soul.

I gasped and the children paused in wonder, but our young guide kept moving us forward, and in the next band of tiles, the one made of glazed ceramic, the room dimmed. The liquid flame of the chandelier became drawn out and stretched away from where it hung in space, translated through the crystals so that the entryway became a living world of color that shimmered and danced like the northern lights. The inner warmth of the walls gave way to delicate, incandescent fractures in the wood, smoldering and cracking like dying embers. The curios and end tables held different objects in this version of the room: a small silver harp with lines of thin shadow instead of strings, theater masks that shuddered under the weight of the emotion in their expressions, a leathery flower that grew from a pot of diamonds, a trail of black ink in a water-filled glass vase that twisted itself into the shape of a face, staring pensively at us with a gaping mouth as we passed. The mosaic on the floor withdrew into itself, the vibrancy muted in a faint red sunset flecked with blue and gold that inspired a feeling of melancholy I was not unfamiliar with.

At last we crossed over the center of the room, and as we did the pieces of glass and metal in the mosaic flared with a pale, cool light that cast all else into shadow and reflected off every surface like a million distant stars. We were lost in our own private universe, a singular nocturne that would not end so long as we stayed in the circle at the center of the entryway. For a moment I felt at peace and marveled at the power of true silence, for all sound had been extinguished. But the boy pulled us onward, and we passed across the other half of the room, into dusk, into dawn, and back into the true emptiness of the place.

It was a strange house. As feeble a thought as this was, I could not find any others to adequately describe my opinion of the House of Darkling. The little silver cross that hung below my throat was even less comforting than before.

The boy in the black waistcoat continued to guide us through the manor without slowing down. I would have worried about getting lost in a house with so many twisting corridors, but as I was being strung along by two boys who currently had more in common with a pair of excited bloodhounds straining against their leashes than with the polite, refined young men I was striving to create, I remained unconcerned.

We were led down a tall, mirrored hallway with flickering gaslights, past oval windows covered in silver latticework and a collection of heavy oak doors. The door at the end stood open, a curved wall of coarse stone panels visible beyond the threshold. The boy took us inside.

"Children?" Lily Darrow rose from a plush green leather chair at the center of a magnificent library. The room was entirely round and four stories tall, with each subsequent ring of bookshelves smaller than the one beneath it, leading up to a domed glass ceiling, beyond which the moon hung ominously between the clouds. An ornamented footbridge led from the fourth level to a closed door. Lily opened her arms, and the boys were quick to enter her embrace. She squeezed James and kissed Paul on the forehead.

"You've come back to me . . . it's been so long." Her eyes trailed away and stared into space, until Paul put his hand on her shoulder.

"But, Mother, we were here just yesterday."

"Of course, yes. Time passes differently here. Days and years can become so confusing." She shook the thought away. "I see you've met Duncan?" She gestured to our young guide. Now that we were inside, I could clearly see that the discoloration of his skin was not simply a trick of light in the orchard. His complexion was indeed a soft shade of orange. The boy bowed out of the room and winked at us as he left. "He serves the master of the house. Good help is difficult to find, and so Mr. Whatley grows his own." I connected Duncan's appearance to the fruit in the orchard, and how it had wandered off during our previous visit.

"This Mr. Whatley grows *people?*"

"Duncan is not a person. Not yet, at least. Perhaps someday." She took a breath and smiled, seeming to become more like herself again. "We have much to do. I expect you'll be staying the night?" She glanced in my direction expectantly, and I pressed my lips together in a flat, expressionless smile.

"I'm afraid we didn't bring any other clothing," I replied.

"Of course you didn't. People would become suspicious."

"Just as they would if we didn't return home in a timely fashion."

"There's no need to worry. An entire day may pass for you here while a minute passes for everyone in Blackfield."

I suppose this was meant to alleviate my concern, but it only made me feel very sorry for Lily. If what she said were true, then our last visit must have taken place years ago. She seemed much the same as before—but then the dead could not be expected to age—regal, beautiful, but with a solemn undercurrent of fragility, as if the weight of her own virtues might cause her to collapse.

Paul and James looked in my direction and then back to their mother, sensitive to the subtle power struggle embedded in our exchange. I was again conscious of the silver cross hanging from my neck, completely useless against the decidedly unsupernatural force of Lily Darrow's verbal persuasion.

"Then I suppose it's not a problem."

"Splendid. Would you care for a tour?" It wasn't a question. She twirled on the spot and waved her arms at the shelves of books. "This is the library, naturally. Charlotte, you're more than welcome to use it whenever you'd like, but do be careful. The books here have a reputation for their cunning. Some readers enter for an evening's diversion and are never heard from again."

"Mmm." I could not stop myself from delivering a rather patronizing smile, but the other woman failed to notice.

"At the top of the library is Mr. Whatley's study. As I said, he is the master of the house, and always very busy. Do not disturb him unless you've been invited to do so. I expect you'll be meeting him soon enough." Lily looked away from us for a moment and seemed to flinch, but it was a quick movement, and I could not be sure that it wasn't caused by something mundane like a speck of dust caught in her eye. I nearly asked about Mr. Whatley and his connection to our hostess, but I held my tongue. That was a conversation that did not need to take place in front of the children, who looked up at their mother with rapt attention and an almost luminous affection. There was not a moment when one of them wasn't holding her hand or placing his forehead against her. I did not even toy with the idea of discouraging that sort of behavior. If my mother had suddenly returned from the dead, I would most likely do the same, so long as my mother still looked as graceful and alive as the former mistress of Everton.

Lily swept out of the library, the boys trailing behind her. I followed suit, and as I struggled to keep up with them, I was overcome by the suspicion that the day was going to feel much longer than it actually was. As we passed the large oval windows in the hallway, I took the opportunity to survey the estate. There were hills in the distance, speckled with thin, barren trees. A light mist roiled close to the ground, and far off a stark, short metal gate marked the edge of the estate.

We continued down the hallway and turned a corner at a marble sculpture of some amorphous, many-headed creature with knots of tentacles twisting out from both ends of a sleek, tubular body. I was glad when the boys passed it without really seeing it, as it was the sort of thing that would give James nightmares, if I didn't suffer from them first. I suddenly wished that I had brought some holy water from St. Michael's Church. Even if it were useless, it might have improved my appraisal of the situation I had allowed myself and the children to fall into.

Lily opened a set of large doors trimmed in gold leaf and took us inside a cavernous ballroom lined with rough stone pillars that could have been plucked from the bowels of the earth. The floor was a smooth black and white marble chessboard. The walls were gilded in silver and set with exotic glittering jewels of every imaginable color. Red velvet curtains clung to the sides of the windows.

"We don't entertain nearly as much as we'd like." Her voice echoed through the massive chamber. I estimated that Everton would fit comfortably within the ballroom twice over. "But we expect to hold a ball sometime in the near future. Have you learned to dance yet?" She lifted James into her arms and swung him through the air. He threw back his head and giggled with abandon.

Paul looked at her strangely. "Father hasn't held any parties."

His mother set James back down on the floor and seemed to notice that both boys were dressed all in black, still mourning the death that hadn't taken.

"Yes, of course. How callous of me."

"Can't we bring Father with us?"

She was quick to respond. "It's quite out of the question, and any mention of this place will close it off forever."

Paul stepped toward me, perhaps taken aback by the unpleasant reminder that mothers could be bossy.

"Don't worry, Mother," James said. "We can keep a secret. Paul brought a hedgehog into the house and kept it in the wardrobe for a whole week before Mrs. Norman found it and screamed like a girl, but I didn't tell a soul."

Lily patted her younger son on the head, visibly aware of the emotional divide that had appeared between her two children. "Thank you, James. Shall we continue?" She led us out of the ballroom and into a labyrinth of tight, narrow corridors, twisting and turning through the house, past the dining hall and the kitchens, the parlor, the greenhouse, the craft room, the baths, until the children were lagging as far behind as I was, perspiring and out of breath. When she realized she was twenty feet ahead of everyone else, Lily stopped and folded her hands with the graciousness of every great hostess. "As you can see, the house is rather large. Perhaps we should survey the grounds?"

I began to sigh, feeling the burn of exhaustion in my legs, but masked it with a carefully timed cough. Lily placed an embroidered silk handkerchief into my hand. "Are you all right?" she asked.

"Yes, thanks. It must be dusty," I answered, and when she looked personally affronted, "in my room at Everton. With my schedule I'm afraid I've let it become a bit untidy."

Lily pursed her lips and turned to face the wall behind us. Much like every other room in the house, it was paneled with wooden rectangles of various sizes. She pressed against one the size of a small door, and it swung away to reveal a stable with a gray open carriage. A silver horse was attached to the reins, its sleek body covered not in hair but in flower petals.

The boys both rushed over to the animal while I fingered the other wall panels in the hallway.

I pressed against a smaller one, and it clicked open to display a stuffed miniature satyr perched in a birdcage. "You're living in a cabinet of curiosities."

"But in a cabinet of curiosities, things stay in one place. The House of Darkling is always shifting to provide you with the things you want most." She said this without any inflection in her voice, her eyes drifting from me to her children. James patted the horse on its flank while Paul ran his fingers gently over the delicate petals that sprouted out of its skin.

"His name is Specter," Lily said softly.

The name was very appropriate. The animal was like something out of a dream, tall and ethereal, glowing like the perpetual moon that hung low in the sky above. Specter snorted and nodded at the carriage.

The seats were thickly padded and covered in a soft, smooth material that looked like leather but felt like velvet. James sat snugly against his mother, and across from them Paul, back to his sullen, gloomy self, sat as far away from me as he could manage. The carriage set off through the dark interior of the house, exiting beside the orchard.

As we rounded the side of Darkling, the fruit trees fell away and a large pond became visible in the distance. A lonely tree jutted out over the water. A rowboat drifted listlessly from a small, battered dock on the length of rope that tied it in place. The water at the center of the pond suddenly began to bulge with the release of air bubbles, but no one emerged from beneath the surface. I warmed myself against the chill night air, and despite himself Paul scooted closer to my end of the carriage.

The front of the great house was naturally more elaborate than the back. A circular driveway framed a fountain unlike anything I had ever seen before. Metal rods protruded out of a dark hole in the earth, all of them different heights, while pale blue swaths of liquid light bounced from one pole to another, cascading back into the black pit in a shower of electric sparks.

"That's the Star Fountain," Lily explained.

"It's beautiful. What is it made out of?" I asked.

"Stars, of course."

"Of course." I could not take my eyes off the fountain. It was like having the creation of the universe in the middle of one's yard. Just who was this Mr. Whatley?

Specter trotted diligently away from the house, leading us over dark green hills flecked with drops of dew. We passed a squat iron fence that ran the length of the property, barely tall enough to keep out small animals. Lily observed it with narrowed eyes as she addressed her sons. "Stay back from the fence, and under no circumstances are you to leave the property."

"Why not, Mother?"

"The neighbors don't care for humans."

A half mile away, the fence became a formidable, ornate gate twined with ivy. It was closed. A thick fog roiled ominously just beyond the property line. James pointed it out to his mother. "It's just like in the orchard. Does it go all the way back to Everton?"

"No." She did not elaborate any further, despite a lingering look of curiosity on her younger son's face. But Specter whinnied, and James forgot all about it. Paul did not. He looked toward me with a dark expression.

"Do you ever leave this place, Lily?" I asked as carefully as one might speak to a dangerous animal that was at an advantage by having very large, sharp teeth.

"No. The estate is safe because that is what Mr. Whatley wishes it to be. The place beyond the gates is not quite as predictable."

"And what place might that be?" I asked.

Before she could answer, Specter returned us to the front of the house. She looked as if she were about to reply, but then thought better of it and stepped down out of the carriage.

"I'm sure you must all be exhausted. Let me show you to your rooms." Lily entered the house and led us up the grand staircase, crossing over the rings of the floor tile, from sunrise to sunset, into the eastern wing of the mansion.

She took us into a room adorned in red and gold, with two beds set against separate alcove windows, two wardrobes, and a coffin-size toy chest. "Boys, you'll be sleeping here."

James jumped onto one of the beds, claiming it as his own.

Paul walked over to one of the windows and peered outside. "Does the sun ever come up here?"

Lily shut the drapes and turned Paul to the bed. "There's nothing more beautiful than the night sky."

The boys undressed, and I hung their clothes in the wardrobes for when we would return home. *Whenever that might be,* I thought cynically.

Lily handed the boys fresh sets of pajamas. "I picked these out myself."

James pulled his over his head immediately, but Paul stared at the clothing with suspicion. "From where?" he asked.

Lily wore a bewildered expression. "A catalog. You've grown very curious in the past year."

"I've grown up a lot in the past year."

His mother smiled weakly and kissed him on the forehead. "Would you like a bedtime story?"

However much Paul had grown up, it was not enough for him to reject being read a bedtime story curled next to his mother. He jumped into bed next to his younger brother and waited for Lily to join them. I immediately felt out of place, but was not sure why. It could not have been that I was jealous. Why should I have been? I wanted the boys to be closer to their mother. That was why I had gone against my better judgment and taken them back to the House of Darkling. That was the point. But suddenly I felt as if I were intruding upon something very private and intimate. I rose to leave the room, but Lily asked me to stay. She ran her fingers through James's hair and did not look up. I sat on the bed opposite the Darrows and waited for her to begin. She reached across the nightstand and grabbed hold of a knob set into the wall. An alcove swung open, and from it she extracted a book entitled *Laurel Parker Wolfe's Tales of The Ending*. She began to read:

The Sleeping King

Once upon a time, there was a castle in the sky and nothing else. From every turret and tower, only darkness could be seen. This suited the king quite well, for while his kingdom consisted of only the castle and the void, he had very few responsibilities. He was very old and tired, being immortal and having been king since before the beginning of Everything, and he had little to do but sleep in his chambers. But this was often easier said than done, for the king had five young sons, who took great pleasure in having noisy brawls in the stairwells.

One day, after the king had been stirred from an especially good dream, he banished the five princes from the castle and forced them out into the void. The princes found this to be a most unfortunate fate, for there was nothing but blackness and oblivion, and it was certainly very dull. For a long time they amused themselves with more fights and brawls, but after an aeon or two they grew tired of even this diversion and stood around in the dark looking for something to do.

The oldest of the princes was eager to return to the castle, for there were comfortable beds and large banquets every evening. He tried to enter, but the doors were firmly shut against him, and the servants had been given strict instructions from the king not to allow the princes back inside.

"We must find a way to appease Father," he said, and after he and his brothers had thought long and hard, they decided that the best way to win favor with the king was to flatter him with achievements and gifts. The oldest prince, having come up with the idea, was the first to attempt to win his father's forgiveness.

"I shall light the void for him, so that he might see his kingdom." With that, he began to cry, and every place his tears fell a star was born. He plucked out his eyes and threw them as far as he could, leaving behind a trail of glittering galaxies. When he was finished, he had his brothers place him beneath his father's tower, for he could no longer see, and he called out to the king. "Father, see what I have done for you!"

The old king, who had enjoyed an unbroken sleep much longer than he was used to, came to the balcony and was blinded by the unusual brightness.

"Bah! Now there is work to be done! Someone must keep the stars in the sky, and take them away when they burn out! Go, my son, and tend to your creation."

The oldest prince was most dismayed, but did as he was told and left to lord over the stars.

The second oldest prince, being much less intelligent than his older brother, learned nothing from this exchange. As soon as his father went back to sleep, he declared his own ambition to win his father's approval. "I shall make a ground, so that he may travel his kingdom and have something to do besides sleep!"

With that, he tore the bones from his body and ground them to dust, scattering them across the void and creating land. When he was finished, he had his brothers place him beneath his father's tower, for he could no longer walk, and he called out to the king. "Father, see what I have done for you!"

The old king, who had only just managed to get back to sleep, was unpleasantly reminded of how life had been when his sons were allowed to live in the castle, and was hardly in the mood to be impressed. He came to the balcony and was shocked by the vastness of his kingdom.

"Bah! Now there is work to be done! Someone must scout the land and find out where it ends! Go, my son, and tend to your creation."

The second oldest prince was most dismayed, but did as he was told and crawled across the land.

The middle brother was a very arrogant creature and, having lived in the shadow of his older brothers for so many years, was eager to succeed where they had failed. As soon as his father went back to sleep, he began preparations for his own creation.

"I shall make a sea, so that the crashing of the waves might soothe him as he sleeps." With that, he took a knife and cut deep into his breast. The blood from his body pooled over a portion of the land, until the castle stood on the shore of an immense ocean. When he was finished, he had his brothers place him beneath his father's tower, for he was very weak, and he called out to the king. "Father, see what I have done for you!"

The old king, who was now growing rather irritable at having been awoken so many times, stomped onto the balcony and was shocked by the appearance of the sea.

"Bah! Now there is work to be done, for the closeness of the water will only bring storms and flooding! Someone must sail the seas and warn us of bad weather! Go, my son, and tend to your creation."

The middle prince was most dismayed, but did as he was told and traveled across the ocean.

The second youngest brother was more cunning than all the rest, and while his brothers had failed, he had devised a scheme that would not only please his father but also improve his station in life. As soon as the king went back to sleep, he began to set his plan in motion.

"I shall give him subjects, so that they might worship him." The prince said this with a sly smile, and created the first subjects from his own flesh, until there was nothing left of him but tendon and bone. When he was finished, he had his brother place him beneath his father's tower, for he was but a skeleton, and he called out to the king. "Father, see what I have done for you!"

The old king was growing angry. He threw himself onto the balcony and was shocked to find that he now had actual subjects to govern.

"Bah! Now there is work to be done!" he exclaimed. But before he could continue, the second youngest son interrupted his father.

"Yes, but I am happy to do it, Father! I will govern your subjects while you sleep!"

The king said nothing for a moment, and then his face

twisted into an expression of bemused spite. "Ah, but as I am the king, there is no need for you to concern yourself with governance! Although someone will need to look after my subjects. They are ephemeral things, and even now they are dying. Go, my son, and tend to your creation."

The second youngest prince gaped for a moment, and then smiled. "A Lord of the Dead is a king of all things, and the realm has room for but one ruler. I shall return when the dying is done, and on that day my father may find himself unable to ever sleep again." With that, he left to walk among the subjects of the kingdom as Death.

This left the youngest prince outside the castle, but no longer in emptiness. He was surrounded by land, sea, stars, and the specter of Death, each of which represented the failure of one of his brothers. Being the cleverest of the king's sons, he had learned from their mistakes. He had watched his brothers try and fail to win their father's approval even though none of them had attempted to consider the old king himself. The youngest did not wait for his father to return to his room. As soon as the king had sent away the second youngest prince, he called out to the king from beneath the balcony.

"Father, I will not offer you the baubles and trifles of my brothers, but the thing you want most."

This caught the king's attention, and his temper abated. "And what would that be, my son?"

"Sleep."

The youngest prince ripped his heart from his chest and opened it. The spark within became the moon in the sky, and the land darkened with moonlight and shadows. Instead of the dusty lands and the sprawling sea that had formerly surrounded the castle, there was now a black-green hill overlooking an empty moor. The subjects of the kingdom were nowhere to be found. The young prince went back to his place beneath the balcony.

The king was much impressed, but did not fully understand what had happened. "What have you done?"

"I have given you a place to end, my father. Sleep here, for while we are immortal and may never die, you will now know peace until Everything has run its course."

The king said nothing, and the youngest prince was unsure whether he had done something very wise or very foolish, but then his father began to cry. He left his balcony and threw open the doors to the castle. The king embraced his son for a long while, and when he was finished he set the young prince upon his throne. There were banquets and celebrations. The newly created subjects of the kingdom were invited, and the other princes even returned home for a brief while to begrudgingly join in the festivities. But when it was over, the old king returned to his chamber and went to sleep for the rest of eternity. The young prince governed in his stead and remains in his castle at The Ending of All Things, beloved by his people as the wisest and most generous creature in the land.

The boys were already fast asleep by the time Lily finished the story and set the book back on the nightstand. She kissed them both on the cheek and disentangled herself from between the children.

"Sleep well, my darlings."

She turned and left the room. I observed the boys one last time and followed her into my own quarters for the evening, which were decorated in muted blues and deep purples. A single four-poster bed sat at the center of the room, adrift in a sea of azure floor coverings.

"That was quite a story," I said.

"And somewhat strange, even for creation myths. But I thought it prudent to share as you'll be spending more time here. The people of this place have a different view of life and death."

"I'm afraid I'm unclear as to which they prefer."

"A perceptive observation. It would most certainly depend upon whom you ask." Lily lingered silently for a moment before going back to the doorway. "Breakfast is at nine."

"How can you tell when it's morning?"

"You can't. I—" She stopped herself. "I'll fetch you and the children when it's time."

Lily Darrow left and closed the door behind her, leaving me alone to wonder why someone who purported to be the lady of the house was showing her guests to their rooms.

CHAPTER 8

Interrupted Moonlight

I dressed for bed, but couldn't sleep. The House of Darkling was flush with ambient noises: creaking floorboards, raspy breathing from down the hall, a scuttling sound just beyond the door to my room. These, combined with the occasional smell of ammonia, were enough to keep anyone awake. I wondered if the children were having any trouble sleeping. At least they had each other.

The wall opposite my bed was made up of wardrobes from different eras, all of them carpentered together into an oversized curiosity chest with half-moon handles on each of the little doors. I opened them one by one and explored the many novelties of Mr. Whatley's collection. There was a hand mirror that sapped what light there was from my room and used it to illuminate the world beheld in the reflection, a glass eye that rolled in one continuous figure eight, something mysterious in a velvet purse that pulsed like a human heart, a pedestal of crystal phials glittering with liquid light, and a wax dollhouse in a constant state of melting as its tiny wax occupants were crowned in flames instead of hair. I paused at this last compartment and they seemed to notice that I was staring at them, for the largest one, whom I assumed to be the patriarch of the house, leapt down from the opened alcove and onto the floor. Four other candle people followed, and they marched in a single-file line to the door of my room, waiting patiently for me to open it.

I wondered at Lily's comment about the house knowing what its inhabitants wanted most, for I found that the natural urges of the body required me to turn away from the dollhouse and leave my room in search of a lavatory. If there was one thing I had not wanted to do, it was to traipse through the house at night (whenever that might be) without Lily Darrow at my side. She had assured us that it was safe, but the strange noises emanating from every nook and shadow told a different tale altogether. There was an elaborate beauty about the place, but it was so bombastic that I could not shake the suspicion that it hid something more sinister. Lily was not being entirely forthcoming about how she had found her way here, to say nothing of the enigmatic Mr. Whatley, who had yet to introduce himself. I made up my mind to take the children back to Everton as soon as they'd had breakfast, but for the immediate future, I had to find the lavatory. I pulled on a housecoat from the wardrobe and opened the door.

The wax men stuck their flaming heads around the lip of the door and looked in both directions before jumping out into the corridor. They waved me onward. The hallways were empty but filled with the same noises that had disturbed my sleep. Trailing behind in the shadows of my new acquaintances, I went from one door to another, attempting to recall which of them led into the lavatory. The first one I tried opened into what appeared to be a small earthen burrow, the kind dug out by rabbits and voles. But this room was nearly as large as my own, and I crossed myself, thankful that it had been unoccupied. The next door was the correct one, and when I was finished I found myself to be quite awake.

Normally in such a situation I would read until I fell asleep, but as it was I had not thought to bring along a book. I remembered the large, impressive library at the other end of the mansion. Surely I could find my way there without any trouble? While it was true that the house was eerie and strange, it had so far only proved itself to be odd, rather than dangerous. Besides, what better way to uncover the true nature of the place than to explore it alone? I would simply collect a volume or two from the library and return to my room.

"Could you please take me to the library?" I whispered to the lead candle man. He nodded briskly and took off down the grand staircase.

I could not ignore the number of small sounds that seemed to come from all corners of the house. Dripping water, something heavy dragging along uneven floorboards, the clanking of dishware; none of them were very loud, but taken altogether they sounded as if there were a great deal of activity occurring just beyond whatever closed door I happened to stand next to. The sounds followed me down the hallway with the large oval windows looking out over the estate. The metal gate at the entrance was barely visible in the mist, but still closed. I pushed open the doors at the end of the corridor and entered the library. The wax men stayed behind in the hallway, obviously sensitive to the realities of vast quantities of paper.

I wasn't exactly sure what I was looking for. The book titles I had examined in the parlor weren't even in English, but then I supposed that if Lily could read them, then so could I. The first circle of the library was by far the largest, and I started there. Each of the shelves was labeled with a small silver plaque, some of them with familiar subjects, like agriculture, astrology, and astronomy, and others with more abstract areas of interest, such as death, demagogy, and demonology. I stopped at one of the larger sections in the Es, labeled "Every Place There Is," which I interpreted as Travel, and took away a book entitled *Balthazar.*

I opened the front cover, looking for some sort of description, but found only lines of elaborate calligraphy in a language I could not understand. But that did not seem to matter. The library disappeared completely, and I found myself on a low sea cliff overlooking a smooth, sandy beach, book still in hand. I nearly stumbled over the precipice in shock and wonderment, but quickly caught myself. Lily had warned me about the cunning nature of Darkling's literature. As I regained my composure, I turned around and saw a magnificent scarlet-colored castle, or perhaps a fortress, clinging to the edge of the rock. Women paraded along the walkways with pastel parasols, while the men wore expensive-looking suits and black top hats. There was a breeze coming in from the ocean, and the calls of seagulls overhead. I closed the book, and the scene at the beach disappeared with it. I turned around to observe the library, but it was the same as it had been the moment before. I placed the book under my arm, careful not to open it, and removed another book from the shelf, this one entitled *India.* The candle men were still waiting for me when I returned to the hallway.

"Back to my room, please," I said. They took me through the House of Darkling a different way than we had come, into an indoor forest with branches made of bone, past a bar whose walls were built out of packing crates, and into a room so dark I began to feel claustrophobic, staying close enough to my guides that I nearly stepped on them when they came to a sudden halt. They huddled together and extinguished themselves, leaving me alone and anxious in the chamber until another light appeared before us.

A candelabra lit with quivering flames hovered in the emptiness, revealing nothing until it crept closer and a small hand appeared wrapped around its brass base, followed by the mischievous face of the boy, Duncan. For a moment I was sure that he had seen me, but he continued forward without a word. A stranger followed behind him. Even in the gloom I could tell that it was a large man, and he held a hat in front of his chest.

I followed them. The candle men grabbed hold of my robe in an effort to stop me, but I shook them off. If I was going to protect the children, then there were secrets here that I had to learn.

Duncan strode slowly through the house and paused before a marble bas-relief sculpture set into the wall, which depicted a litany of faces (human and otherwise) agape in agony.

"Oh yes, please. Please . . ." said the man with a hint of desperation. His eyes were small and watery, set too deeply in a fat, chinless face, with a wattle that trembled as his body shook with excitement. Duncan's expression of bemusement never changed as he pressed a finger into the eye socket of one of the smaller characters from the sculpture, pushing it back until it clicked into place. The wall swung open slowly, heavy with the weight of the marble, and the boy stepped aside. He looked back in my direction and brought a finger to his lips before joining the stranger in the secret room, leaving the door open for me to follow. I accepted this rather blatant invitation and trailed behind them.

I entered a circular chamber enveloped in concentric rings of billowing silk veils. They turned slowly in place, so that instead of walls there were only spinning layers of gauzy partitions, with gaps at random intervals in the fabric. To move from one ring to the next I had to step quickly through the openings until I stood just beyond the center of the room, where Duncan was strapping the large man into a metal chair. A wheeled table stood beside them, and on it a silver tray that held a smoky-colored phial with a white label I could not make out, a syringe, a set of forceps, and what looked to be a single lump of sugar.

"Yes, yes . . . I've been waiting so long." The man closed his eyes. Tears streamed down his corpulent cheeks as he relaxed into the chair, and the boy removed the stopper from the phial to extract the contents with the syringe. He injected a black liquid into the center of the sugar cube and set the needle aside, using the forceps to place the modified confection into the open, eager mouth of the stranger.

The man bit down with a crunch and immediately strained against the chair's straps as his entire body began to convulse. Duncan ignored this and tidied up the tray, sealing the phial and capping the syringe before glancing once again in my direction with a sly, knowing look. The man in the chair had stopped moving. The boy initiated the process of releasing him as I backed out of the room to find the candle men still waiting for me, their flames reignited and beckoning me from the darkness.

I could not be sure of what I had just seen, but it was most certainly sordid and secretive. Why Duncan had allowed me to witness such a thing was even more vexing than the fact that such a room existed within the confines of Darkling. I was being toyed with, and I was not pleased.

We soon reached the wing where the children and I were to spend the night. Moonlight streamed through the window at the end of the corridor. I had opened the door to my room when a shadow passed over the wall. The flames of the wax men sputtered out, and they ran back to their alcove.

I spun around, but there was nothing behind me. It happened again, and this time I noticed something moving beyond the window, interrupting the moonlight. Curiosity got the better of my fear, and I padded quietly to the end of the hallway to investigate.

Below the window was the pond, and an elderly man whom I could only assume to be the groundskeeper was shoveling wet, viscous slabs of something that looked like meat from a wheelbarrow into the pond. For a moment nothing happened. The meat plunked into the water and sank immediately. But then something bubbled and bulged beneath the water as it had during our tour of the estate, and a tentacle emerged like a headless snake, and then another, and another, until a half dozen of them swayed in the water, twisting and curling, finally snapping at the hunks of meat already in the pond. The old man wiped his brow with his shirtsleeve and continued emptying the contents of his wheelbarrow. The limbs of the creature submerged in the depths of the water shuddered hungrily.

I backed away from the window, my heart beating against the silver cross I still wore. I did not scream. I did not swoon. But I felt with complete certainty that I had to get the children out of the house as soon as possible.

"Don't be frightened." A voice came from behind me. I whipped around.

Lily Darrow stood at the other end of the hallway, staring at me with calm reserve.

"How could you invite your children to such a terrible place?"

"I'll admit that it is strange, but terrible . . . no."

"The thing in the pond—"

"Was eating." She approached the window and looked out over the estate. "Just because it does not look or behave as we do is not enough to make it evil. It would never harm you or the children." The shadows of the tentacles in the pond passed over us, and she observed the books under my arm. "I see that you've been to the library."

"Among other places," I said with a small measure of disdain, but I would not reveal to her what I had seen. Perhaps Lily herself was unaware of the kind of business that this Mr. Whatley trafficked in. "I couldn't sleep."

"Neither could I. I've been worried about the children."

"As have I."

"I would never let anything happen to them, you must realize that."

"And how would you protect them from things I can scarcely find the words to describe?" I gestured to the window.

"I cannot, but the master of this house is perfectly suited to do so."

"I find myself growing exceedingly suspicious over the arrangement you've made with this Mr. Whatley, who, I might point out, has yet to introduce himself."

"He's a very busy man. But he'll be at breakfast tomorrow. When you meet him, you'll understand why I agreed to stay. Please, if you still don't trust me after tomorrow morning, you can take the children and never bring them back." She gently touched my arm and looked into my eyes. She was a cipher of a woman, an odd amalgamation of strength and fragility, and I hoped that would be enough to keep whatever lived in the House of Darkling at bay.

"Then why do you worry?"

"They've grown." She softened a little, and I could not keep myself from doing the same.

"Children have a tendency to do that when you're not looking."

"So much time has passed. Perhaps I should have let them go. I've been terribly selfish."

"Nonsense." I put my hand over hers and smiled in sadness. "Any chance for them to know you is too important to ignore. I wish I had known my mother a little better, before she died."

We stood facing one another in silence, the other woman's head tilted to one side, as if she were deciding something. Then she embraced me softly.

"Until tomorrow."

She turned and left the hallway. I realized that I had no idea where she slept, and I wondered again what she had been doing up while the rest of us were in bed.

The noises in the house never subsided, but I was able to escape them with the help of the books from the library. The lines of strange calligraphy in the volumes translated themselves into the sights and smells of India. I wandered through the streets of Lucknow and Bombay, traveled through the courtyards of the Taj Mahal dressed in nothing more than my nightgown, a barefooted ghost unobserved by all. Each page took me to another part of the country, and I explored each of them until my legs were ready to give out from under me. I closed the book and returned to my room at the House of Darkling, where I immediately dropped onto the bed and fell into a deep sleep.

I dreamt that my mother walked along a windswept moor in nothing but a nightgown identical to the one that I wore, still dead but walking all the same. I tried to convince her to come back inside, to a house in the distance, but she told me to let her be. The wind continued tearing at her, stripping off her clothes, her hair, and then her flesh as I looked on in horror, helplessly grasping at her against the storm, crying out as she literally ran through my fingers.

I was already dressed when there was a sharp knock at the door to my room.

"Yes?"

A maid entered. She was young, with the same sallow, peach-colored complexion as Duncan. She motioned for me to join her in the hallway. I checked on the boys, but their room was empty. My chest tightened. I swept down the grand staircase, across the segmented foyer of the entryway, lights flashing and dimming with each step, and found the dining hall at the other end of the house.

When I entered I felt as if I had stumbled upon some medieval banquet. The massive table was laid out with slabs of meat still on the bone, platters of sliced fruit, tureens filled with egg and cheese, urns of coffee and tea, great heaps of fish, and a number of other delicacies that I could scarcely identify.

James and Paul were seated next to one another, across from their mother. A pale teenage girl with sleek blond hair sat next to Lily. The heads of the table were occupied by two gentlemen. The first I recognized as the large man from the night before, seemingly recovered from the previous evening's indulgences as he dined on a tray of sausage and ham. The second I could only assume to be the oft-mentioned Mr. Whatley. The two men stood from their chairs.

"Charlotte, so good of you to join us," said Lily. "May I introduce you to Mr. Samson"—the heavyset gentleman bowed his head, still chewing—"and of course, Mr. Whatley."

I nodded congenially. Mr. Whatley was imposing, not in

terms of weight or girth, but in proportion, not quite a giant, but oversized compared to what one would think of as normal. His substantial hands picked up a napkin from the table and dabbed it at the corners of his mouth, his thin lips framed by a rugged face, the kind that is never completely clean-shaven. He had a windswept look about him, his hair wild and disheveled, his clothing very fine but rumpled, his shirt not entirely tucked in, his collar askew, yet the most interesting thing about him was his eyes—so dark that no light escaped them, giving off no reflection. They were unreadable, and as we looked at one another from across the table I felt a swell of apprehension. He was not a man to trifle with.

"Welcome, Mrs. Markham." His voice was deep and commanded the same power as his eyes, yet there was a swagger to it, as if he couldn't be bothered to take anything seriously. "Please. Sit."

It sounded less like an invitation and more like a command, and so I hovered for a moment just to see what he would do. Whatley had gone back to his breakfast, and when he noticed that I had not complied with his request, he leaned forward and spoke to me again.

"So good of you to bring the children." He gestured with his hand at the chair Lily had offered me.

"Children need their mothers, little boys most of all," I said. I nodded imperceptibly to Mrs. Darrow and took my seat next to James and Paul. I did not wish to come off as impertinent or as a troublemaker, at least not just then. I wanted to test him, and so I had. He seemed patient, the sort of predator that prefers to lie in wait.

"Alas, there is not a strong maternal feeling among the people of The Ending, Mrs. Markham," said Mr. Samson between bites.

"Then I am sorry for you." I placed my napkin on my lap and began to serve myself.

Mr. Whatley smirked at me, his thin lips pulled to the left corner of his mouth. "Are you now?"

"Yes. There is nothing like a mother's love. One must value it while one can." I nodded to the boys and to Lily.

"So long as it benefits the child?" said Mr. Whatley in a more serious tone.

"Naturally."

"Then it's for the best that most of ours depart. Some mothers have a hunger for their children that can't be satisfied by love." He said this with relish, his face an expression of mock sympathy in everything but his eyes, which observed me without emotion like a reptile's. "It's not without precedent, even in the world of the living."

Samson cleared his throat and brought a napkin to his lips. "Come now, my friend. Must you use that phrase? 'World of the living,' indeed. We are just as alive, are we not?"

"Perhaps even more so, as we do not die. But then again, most of us do not exactly live, either."

The large man chortled at this. "Conserve some of that wit, Whatley, for when I finally convince you to join us."

"Please, sir. No politics at the table." The pale, blond girl seated next to Mr. Whatley spoke up with refined enthusiasm. She was severely beautiful in a cold sort of way, with arched eyebrows and an upturned nose. Her eyes were so pale that they were colorless, and they shone with enough light to compensate for the dark opacity of the man who sat to her right.

"You have my apologies, my dear."

"Quite all right, Mr. Samson. My father hardly needs the encouragement; he can be ever so boorish as it is. I've tried to train him the best I can, but he's simply hopeless."

"I prefer impertinent," said Mr. Whatley.

"It's all the same to me. It will never do at all if you hope to marry me off."

"Perhaps I don't want you to marry, Olivia."

"Of course you do, Father. Don't patronize me. I simply detest being patronized. You want me married as much as I do or you would never have procured a governess, let alone a human governess." She looked at Mrs. Darrow and smiled gratefully before patting her hand. "Father demands the best for me."

"The best?" I asked. It felt a strange sort of thing to say, using mankind as an indicator of quality, like the mink in a fur coat, or a particular kind of tea.

"Humans are the height of fashion."

"For now," said Mr. Whatley dismissively.

"Whatever for?" I asked. I was most confused.

Mr. Samson folded his hands together and placed them beneath his lack of chin. "We are immortal things, Mrs. Markham, and there is nothing duller than eternity. To pretend for a time that we know what it is like to be mortal is a mercy, however short-lived it might be."

"One must stay current with the trends of society." Olivia sipped on her tea, pinkie extended.

Mr. Whatley leaned back in his chair with lazy pompousness. "On the contrary, I could do without society altogether. It's such a tiresome thing."

"All I require of you is that you're mildly agreeable until after my coming-out ball," said the girl to her father.

"I have already agreed to your terms, my love. Am I not wearing this silly thing?" He plucked at the skin of his face so that it stretched and snapped back into place like a rubber mask. Paul jumped in his chair, while James cackled maniacally at the display. For myself I pushed my plate away, having thoroughly lost my appetite.

"You wear it, but not well," Olivia went on.

"Then you must be more specific the next time you make a bargain. One must be careful with what one agrees to."

"A valuable lesson," said Mr. Samson as he stood from the table.

"Leaving us so soon?" asked Mr. Whatley.

"I'm afraid I must be on my way. Thank you again for your hospitality. You shall not forget what we discussed?"

"I shall consider it, nothing more."

"That will be acceptable. Good day to you all." The large man departed the dining room, leaving a lull in the conversation that I was eager to break.

"I'm afraid the children and I must shortly return to Everton. Their father will soon begin to worry."

Mr. Whatley leaned over the table and sipped at his tea. "Mr. Darrow, you say? What is he like? Lily has been rather cryptic."

Mrs. Darrow jumped in immediately with a flash of an innocuous, sociable expression. "Mr. Whatley, why don't you show them the main collection after breakfast? It is ever so interesting."

"Splendid idea!" If he noticed Lily's obvious intrusion into the conversation at the mention of her husband, he pretended not to, although his eyes remained darkly mysterious.

"What do you collect, exactly?" I asked out of politeness more than curiosity, and in an effort to divert attention from the apparently uncomfortable topic of Mr. Darrow.

"It's better to show than to tell." Mr. Whatley winked at me without any regard to propriety, and I looked down at my plate as I blushed, completely unprepared to deal with such a person. I had expected some cold, hard miser, the sort who would flourish in an eternal night like the one present at the House of Darkling, stifling all beauty and withering all life. But Mr. Whatley was strangely playful and in control of a quiet power that, when taken with his disheveled appearance, was quite striking and a contrast to the beautiful melancholy of the master of Everton.

When everyone else was finished eating, Mr. Whatley stood from the table. "Well then, by now you must have seen some of the eccentricities of the house?" He didn't wait for a response. "A cabinet of curiosities is enough for some. A small wardrobe with antiquities and keepsakes from the places one has been. But a true collector lives and breathes his collection." He began to leave the dining hall, continuing to talk as he went and expecting us to follow close behind, which we did. At the end of one hallway, beneath a portrait of an austere-looking woman with tentacles instead of hands, he pointed out a stone dais that held a statue of a man, the shadow of which passed over a circle of markings with various labels, like CHILDHOOD, YOUTH, and MIDDLE AGE. In another room there was a spinning wheel that spun water, and a vase that, when held and turned clockwise, changed its pattern so that it was always different.

"The House of Darkling is my life's work, full of oddities and marvels, some of them trinkets and some of them more . . . useful." He led us into the library and up the spiral staircase. When we reached the top level of the library, he went across the bridge and, after turning back to us with a dramatic pause, opened the door to his collection.

"This way, if you please."

The room was like a mausoleum, starkly furnished in ivory, opal, and alabaster, with a tall ceiling that opened up into a glass dome identical to the one found in the library. The natural light of the evening sky was enough to illuminate the gargantuan room, which extended along the entire length of the house, branching off every now and then into corridors with similar items on display, galleries within galleries, like chapels in a cathedral.

"A collector is only as good as his collection, they say. This place holds all of my more valuable items. These are my Emotions." Mr. Whatley pointed to the first section. Both sides of the hallway were lined with alabaster statues lit from behind in small pools of light. They were ancient things, reminiscent of the golden ages of Greece or Rome, naked, handsome figures, over four dozen of them, each one in a different pose. I approached one labeled *Envy*. The statue was of a man, his arms folded and his eyes looking sideways at something with an expression of distaste. As I looked at it I began to feel very insignificant. Mr. Whatley had certainly accomplished quite a lot if he had the luxury to work on such an expansive personal compilation of relics and antiquities, whereas what had I done but lose every person I had ever loved? I folded my arms and began to watch Mr. Whatley from the corner of my eye, before Lily pulled me away from the statue. The sensation left me as quickly as it came, and I was myself again.

"It's best not to get too close to some of them," she said.

We continued down the corridor, and I kept an eye on the boys so they did not linger too long before any of the statues, especially the ones like *Lust* that were too obscene to warrant a description. Beyond the display of emotions were landscapes painted on panes of glass. They seemed to provide their own illumination, pulsing faintly in the gloom.

"These are perhaps some of my favorite pieces," said Mr. Whatley.

"What are they?" Paul spoke up as he peered at a painting of a sprawling metropolis.

"Places. Or doorways to places."

Paul reached out to touch the glass picture of the landscape, but Mr. Whatley grabbed his hand away with gentle control. "They're not to be touched, unless you wish to become stranded there without any hope of returning. Besides that, they're incredibly fragile and easily ruined. If you find one that piques your interest, simply ask and I can create a doorway in the orchard, like the one to Everton."

"Are you familiar with Everton, Mr. Whatley?" I asked.

"Only from Lily's stories. I have not yet had the pleasure. Perhaps someday soon you would be good enough to give me a guided tour?"

I was so taken aback by this that all I could do was nod tersely in agreement.

Olivia gave a dramatic sigh. "Father, must you show them everything? My lesson with Mrs. Darrow was supposed to begin twenty minutes ago."

"Whatever love wants. There will be plenty of time to see the rest, and there is still much more to see." He led everyone out of his collection and locked the door behind us. As we went down the staircase to the bottom of the library, Lily pulled me aside and spoke to me as we walked.

"Duncan can escort you back through the orchard, but I hope you'll be able to visit us again soon? Perhaps the day after next?" There it was, laid bare before us—the moment of truth. Would we return? Darkling was certainly a very interesting place, and the Whatleys were odd but not obviously threatening. This did not release them from my suspicions, but I softened toward them. Mr. Whatley appeared to be a man of knowledge, and there was much that could be learned at the House of Darkling, things that would prove impossible at Everton. This alone was worth exploring, and considering it in conjunction with Lily's desire to continue her relationship with her children, I saw little reason to decline the invitation. I could not ignore what I had seen of the creature in the pond, or Mr. Samson's interlude with Duncan, but if there was one thing I had learned as a girl in India it was not to presume to understand a thing before one had all the requisite facts.

"I suppose we could."

"Excellent. I'm planning a surprise for the boys."

"There's no need to go to any trouble. Having their mother back from the dead is more than enough excitement for one week."

Lily lowered her voice and slowed our pace to put some distance between our conversation and the others. "As you can see, my position here is a professional one, just as yours is at Everton."

I gulped down a knot of guilt that rose in my throat, remembering the way I felt when seated next to Mr. Darrow in the music room, alone in the middle of the night . . .

"Can I count on you to return?"

"I said I would return with the children and I meant it. I don't entirely trust this place, but I understand that you do. For now, that's enough."

"Good." She squeezed my wrist. At the bottom of the library we bade the Whatleys good-bye. Olivia went to prepare for her lesson, and Mr. Whatley, after taking my hand into his own large fingers and kissing it, nodded to Lily and began wandering aimlessly through the house, stopping every so often to admire the pieces of his collection that decorated each interior. Lily escorted us across the foyer of the entryway, a kaleidoscope of rooms within rooms, to the back entrance into the orchard, where Duncan was waiting for us. She kissed the children goodbye and watched from the steps of the great house as we disappeared through the trees.

CHAPTER 9
Bazaar and Bizarre

I had never been to a village bazaar before the one in Blackfield. Mrs. Mulbus spent the whole week leading up to it baking mincemeat pies, spice cakes, and chocolate biscuits, too busy to even bother shouting at Jenny, who sulked from the lack of attention and loudly broke a number of dishes with more than a little dramatic flair, all the while looking over her shoulder at her tormentor with something like desperation in her eyes. When she could be bothered, Mrs. Mulbus would tut quietly to herself, and Jenny would happily scowl back at her with affectionate venom.

When I passed by Mrs. Mulbus's table with the boys and Mr. Darrow, she snuck some biscuits into the hands of the children, thinking I hadn't noticed. I was too struck by the normality of it to say anything. Following the discovery of Darkling, it seemed a long while since I had been plagued by something as simple as the children spoiling their appetites. The boys ran ahead of us and crammed the biscuits into their mouths, gulping down crumbs and wiping the bits of chocolate from their faces onto their gloves, as pleased with their own cunning as they were with their secret snack.

Autumn was ending. There was very little green left in all of Blackfield. The surrounding forests shook in the breeze like dying embers, brilliant patches of gold and red erupting from the trees as showers of sparks into the ashen sky. James kicked through the piles of parchment-colored leaves that littered the grounds of St. Michael's Church. Mr. Scott walked arm in arm with Cornelia Reese, who was not only the richest woman in the village but also the catalyst for the bazaar itself. Having come from the city, she made no effort to hide her displeasure with the quaint nature of our little church, and she told anyone who would listen—Mr. Scott most of all—how she intended to see to it that St. Michael's be cultivated into a proper place of worship befitting the level of patronage she could offer. And so, every Sunday for the past few months, poor Mr. Scott had reminded everyone who could hear him over the din of birdsong wafting down from the rafters to do their part. The turnout at the bazaar spoke very highly of his place in the esteem of the villagers, for although many people could not stand to see Cornelia Reese succeed, it was apparent that this sentiment had been overcome by those who wished to see the vicar prosper.

There were other tables from Everton in addition to the cook's. Ellen and some of the other maids had a display of handmade dolls with simple button eyes but exquisitely detailed dresses. Mrs. Norman sat enclosed in a small tent, looking haughty and mysterious in a cloth turban that was woefully inaccurate if she intended to conjure the image of an Indian swami. Some of the villagers, Cornelia Reese in particular, seemed mortified by the idea of having a fortune-teller on the grounds of the church. They glared at Mrs. Norman as they passed by her booth, some of them more than once to make their opinions known, and all of them crossed themselves with exaggerated devotion. If Mrs. Norman noticed, she neglected to give them the benefit of a reaction, for hers was the busiest of all the tables, and by the end of the day no one had contributed more to the proliferation of St. Michael's Church than the housekeeper from Everton.

The bazaar was a boisterous affair, despite the occasional social posturing. Mr. Watersalt, the carpenter, had built a small puppet theater next to Ellen's table and was demonstrating the usefulness of her handmade dolls with a bit of theatrical flair and a vast assortment of tiny, high-pitched dolls' voices. Mildred Wallace, who was usually too concerned with the lives of others to enjoy her own, tried to show anyone who would listen the ornate clock her husband had constructed that, on the hour, displayed a whole array of carved, lifelike figures that very much resembled herself. Even Mr. Darrow seemed to forget his melancholy. He greeted everyone he passed with a dashing smile and carried James on his shoulders until the boy was persuaded to join a group of children in a complicated game of tag that mostly involved running in circles around the church and screaming as loudly as possible.

"It occasionally astounds me that he can be so happy," Mr. Darrow observed.

"Children are more resilient than we are, but they do still need us to set an example," I said, obliquely referencing Mr. Darrow's unfulfilled promise to spend more time with his sons.

"You are a wise woman, Mrs. Markham."

"You flatter me, Mr. Darrow."

"Perhaps I should do so more often."

We gazed at one another, lost in the moment until Constable

Brickner cut between us. Mr. Darrow shook his hand with enthusiasm, much to the other man's surprise, for he was immediately suspicious of such goodwill. Together they went to the Larken brothers' table, which was copiously populated by both many kinds of ale and the majority of the men of the village. I asked after Susannah, since I hadn't yet seen her at the bazaar, but Lionel had lost track of her the hour before last. Mr. Darrow found Fredricks, who was well ahead of everyone else in his enjoyment of the festivities. It was then that Mr. Darrow took his leave of us to purchase a pint for his old friend and confidant.

That left Paul and me to wander the grounds of the church alone. We drifted away from the noise and the laughter and the scent of food, into the graveyard. The tombstone of Lily Darrow was unchanged from our last visit, and yet it meant so many other things than it had before. Paul touched the chiseled numbers that marked the date of her death.

"It's still here."

"What did you expect to find?"

"I don't know . . . maybe a crack running through it? Just something different."

We stood beside one another in silence. I didn't know what to say. I placed my hand on his shoulder, and he continued.

"I wanted to see her again so badly. I dreamt of her every night, and every morning I would wake up and remember that she was gone. It made me sad, but it was worth it just to pretend for a while that everything was all right. But somehow this is worse, because it's real, and I still have to leave her. I can hug her, but she's still dead and Father is alone. We can't take her back with us, and everything is still broken."

"Would you rather that she never came back?"

"No. I don't know. I wish nothing ever had to change."

"That's all life is. It must change, or else we never would."

Paul looked so sullen, his bright blue eyes dull with a sadness that resembled his father's more and more every day. I ran my fingers through his soft black hair. "We don't have to go back, you know, not if you don't want to."

"Yes, we do. I'm not ready to say good-bye, and neither is she." Paul stood from his mother's grave and returned to the bazaar without any pretense of enjoyment. I followed behind him, until Roland caught my gaze with a friendly, nervous wave. He was dressed in his best Sunday clothes, and he had attempted to slick down his dark hair with copious amounts of pomade, but instead of refining his appearance the waxy substance sharpened the strands into asymmetrical spikes that lent him a feral, yet also innocent look.

"Good bazaar, eh?"

"I can see that you've dressed for the occasion."

"A fellow's got to look nice once in a while, or he's not much of a fellow at all. Is Mrs. Larken all right?"

"I suppose so. I haven't seen her in a day or two—" He ran past me, toward a disheveled young woman with wild red hair. He slid an arm beneath her and sat her on the ground. Her hands were bleeding.

"Susannah?"

"Charlotte!" She smiled at me with relief, and patted Roland's arm. "I've so much to tell you!"

"What on earth has happened to you?"

"You're going to think I'm insane." She put her head in her hands, smearing blood onto her forehead. It was difficult to get the groundskeeper to leave her side, but eventually he relented and agreed to fetch Lionel, occasionally glancing back at us with a dark expression. I took Susannah into the church and sat her down in a pew before the altar.

"I could never think you mad," I told her.

"At least that makes one of us."

"Let's start at the beginning. What happened to you?"

She sat back in the pew and smoothed down her hair before taking a deep breath. She told me her story.

"I'd brought along a special cask of ale for the reverend. Lionel forgets himself sometimes when he starts drinking with the boys, and I didn't trust him to keep it set aside, so I hid it in the cellar of the church for safekeeping. But when I went down to retrieve it, the room had *changed,* Charlotte. There was a door where there had never been one before. For a moment I thought I had gotten turned around and discovered some new chamber beneath the parish, but no . . . it was the same old stone walls, and the cask of ale was on the table right where I had left it.

"There was nothing special about the door aside from the fact that it hadn't existed just a few hours before. It was made of cherrywood, with no special markings and a plain brass doorknob to match. I was about to leave, but then it opened inward by itself. I didn't want to know what was inside, you must believe me. I tried to go back up the stairs, but there was a darkness on the other side of that door that spilled into the cellar. The entire room went black, and soon I couldn't tell which way was up. I felt along the walls trying to find my way out, and then I saw a light.

"I went toward it, desperate to get out of that accursed place, but was disappointed to find myself staring into a mirror. I spun around in an attempt to locate the source of the light, but the rest of the room was still awash in gloom. I pressed my forehead against the glass, starting to feel exasperated, when a pair of black hands slid around my throat. Gloved hands. *His* hands. I tried to scream, but he was already choking the life out of me. I tried to thrash against him, but I could find no one behind me, just the hands closing tighter around my throat, and yet, I wasn't dying. In fact the light before my eyes multiplied, and I was surrounded by a half dozen similar mirrors. My reflection was different in each of them. In the closest one, I was drowning underwater. In the next, I was burning alive. There were scenes of me with my throat slit, being mauled by a wolf, shot in the head—every terrible way that I've ever been afraid to die, forced upon me. I felt myself growing faint. The hands were tightening their grip around my throat, and the mirror images multiplied again.

"I saw a vision of myself the same way I had seen Nanny Prum . . . coming apart from the inside. In that moment, even as I began to lose consciousness, I felt something rise up out of me, from some deep place I didn't know I had. I stopped trying to pry the fingers from around my throat, and with all my might, I punched my fist through the looking glass.

"Every mirror shattered at once. I grabbed ahold of a glass shard and cut at the hands still clutching my neck. They shuddered and fumbled against me, trying to regain their grip, but then stopped altogether. We were no longer alone in the darkness. There were other women with us, visions of myself flayed, burned, bleeding . . . all of them stepping through the broken glass to lunge at the man in black with a fury I could never have dreamt I was capable of. I turned away and ran into the gloom that surrounded us, until the world felt solid beneath my feet once more and I could feel the cool stone walls of the church cellar. I turned around to close the door, but in its place was nothing but a pile of soot and cinders."

She stared at me when she was done and waited for me to say something. I didn't know what to believe until she unclenched her bloodied hands to reveal a small shard of mirror glass.

"I didn't dream it, Charlotte. It *happened*. What do I do?"

My mouth tasted like ash. My mother, my father, Jonathan, Nanny Prum, and now Susannah . . . all of them set upon by a mysterious man in black.

"Be careful. Be watchful." Mrs. Norman's warning became my own. "It's time for you to find your husband and to tell him what's happened."

A man waits for you. He watches you.

But why? What did he want from me? The specter of Death had hung over my life since I was a girl, taking everyone I had ever loved. But then, with a wave of triumph, I remembered: Death is not an absolute. I knew someone who had fought against it and won, and I realized that with her help, I would be able to put an end to this horror once and for all.

CHAPTER 10

A Dangerous Game

The next afternoon, I took the children back to the House of Darkling. A young man of sixteen or seventeen years was already waiting for our party on the other side of the swirling mist. He bowed before us in greeting, and I nearly introduced myself to him. But Paul touched my arm.

"Is that Duncan?" he asked.

I observed the young man's face as he rose back to full height. There were certainly traces of the impish, mute little boy in the appearance of the stranger, as they both wore the same frozen, knowing smiles, but we had only been gone a matter of days and the pigmentation of this young man's skin was more like that of a human, whereas Duncan had retained a distinctive shade of orange. I could not believe that the two were the same until the young man brought a finger to his lips.

"Have we really been gone that long?" I said softly, my mind wandering to thoughts of Lily Darrow, alone in Darkling for what must have felt like years, though it was probable that the Whatleys kept her busy with Olivia's education, and there was certainly enough mischief to keep her occupied were she not otherwise indisposed. I wondered how she passed the time, and then I remembered the room with the gauzy silk veils, and Mr. Samson strapped to the chair. I shivered against the coolness of the air and warmed myself by keeping pace with Duncan.

"How do you know when we're coming through?" I asked.

He gestured to the trees with long, spindle-like fingers, and as he did, the branches twitched and swayed. The hanging pieces of fruit turned to face us, drawn to Duncan's presence. He escorted us the rest of the way out of the orchard and into the house, leading us past a room filled with the softest, most beautiful music I had ever heard, though there were no obvious musical instruments visible in the space. We found another room whose windows looked out onto a sunlit mountaintop that was, as far as I could tell, nowhere near Mr. Whatley's estate. Another room was shaped like the inside of a gazebo and made entirely of glass, and as we passed through it, I was certain that I could see the town of Blackfield in its reflection. I had no time to dwell on this, for Duncan guided us briskly through the house, the slow, languid pacing of his youth replaced by the urgent certainty of adulthood.

We found Lily and Olivia in a small parlor, both of them seated before easels with panes of painted glass identical to the ones in Mr. Whatley's collection. Lily was helping the girl mix a particular shade of green for a rolling hillside when we entered, and as she saw us, she dropped her palette in a splatter of paint. She could say nothing for a moment as she extricated herself from behind her canvas, kneeling down to hug both of the children with an audible sigh of relief. When she rose she greeted me with a polite peck on the cheek.

"You've returned," she said, slowly recovering from her daze.

"Of course, Mother. We missed you!" James buried his head in her skirts.

She smiled weakly and stroked his cheek before turning to her pupil. "Olivia, will you excuse me for a moment? There's something I want to show the children."

The girl nodded with her typical cool indifference, too involved in the creation of her landscape, which seemed to move even as she refined the details.

Lily led us from the parlor, across a drawbridge set between two cascading, lavender-scented waterfalls, through a room where it was snowing and I had to pull the boys apart as they pelted one another with balls of ice, and finally into an empty banquet hall that could have been lifted from some medieval castle, the ceiling supported by roughly hewn wood beams, and the walls made of crumbling, porous stone. There was a door at one end, a ghastly thing forged from black wrought iron that snaked around the frame like ivy, with a silver knocker set in the center.

Lily stood before it. "Now, tell me what you see."

"It's a door," said James.

"Yes, but what kind of door?"

"A heavy one, made from oak," answered Paul. "With metal rivets set in the wood." His little brother shot him a look unique to siblings, a combination of disbelief and pity that he could possibly be related to someone so dim.

"That's not it at all. What about the gargoyles?" James pointed to the top of the door, where I could see nothing but black metal loops like vines.

Lily stepped between them. "The door is different for everyone. To some it might show the thing you need most, to others, a version of your life that you did not live. Some say it can even tell the future. Shall we find out what it has in store for us?" I was about to object, for there are some things that children are not prepared to know, but she had already opened the door. There was darkness on the other side of the threshold, and it descended upon the stone hall to surround us in a singular void. I could still make out the Darrows as a dozen points of light circled around them, taking the shapes of framed paintings.

The first depicted Lily in a sickbed at Everton, one hand to her forehead, the satin sheets rumpled and positioned like something out of a romanticist's studio as a doctor took her pulse. Suddenly the picture came to life, startling the four of us as the doctor's voice echoed through the abyss, hollow and distant.

"Madam, I do believe you shall recover!"

The scene ended, and the trio proceeded to the next moving frame, where it was Christmastime at Everton. The house was decorated with an attention to detail that I could never hope to match. Lily sat by the fireplace observing her family. An older version of Paul carried a little boy in his arms, and the woman who might have been his wife held a little girl by the hand as they helped the children choose their toys from the magnificent Christmas tree. A teenage James was on the other side of the room, trapping a giggling young woman beneath the mistletoe and kissing her scandalously on the cheek. Mr. Darrow joined his wife by the fire and took her hand in his. I blushed. These were private moments, and yet they would never, could never happen.

My discomfort was readily visible and threatened to change into something else altogether. I could not put into words the anger I felt in that moment. I had been betrayed. The children were supposed to say good-bye to their mother. That was what I had brought them for, but instead Lily allowed them to wallow in their loss, to obsess over the things that could never be, the lives that could not be lived. And yet, was I so very different? Did I not dream of Jonathan or my mother or father every night? My anger shifted to myself. There was a danger in what we were doing.

I backed away from them and sought my way out of the room. There was another point of light in the distance, and I moved toward it, hoping for some sort of exit, but unfortunately it was another of the floating frames. Then I realized that was wrong. I could see myself in its surface, fractured a million different ways. These were not paintings; they were mirrors, and a piece of this one was missing. Even in the splintered looking glass I could see the look of understanding as it crossed my face, curdling into revulsion, and then anger.

I remembered the blood on Susannah's hands, and the sound of Nanny Prum's scream as it cut through the night all those weeks ago. But most of all I remembered the man in black; the phantom from my youth who had followed me into adulthood, striking down everyone I had ever loved.

A man waits for you. He watches you.

Were the specters from my past and present one and the same? How had a relic from the House of Darkling found its way into the basement of St. Michael's Church, and why had it been used against Susannah?

I willed myself out of the darkness, groping about for solid walls until I felt the edges of the door and slid back into the empty stone room. Duncan was waiting with a small piece of parchment that declared Mr. Whatley's desire to speak to me in private.

The young man led me deep into the great house, down many flights of stairs to a room that resembled a Turkish bath.

Despite the copious veils of steam wafting through the air, I could see Mr. Whatley at the other end of the chamber, half-submerged in a murky mineral bath. He tilted his head back until the ends of his hair trailed through the water. The pool was large, and ripples formed where it was impossible for him to make them. I noticed something gliding beneath the water very much like an eel or a snake, and then I realized that it was a tentacle. There were at least a half dozen of them traveling away from Mr. Whatley's body, dipping in and out of the water in a languid, thoughtful sort of way. Yet his face was still human, as rough and wild as it had been upon our first meeting.

"Ah, Mrs. Markham." He smirked at my discomfort in seeing him in such casual repose.

"Mr. Whatley," I said sharply. I took a breath in an effort to calm myself, and he pointed for me to sit on a marble bench at the edge of the water with a hand that still resembled a man's. I knew I should have been horrified to see such a creature, especially on so intimate a level, but I felt nothing like terror, as I was too angry to have any fear. It had burned away the moment I found the shattered looking glass and connected the specter of the man in black to the House of Darkling. Who else but a collector such as Mr. Whatley would have possession of an oddity like the mysterious, ever-changing door?

"I know I should apologize for calling on you in what I'm told are improper conditions in your culture, but I won't."

"Should I be impressed by your rudeness?"

"Perhaps. I only share my daughter's interest in the human fashion where it suits me. Otherwise I am only ever myself."

"How lucky for you. May I ask the purpose of this meeting?"

"It's rare that both Lily and the children are preoccupied. What did you think of their little game?"

"I found it somewhat less interesting than the one you're playing."

"Is that so?" He splashed at the water, playfully distracted as I narrowed my eyes at him.

"I think it unlikely a collector such as yourself would let any of his antiquities be put to work without some notion of how they were to be utilized."

"It sounds as though you believe part of my collection has been put to ill use," he said with his sideways smirk.

"There are things happening in Blackfield that defy explanation, unless the answer lies in our recent excursions to the House of Darkling. The timing is rather suspicious."

"Perhaps the two are merely a coincidence?"

"Or it is as I've said, and a game is being played."

The master of Darkling tilted his head to one side in a brief moment of contemplation. "On that point I must disagree with you, for a game cannot be played alone. There must be two players." He stared at me from across the water, something hungry in his gaze that weighted the statement, twisting it into a kind of invitation that hung in the air with the currents of steam, chilling the heat of my anger and confidence until I began to shake. I folded my arms in an effort to mask my nerves. I had not been entirely prepared for his boldness, but I refused to be intimidated by him. I thought of Susannah, and straightened myself as I replied.

"I would imagine there to be stakes involved?"

"Naturally. If you are able to prove a connection between Darkling and Blackfield, then I can promise you that whatever is happening will come to an end."

"And if I fail?" I kept my voice even.

"I do not enjoy being accused of treachery in my own home."

His expression suddenly grew dark, and the water became still as if in response to the change in his temperament. "If you fail, I will take something from you of my own choosing to add to my collection. Are you sure enough of yourself to take such a risk?"

I stood from the marble bench and knelt down to the lip of the pool, lowering myself over it to look into the black pits of his eyes. "That would depend on the rules."

"The only rule is to win."

"Very well." I rose and flicked the condensation from my hands. "Then how do we begin?"

"With a question: Do you think you'll continue to bring the children here?"

"After today I'm not inclined to."

"They'll come to hate you for it."

"That is a sacrifice I'm willing to make."

"How brave of you. I doubt that would please Mr. Darrow."

"I was under the impression that you've never had the pleasure of his acquaintance?"

"I feel that I know him already. It is a very familiar story, is it not? The widower who hires a beautiful young governess to tend to his children. The secret romance, social barriers broken, a spectacular wedding at the end. They all live happily ever after."

I tried to read his face to gauge the intent of his words, but the steam was too thick and his eyes retained their vacant, unreadable blackness. I folded my hands and walked along the edge of the shallow pool.

"It may be a familiar story, but it is not one that I've had the privilege to live out. I know very little of happiness."

"And you won't if you do not let Lily and the children end on their own terms. They must be the ones to finish it."

"You insult my integrity. My only interest is in the well-being of the children."

Mr. Whatley dipped beneath the surface of the water and swam to the other end of the pool. Duncan stood near the stairs with a robe. Whatley stepped out of the pool, his entire body unabashedly visible to me, completely human, completely male, muscular and imposing. I felt myself blush and was glad for the darkness. He stepped into his robe, and Duncan handed him a cigar.

"Do not insult my intelligence. You would be a fool not to hope for such a union. Besides, what the children need is a mother. Preferably one who is of the living."

I could not argue against that. I thought of Mr. Darrow and our conversations in the music room, and our midnight tea parties. With a shock of revulsion I wondered if our relationship was genuine, or if it was something I had, on some subconscious level, planned from the start as a game of my own. The gentleman bit off the end of the cigar but did not seem to spit it out. Duncan lit the tip of it, and Whatley deeply inhaled the smoke.

"And what of Lily?" I asked. "Will she live happily ever after as well?"

Mr. Whatley pulled the cigar out of his mouth and smiled again. "Perhaps. But ever after is a very long time. Good luck to you, Mrs. Markham. It's your move."

Duncan was suddenly at my side. Mr. Whatley disappeared into a tunnel that continued on deeper into the baths, the glowing end of his cigar sliding away with him into the gloom.

CHAPTER II

The Stolen Sun

Duncan led me to the entrance of the baths and watched as I walked up the stairs to the rest of the house. I passed by the library, rising four floors into the air, perpetual moonlight bathing the books in a soft blue glow. I could not hope to match Mr. Whatley unless I knew more about what I was involving myself with. I ran my fingers along the leather spines, and noticed a small stack of books next to the plush leather chair that Lily had been sitting in the first time we found her in the room. One of them was entitled *Dreams of Blackfield*. I closed the door to the library, took to her chair, and opened the book.

My eyes trailed over the lines of unintelligible calligraphy, and suddenly I was in Mr. Darrow's study. The man himself was slumped in his chair, quietly taking an impromptu afternoon nap. I found myself pushed toward him, nearly against my will, gliding across the room until I was at his side. He opened his eyes.

"Charlotte?"

"You can see me?"

"Yes, of course." He rose from his chair and stood very close to me. I could feel his breath on my face. "I always see you here." He touched my cheek with trembling fingers, and I sighed with relief.

"Mr. Darrow—"

"Henry. My name is Henry."

"Henry."

He pulled me against his body and kissed me deeply on the lips. I returned the gesture and ran my fingers through his golden hair. He pushed me against the wall and jolted me out of the reverie. I was back in the library.

"Oh dear." I set the book on top of the pile, thought better of it, and set it back in my lap. Flushed with excitement, I had no idea how real my experience inside the book had been. What would happen the next time that we saw one another? It was difficult not to be attracted to Henry Darrow. He was very handsome, sensitive, and financially secure. Yet the attraction felt wrong, and it could not be blamed on the fact that Mr. Whatley had pointed it out. The dream of becoming the next Mrs. Darrow had begun the moment I met him, as had the loathsome idea of coming off like some sort of temptress, some fortune-seeking harpy who was using her position with the children to secure the good favor of her employer. I was not that woman; I refused to be, and so long as I could not be sure of my own intentions, I would refuse myself any happiness just to ensure that my actions were entirely pure and unquestionable.

I went through the other titles in Lily's collection: *Ode to the Balthazar, Eternal Death, Human Fashions,* and *Mysteries of The Ending.* I took this last one with the other I had just read and carried them upstairs to add to my growing collection. As I passed the boys' room, the door was open and I saw the children settling in beside their mother for another bedtime story. I was about to return to my own room, but Lily saw me standing in the hallway and gestured for me to sit down with them. She began to read:

The Stolen Sun

Once upon a time, there was a caravan of gypsies traveling through the countryside. The youngest member of the clan was a girl named Spada. She was as inquisitive as she was beautiful, and each time the caravan stopped to set up camp, she would start out into the surrounding woodlands to see what sorts of interesting things she could find. As the forests could be dangerous, her mother and father would have to go after her before she got lost and left behind, for winter was coming and the caravan had to make it over the mountains before the first frost.

One day, the gypsies set up camp after an especially long trip and Spada went into the forest in search of something to eat. Her parents were busy tending the horses, as they had briars caught in their hooves, and in no time at all she was as lost as she could be, wandering through the woods as the sun began to set. There was a chill in the air, and Spada, who was usually fearless in the face of everything, grew worried that she would be unable to find shelter for the night. No sooner had she almost given up than she found a magnificent house in a clearing.

It was ancient, made of rough, large stones and timber, but the windows were full of light and the smoke coming from the chimney was sweet with the smell of baking. She approached the house with little hesitation and pulled the rope next to the entryway. A short, squat man with curling whiskers answered the door and was more than happy to take in the lost gypsy girl.

"You may stay the night," he said. "But you must stay the entire night, for the forest is dangerous and I'm certain your family would rather have you lost than dead."

Spada found the sense in this, and agreed to spend the entire night in the strange little man's home. He led her through the house to a large dining room, where they dined on many succulent dishes, and to a room with high ceilings where she was given a comfortable bed. She quickly fell asleep beneath a pile of soft blankets.

The girl slept for quite some time, so long in fact that she was surprised upon waking to see that the sun had still not risen. Spada found this to be very strange, and she left her room to learn how much time had passed. She located the little man in a parlor with a great black fireplace and told him of her concern.

"But my dear," he said, "you've been here but an hour. I suppose you've enjoyed it so much that it must have seemed longer."

Spada found the sense in this and was about to return to her room when the little man invited her to a game of cards. No longer tired, the girl played with him for quite some time until they were both feeling hungry again, and the little man called for his servants to prepare the dining room once more. Spada and her new friend ate many succulent dishes, and when she asked to retire for the remainder of the evening, she was led to another bedroom altogether, with an even larger bed and pillows so delicate she felt as if her head were resting on air.

When she awoke Spada was certain she must have slept at least half the day away, but when she looked out the window she was dismayed to find that the sun had still failed to rise. She rushed through the great house and found the little man seated in a study filled with books and paintings. She told him of her concern.

"I agree that the night seems very long indeed," he said. "But that is only because we have done so much in such a short time."

Spada found the sense in this and was about to return to her room when the little man suggested that she join him in playing music. Coming from a family of musicians, the girl found this to be a very practical way to pass the time, and together they played and sang until their fingers hurt and their voices were raw. The little man called to his servants to prepare the dining room, and for the third time that evening Spada feasted on many delicious dishes. When they were finished the little man excused himself for a moment and left the girl alone in the company of his butler.

The servant, who always observed his master with a small measure of disdain, began speaking to the girl in a hushed whisper as soon as the little man had left. He warned her that she had been tricked, and that the little man had stolen the sun from the sky and hidden it somewhere in the house to keep her with him for one long, eternal night. Spada thanked the butler for telling her, but found that this information neither frightened nor upset her. In fact, all she could feel for the master of the house was sympathy and a little pity.

"He must be very lonely if he is willing to go to such lengths to keep me here," she said. "If the sun is in the house, then I shall find it and prove to him that he does not need to use such tricks to make us friends."

The little man returned to the dining room and escorted Spada to another fantastic bedroom, this one with a bed lined in lullabies. She slept very soundly, but when she awoke she did not go in search of the little man. Instead, she went through the house and examined every reflective surface in search of the sun. She peered into mirrors and silver goblets, golden doorknobs, and gilded cages, looking carefully for anything that contained the sparkle of daylight. When she had satisfied herself that every reflection in the house was natural, she found the little man waiting for her in the kitchen wearing a ridiculous chef's hat. Neither of them brought up the unending night. Instead they baked all of Spada's favorite pies and cakes and ate everything that they made until their stomachs were ready to burst.

In due time, the little man escorted her to a new bedroom with a plush, delicate bed lined with dreams. This time, before he left her he paused at the door and wished her a pleasant evening. She drifted off to sleep.

When she awoke, Spada set off into the house in search of every candle flame and burning fireplace that might contain the stolen sun. She peered into every gaslight that lined the hallways, and into every room with a blazing hearth, and when she was satisfied that she had examined every available source of firelight, she found the little man in an empty ballroom. He wore his best dancing shoes and seemed eager to teach her his favorite steps, but the look of defeat on Spada's face was enough for him to ask her what was wrong.

"I know that you have stolen the sun," she said without any anger or accusation, much to the little man's surprise, "and I've been looking for it in every place I could think of. I was certain that if I could find and return it, you would see how you did not need to trick me to win over my friendship. I would have given it freely, and do still."

The little man was very clever and usually good at anticipating every possible outcome of a situation, but Spada's declaration caught him off guard. His eyes glistened with tears more brightly than was possible, and Spada discovered that he had hidden the sun not in his house, but in his heart. So great was his affection for the gypsy girl that he could no longer keep it to himself. His chest welled with emotion, and as it did the ballroom filled with sunlight, which streamed out through the windows of the house and into the sky above the forest, calling to the gypsies still searching for the lost Spada.

When the girl's family arrived at the great house, they were invited into the ballroom, where everyone played music and danced and sang, and Spada never left the little man's side, not even when the sun had set and the first frost of winter licked across the earth. The mountains would wait until spring, for a true friendship was as rare as the sun in the sky.

"Was that a true story?" James yawned and lifted his head from his mother's shoulder as she finished. Lily closed the book and set it on the nightstand. Paul, who was wide awake, kept his head in her lap and stared quietly into space.

"Every story starts with a bit of truth, no matter how small," she said.

"Then they probably changed the ending to make it happy," said the boy as he stretched his arms over his head. "Her family wouldn't have been glad at all. The little man tried to steal her away."

Their mother was becoming visibly uncomfortable. Children were supposed to fall asleep with a bedtime story.

"I suppose he must have been very lonely," said Lily.

"Lots of people are lonely," said Paul without moving. He blinked and sighed. "That doesn't make it all right to do something wrong."

James sat up and reached over his mother to pick up the book of fairy tales. "Do you think they were all dead? Did the little man kill them?"

"Why would you say such a thing?" Lily asked with surprise that bordered on horror. "Winter was coming. They might have died if they went into the mountains. Perhaps he saved them." She kissed him on the forehead and began to extricate herself from her sons. "Although that's a very interesting interpretation."

She brushed the side of Paul's face, but stopped when he said: "Perhaps he was collecting the gypsies." Her eyes flashed and revealed something secret, but it happened so fast that it was difficult to read. She kissed him on the cheek, and together we closed the door to the bedroom. We stood facing one another in the hallway, and Lily observed the books clutched under my arm.

"You returned to the library."

"Yes, the books here are quite fascinating, as was the fairy tale."

"Some stories are truer than we realize, and others less than we might wish," she said.

A silence passed between us, unbroken until I lifted the books to keep them from slipping, minutely aware that I had tactfully placed my arm to hide the title of *Dreams of Blackfield*.

"I hope you don't mind that I've taken them?"

"Not at all. In fact I encourage your curiosity. The more you know about this place, the more comfortable you'll feel bringing the children."

Moonlight came in through the window at the end of the hallway, broken up only by the shadows of the languid tentacles rising from the pond outside.

"Mr. Whatley asked to speak with me today."

"Did he?" Lily's voice was unreadable. "Whatever for?"

"He wanted to know if I would continue to bring the children," I said, leaving out the bargain I had struck with the master of Darkling. Lily waited for me to go on as I struggled to find the right words. "I said that I would, for now."

"Splendid!"

"I'm not so sure that it is." I tightened my grip on the books. "How much do you know about Mr. Whatley?"

"I believe that he's some kind of politician."

"But what sort of man is he?"

"I should think you'd be aware by now that he's no man at all."

"Yes, of course, but has he ever given you any reason to fear him?"

"We made a bargain, and whatever he might be, he keeps his promises."

That did not answer my question. I attempted a different tactic. "I worry that Darkling could be harmful to the children."

Lily narrowed her eyes and folded her arms. "I'm not sure I understand."

"Mourning is difficult enough by itself, but to extend it indefinitely . . . they might never recover."

"I see." Her voice was a piercing whisper. "Then why bring them at all?"

"Because I understand what it means to lose a loved one. You can all heal together, but at some point it will have to end."

She held my gaze for a long while, until I began to feel uncomfortable and looked away. Lily's ire deflated, and suddenly she looked small and weak. "What do you propose?"

"An end to it. Three additional visits. No more than that."

Even in the dark I could see that she went pale. "I'm tired, Mrs. Markham."

"I did not mean to overstep myself—"

"You've made your point. I shall consider it carefully."

Lily left the corridor for her room, a place I realized I had still not seen. I hoped she would think on my proposal. To protect the Darrows, I had to sever the ties between Darkling and the world of the living, but I could not do so until I more fully understood the connection.

I continued down the hallway and found my own room, too tired to explore the mysteries of the books from the library.

I dreamt of Sundays with my father. In the years after we returned from India with my mother's body, we had started to spend time together on the Sabbath day locked away in the conservatory, reading books, playing chess, and telling each other stories both fictional and true, no small number of which pertained to my late mother.

"The end is nigh, my peppercorn." That was his my father's pet name for me, his peppercorn, for he felt that I was very beautiful, but rather fiery if not handled with care.

He lit his pipe and began to smoke, which meant he was growing tired and that we would soon be off to bed. But the smoke did not disperse into the air to attach itself to his hair and clothing. It circled around his head before gathering beside him, a cloud of noxious fumes taking the shape of a man. My father grew weary the more he smoked, and the cloud became more substantial. *Black*. It watched him sit back in his chair as he dropped his pipe and stopped breathing, eyes open, mouth slack.

It lingered for a moment beside his lifeless body before scattering through the air to attach itself to everything in the room, a memory extinguished and remade.

CHAPTER 12

Mysteries of The Ending

The next morning Lily did not come down for breakfast. Instead, she gave Duncan a note for the children, which mentioned something about an upset stomach and resting for their next visit (which she hoped would be soon). I held my tongue, while Mr. Whatley tipped his glass in my direction and stared at me from across the table with the devilish smirk that seemed a permanent fixture on his rugged, impish face. We did not linger after our meal.

As we approached Everton, I was so lost in thought that I did not notice Mr. Darrow standing at the door of the house waiting for us, and I had no time to prepare myself for our first encounter since I had inadvertently invaded his dream.

"Hello, boys!" Mr. Darrow lifted James into the air and tussled Paul's hair with his free hand. "Having fun with Charlotte?"

"It's a lovely day, so I thought we'd go for a walk." I spoke up before the boys could respond to their father's question. Adults are much better liars than children.

"Splendid idea! I wish you'd thought to invite me along. I

ended up falling asleep at my desk." He looked at me and blushed when he noticed that I was looking back at him. He turned his attention to the boys. "Are you finished with your lessons yet?"

My stomach tightened. Our lessons seemed such distant things. What kind of governess had I become? I chastised myself, but not too severely. The boys were young and would recover from whatever lapses these interludes with their mother had caused in their education. Some things were more important than arithmetic, such as being available to their reclusive father.

"Yes, I believe we are for the day." The boys turned to one another, beaming at their good fortune.

Henry clapped his hands together. "Excellent! I believe we have an appointment by the lake?"

The boys rode their bicycles ahead, flicking the bells on their handlebars with gusto at every passing pedestrian as I rode next to Mr. Darrow. We traveled past the bakeshop and the butcher, the blacksmith, and the sweets shop that sold the caramel toffees the boys loved so much, past St. Michael's Church and the vicarage. We continued on until the barren autumn spokes of the forest obscured the village of Blackfield, and we found a grassy clearing overlooking the lake. Everton was visible across the water.

It was unseasonably warm, as if summer had decided to make one last appearance before the onset of winter. I removed a picnic basket from its perch on the back of my bicycle and began to set out our lunch, but while my back was turned the boys stripped down to their underwear and jumped into the lake.

"You'll catch your death!" I said anxiously, but Mr. Darrow laughed and sat down on the blanket.

"More for us, then," he said.

I looked up and smiled uncomfortably.

"Is everything all right?" he asked.

"Yes, I'm just afraid I haven't gotten much sleep lately."

"You're working too hard, and that's not good for anyone. Especially the children."

"They are very energetic."

"Which is why I want to be more involved, just like this. Spending time with them and getting to know them better. Being a father instead of a distant figure locked away in his office, snoring." He smiled again, and I tried to stop myself from thinking him rather dashing, but failed.

"That's why I so enjoy working for you, Mr. Darrow. You have a true interest in the well-being of your children."

"My name is Henry."

"Sir?"

"You can call me Henry, if you like. We're outside. There aren't as many rules out here."

"Mr. Darrow, I am still your employee."

"Nonsense. You're part of the family. Since I can call you Charlotte, it's only fair."

"All right then, Henry."

"Charlotte."

We stared at one another comfortably, wordlessly, at complete ease in each other's company. Then the boys plopped down on the blanket, wet as dogs.

"We're hungry!"

"What have I told you about toweling yourselves off?" I said with a bemused expression.

"But I'm wet like a fish!" James sucked his cheeks between his teeth and puckered his lips. "Phfee?"

I grabbed the nearest towel and locked the boys' heads in the crooks of my arms. Henry watched in amazement as I wrestled them dry.

"There! Almost passable. At least it'll do for now." I released them and turned around to serve tea from a sealed flask when I heard a pair of giggles followed by the appropriate splashes.

I turned to Henry. "You couldn't have stopped them?"

"I wanted to see you dry them off again. It was quite impressive." He smiled playfully and dashed off to the edge of the lake, calling, "Lunchtime!"

When he finally succeeded in getting them out of the water and dried off on his own (I refused to help him), he walked back with the boys, his gaze carefully fixed in my direction. I suddenly felt my heart very acutely, beating against the confines of my chest, and I was glad that he happened to be out of reach lest I might have re-created the scene from his dream and made a fool of myself in front of the children.

It was a relief to bask in the sunlight again after so much time at the House of Darkling. I spread my dress over the blanket on the ground and took in the mild air of the lakeshore. Henry removed his hat and sat down with a pleasant sigh and a half smile, seeming to lose his perpetually tortured expression.

He spoke without opening his eyes. "Would you care to take the boat across the lake?"

"What a lovely idea. You prepare the vessel, and I shall untangle the children."

They had started fighting after they left the water, and it was no small task to separate them. Paul had already directed a few choice blows into his brother's shoulder and thigh, and James was insistent that there be retribution. But when I threatened to drown them both like unwanted kittens, they believed me and sat quietly on opposite sides of the boat. Henry pushed us off, and we began to glide through the water.

The lake was surrounded by great hills and a smattering of trees. The steeple of St. Michael's Church was visible in the distance, and trails of smoke from the cottages in the village laced the air with the smell of freshly baked pies and roasted nuts. The boat rocked gently against the tepid current.

"So tell me, boys, what have you been learning from Charlotte?"

"If we don't do our lessons, she's going to skin us like a pair of Indian tigers!" James said excitedly, thrilled to be compared to anything as vicious as a tiger.

Henry smiled broadly and began to chuckle.

"One must be firm with children, Mr. Darrow."

"Oh absolutely!" He had to stop to catch his breath. "Boys, I was unaware that I had unleashed such a force of nature upon you. Your mother would be very pleased."

James spoke up before Paul or I could think to stop him. "But she is, Father!"

Paul immediately stood up and lunged at his brother. The boat leaned precipitously to one side, and then turned over completely. I took Henry's arm instinctively as we fell into the water, a plume of spray ascending into the air when we splashed into the cold lake. We were still near the shore, but I grabbed James anyway and lifted him to my side, scrambling out of the water like a drowned rat, our clothes sticking to us uncomfortably and releasing pockets of water with each sloshing step. The four of us collapsed at the edge of the lake. Henry took out his handkerchief, but saw that it too had been completely soaked and threw it on the ground.

"Paul, what on earth has gotten into you?"

The boy looked at me nervously, and then to his father.

"I'm afraid it's my fault, Mr. Darrow. James has been telling fibs, recently—" James opened his mouth to speak, but I gave him a forceful look, willing him to be quiet. He was. "—and I've been trying to break him of the habit. Paul was simply a little overzealous with my instructions."

Henry scratched his wet head, and pushed a strand of sopping dark blond hair away from his face. I thought he suddenly looked very boyish.

"I see. Well then, I suppose we had better get back to the house and change before any of us catch cold." He extended his arm and pulled me up from the ground, but when I stood, I neglected to release it.

I felt an unpleasant combination of euphoria and dread. I could not deny that it pleased me to be walking arm in arm with Henry Darrow. I would never be able to forget my late husband, but Henry made the loss of Jonathan bearable somehow. When I was around him, the pain I always felt transformed itself into something else. He gave me hope that I could be happy again.

But then there was the other part of it, the echo of the conversation I had had with Mr. Whatley. What kind of person was I that I presumed to take an interest in a man whose wife had not been—and was still not quite—dead for much more than a year? I never thought of myself as a schemer or a seductress, but it was difficult to avoid the comparison. A match with Mr. Darrow would be advantageous to say the least. The only thing I could rely upon was the strong arm that looped through my own, and I held on to it more tightly than perhaps I should have. I wondered if this was not lost on the boys, who trailed behind us in silence.

* * *

Lionel Larken was waiting for me in the kitchen when we arrived back at Everton, trying not to come between the cook and the scullery maid, for Mrs. Mulbus held a large paring knife in her hand and was pointing it severely in Jenny's direction while muttering something about a nick in the stew kettle. He looked haggard and tired. After I had dried off and changed, I sat with him in the parlor.

"It's Susannah."

"What's happened? Not another attack?" I felt the color draining from my face.

"That's just it, I don't quite know. I'm not sure that she's been sleeping. I woke up the night before last and found her wide awake, pacing around the cottage. She was staring out the windows with this funny look in her eyes, but she wouldn't tell me what it was all about. I finally got her back into the bedroom, but she insisted upon touching every shadow in the room to make sure there wasn't anything hiding in them.

"But that's not the worst of it. Mrs. Willoughby called on me last night. She said that Susannah had an episode in the shop yesterday. She left her alone again in the afternoon to make some deliveries, and when she came back, the store was in ruins. Susannah said that she thought she saw something like a rat in a pile of scrap fabric. She went to see what it was to get it out of the store, but there was nothing there. Instead, and these are her words, the pieces of fabric started knitting themselves together around her throat, strangling her, covering her nose and mouth, binding her hands so she couldn't struggle. She was able to free one of her hands and took a hot iron to her throat. Whatever was happening to her stopped, and she burned all of the fabric scraps behind the store. My God, Charlotte, you should see her throat. Dr. Barberry said she'll be fine and all healed in a few weeks, but I'm worried for her."

"Do you believe her story?"

"I believe that she believes it, and my wife is no fool. Never was very superstitious. If she said she saw something unnatural, then I believe her. But what do you do for someone chasing ghosts in the night?"

"These things are only happening when she is alone. You must watch her. Never let her out of your sight."

"There must be something else we can do."

"Leave it to me."

That night as I was preparing for bed, I removed *Mysteries of The Ending* from my basket. I remembered Lily's warning, and how the books had affected me back in the library, but my anger and suspicion overpowered any sense of caution. Nanny Prum had died an unnatural death, and so would Susannah unless I could better comprehend Whatley's intentions. To work against him, I first had to understand him. I sat on the bed and opened the book.

As I read over the strange, otherworldly characters, an icy wind plucked at my nightdress. I looked up to close the window, but instead of being in my bedroom at Everton I stood before a crumbling castle with toppled-over towers and a drawbridge that looked as if a very large bite had been taken out of its side. Across it stood a ruinous doorway with a knocker made of chains as thick as my neck.

The book was still open in my hands, and I closed it around my index finger to keep my connection to the place open but tenuous in case it proved to be dangerous. The door was thrown backward before I could even knock, answered by a vile, mad-looking thing shaped like a little girl. Her hair was falling out in clumps, and where her eyes should have been there were two tiny black keyholes set in the gray flesh of her face, both of them oozing a dark, foul liquid I did not care to identify. I gasped with a sharp intake of breath, and she snapped at me with black, broken teeth, almost catching my arm until she was yanked backward by a loop of chain around her throat.

The little girl lay sprawled. The chain that encircled her neck extended across the coarse stone floor and halfway up a staircase, where it was wrapped around the gloved wrist of a woman dressed in an aging ball gown, ratty and frayed around the edges, with holes worn down to the petticoats beneath, and a ring of skeleton keys that clattered at her side. But even so the woman held herself with a composure that bordered on the majestic, and when she spoke it was with a voice as rich as velvet, deeply commanding and aware of its power to instruct and control.

"You do not belong here," she said softly. In her other hand she held a battered candelabra whose candlesticks were lit with tiny blue flames. I stood upon the threshold, still shaking from my encounter with the unpleasant little girl, my insides knotted together with fear.

This was a mistake. I contemplated closing the book and turning back to Everton, to slide back beneath my covers and allow Whatley to do as he would, but what of Susannah and the Darrows? I inhaled deeply, the air stale with decay, and entered the castle.

The blue light from the candles was reflected in the chain held in the woman's hands. It not only bound the strange girl who had greeted me so poorly but trailed away behind her to every corner of the room, lashed to an infinite line of creatures hiding in the shadows, all of them thin and emaciated, some crawling along the floor while others were strung up the walls by their shackles. The lady of the castle noticed my wandering gaze and spoke again.

"You do not belong, and yet still you enter."

"There are things I must know."

"Your questions will have a price."

"I have no money."

She smiled coldly. "I trade in a different sort of currency."

"What sort?"

"Answers for questions. Mr. Whatley is not the only collector in The Ending."

"How do you—?"

"The stench of Darkling clings to you. This way." She descended the staircase and beckoned me into a room hidden behind a tattered curtain, the loop of keys at her waist chiming as she moved. I kept myself away from the walls as I followed, afraid to brush against the rest of her children, who slumped from their chains in a living death, staring into space with their empty keyhole eyes.

I found the woman in a small salon, seated at a table before a window that looked over a nocturnal landscape of mountains pressing into the pale flesh of the moon. She pulled the chain that encircled her wrist, and a serving boy with dirty fingernails set two crystal goblets in front of us, filling them with the scarlet contents of a dusty cask. The scent of blackberry and rye rose from the liquid, though I did not dare to taste it.

"I will give you three answers and three answers only."

I opened my mouth to argue, but glanced again at the chain around the woman's wrist and thought the better of it. She lifted the circle of skeleton keys from her side, unhooked the catch, and placed three of them on the table. The boy with the cask still stood before us, lock-shaped eye sockets staring out the window.

"Your first answer." The woman picked up the nearest key, all rusted brass and crooked teeth, and stuck it into the small, dark keyhole where the child's right eye should have been. I cringed and looked away as she turned it with a click of bone and metal. The boy began to speak with a thin, androgynous voice.

"You cannot hope to stop the master of Darkling. The games he invents are centuries in the making and will end only when they are played out. The most you can hope to do is twist the outcome to your own devices."

When the boy was done speaking, I turned to the woman. "I never asked my question."

"These are the answers you need, not the ones you want. The next answer." She lifted the second key and inserted it into the child's left eye socket. This time he spoke with the voice of an old man, high and reedy.

"We are the things that do not die, born to end with the world, but not before. We are your gods and your monsters, indifferent and unsated, waiting for a close that might never come. '*The Ending, The Ending, full of nighttime portending, the place for the Things Above Death. In great houses they wait for the Season to abate, and for time to give up its last breath.*' "

The woman touched the boy's neck and pushed down the stained collar that crowded against his chains, revealing a third keyhole at the base of his throat. She used the last key. The boy spoke with a voice more appropriate for his appearance, small and quiet, with a singsong melancholy.

"There are only the dead and the damned. Remember that when the man in black comes for you. He is coming soon, Charlotte." With that, the woman collected her keys and placed them back upon the metal circle at her waist.

I felt as if I were going to be sick. *He is coming soon,* but the boy had not said when, and would not. Three answers only. I stared ahead as dumbly as the dirty children, not seeing the lady of the castle until she placed a length of cold metal chain into my hands, the end of it looped around the neck of the boy with dirty fingernails.

"My payment," she said.

"I don't understand."

She ignored me and returned to the entry hall, her children screaming as she dragged them off the floor and down from the rafters, up the length of the staircase into the hidden depths of the castle, illuminated only by the blue glow of the candelabra.

"Answers for questions. You will take him back with you, to watch, to listen. To remember."

That was simply too much. I threw down the fetters she had given me. "I will do no such thing!"

She never heard me, for the world turned over on itself and I was back in my room at Everton. Head spinning, I regained my balance in time to see the end of the chain slip around the corner of my open bedroom door as the boy with the keyhole eyes escaped into the hallway, the rattle of metal muffled by the carpet.

The children.

I dropped the book and bolted out of my chambers. The creature was moving in the opposite direction of the nursery, dashing through the corridor on all fours with such speed I could never hope to keep up. He disappeared down the stairwell, chains slapping against the banister in a dull echo I was sure had awoken the entire manor.

I cornered the creature in the kitchen and grabbed hold of his shackles. "Stop this at once!" I hissed at him, and he responded by pressing his body against the wall, sinking into it as if he were stepping into a bath. He leered at me with a mouthful of rotten teeth as his face disappeared into the skin of the house. I wrenched and twisted the chains around my arms, but still they followed the boy into the walls of Everton. Link by link they slipped away from me until at last the final loop remained, a thin brass key dangling from its end. The teeth caught on the skin of my hands, friction burning as I lost hold of it. Then I was alone in the kitchen, sobbing despite myself.

Numb with exhaustion, I did the only thing I could think of: I made a cup of tea. I sipped it quietly in the dark as I glared at the wall, at yet another problem I had not the faintest idea how to solve. The woman had said that he would only observe us, but that could hardly be trusted. *What have I done?* I was as bad as Lily, stubborn beyond reason and steadfast in a belief that my own abilities were unmatched; a belief that was apparently misguided as I had released something wicked into Everton.

I wondered if Lily felt the same.

Through the window, the grounds of the estate were bathed in moonlight, just like the House of Darkling. With the thought of the place, I set my cup onto its saucer so severely that it fell off the table and cracked into a dozen pieces. I cursed myself under my breath and knelt down to collect the ceramic fragments, so absorbed in my own melancholy and frustration that I didn't notice Henry standing over me.

"Are you all right?"

I stood, holding the sharp pieces too tightly in my hand.

"Yes, I hope I didn't wake you?" I glanced again at the place in the wall where the dirty little boy had escaped, and then into

Henry's soft sapphire eyes. Every anxiety, doubt, and fear that had been building within me melted into the ether.

"No, I've been awake. I had tea prepared, but no one else came down."

"How thoughtful."

"I had hoped you would join me."

"I'm sorry, I didn't realize."

"How could you have known? I should have made my intentions clear."

He gently took the pieces of the broken cup out of my hands, his fingers lingering against my own. Even after he moved away, I could feel the echo of his touch singing through my body. I gasped softly and backed away, but he held my arm, pulling me against his chest and pressing his lips to my own. The song I felt at his touch erupted into a chorus of emotion, the darkened space around us blazing with invisible light. We parted, and I rested my head against his shoulder to catch my breath.

"Henry."

He stiffened at the sound of his own name, releasing me and beginning to stammer. "I'm so sorry—don't know what I'm doing—if I've offended you—"

"You haven't." I tried to take his hand, but he pulled away.

"I've taken advantage. You're in my employ. The children—" He backed away, shaking his head. "Forgive me, but I've made a terrible mistake." Mr. Darrow spun around and nearly ran from the room, leaving me alone with the broken pieces of the cup in the sink, which were not nearly as sharp or painful as the ones I felt inside.

CHAPTER 13

Death Revisited

After a fitful night of straining to listen for the rattle of chains or the scraping of dirty fingernails against the walls, I rose for breakfast. Mr. Darrow was nowhere to be found, nor was he at lunch, yet his presence weighed heavily on me. The dread I felt at the prospect of our next meeting was so suffocating that when the boys asked to go on their late afternoon walk, I was outside waiting for them before they could even find their coats. We left under the pretense of visiting the cemetery, and found the cloud of mist just beyond the cage of roots in the forest.

I did not know what I would say to Lily. How could I look her in the face?

Why should you be ashamed to take what is yours?

I tried unsuccessfully to silence the voice in my mind that had grown steadily louder since my conversation with Mr. Whatley. The tone was selfish and callous, but also powerful and assured, threatening to overrule the well-mannered woman I had always prided myself (perhaps foolishly) on being. I remained undecided about whether or not this was something to resist.

Duncan was waiting for us in the orchard, even taller than before and ever closer to my own age. His skin had lost all of its discoloration, leaving him nearly human in every way but for the impish smile that was imprinted upon his face like a mask.

There were two crisp suits waiting for the boys in their room.

"It would appear that we are expected to dress for dinner," I observed. I attempted to help James change, but he became jealous over his older brother's silver cufflinks, and Paul did not take kindly to having his little brother attempt to strangle him from behind. I split them apart as best I could, each brother taking something from the other—like hair and skin—during the course of the separation, and I threatened them both with a form of Indian torture so terrible that I couldn't describe it to them for fear that it would scar their delicate, youthful psyches.

I left them alone and returned to my own quarters. A dark green gown had been placed over the blank fabric body of the dressing mannequin next to the wardrobe. I slid it off the dressmaker's dummy and held it against my body. It was exquisite and sleek, much more extravagant a thing than I could ever have afforded, let alone purchased from Mrs. Willoughby's dress shop. I thought about Susannah and the promise I had made to her husband. *Leave it to me.* Yet what progress had I made? I still only half understood the game I was playing. I refused to dwell on what would happen to my friend if I failed.

I began to undress, and when I was down to my underthings, Lily entered the room dressed in a slender silver gown encrusted with glittering jewels. She closed the door. I was startled and tried to hide my nakedness by pressing the dress against my body, and I snapped at her. "Lily!"

She did not avert her eyes or apologize for intruding. She

wordlessly walked toward me and took hold of the dress. She helped me into it without a word, her hands moving along my body, finally lacing up the back. When she was finished we turned to one another, our faces mere inches apart. I wondered if she could see in me what had happened the night before with her husband, what I felt for him.

"I wanted to apologize for the way things were left," she said. "You were right to question me."

She tightened the corset of the dress, and I could only muster a reply half above a whisper.

"I only want what's best for the children."

Lily brushed a strand of hair away from my face. "Let me fix your hair," she said. She sat me down in front of the vanity mirror and undid the tightly wound bun at the back of my head, releasing blond hair over my shoulders and combing through it gently, our faces in stark contrast to one another: Lily's, ethereal with her sharp green eyes and midnight-black tresses that took on a blue sheen beneath the gaslights; the pointed features of my own softened by the light flush of my complexion, now even richer in contrast with her paleness. I looked beneath my reflection for any trace of my mother, gathering strength from it. I wondered what Lily saw when she looked at herself.

"We're not so different, you and I," she said. "Either in our current occupations or in the things that we want." Our eyes met in the mirror. *She knows.* I smiled weakly and closed my eyes as the comb ran through my hair, massaging my scalp.

"If you know what I want, then I hope you'll enlighten me, because I'm not so sure that I do."

Lily placed her hands on my shoulders and set down the comb. "We have lost too much. Life has been cruel. But we must not lose our capacity to love. We must soldier on, for life is short and death is long. We must try to love, to move on, to embrace the opportunities presented to us."

I opened my mouth but then closed it again. I couldn't respond, at least not right away. She knew what had transpired between Mr. Darrow and me. I didn't know how, but she was aware and she approved. I doubted whether I would have been as lenient with Jonathan had our places been reversed, but then I could not begin to fathom the things that Lily Darrow had been through.

There was a charged silence between us, long enough for me to wonder if I was mistaken. Perhaps she was speaking more about her own situation than mine. Lily ran her fingers through my hair, gathering it up in her hands and pinning it into place.

"One must make sacrifices to get the things one wants most," she said.

"Do you think so?"

"I know so."

"And what's your sacrifice?"

"Don't you remember? I died." She held a hand mirror to the back of my head, showing how she had styled my hair high onto the top of my head. I didn't fully believe her. There was something else in the mirror's reflection, an expression of anguish highlighted by the glistening of her eyes, as if she were on the verge of tears. "I'm hosting a dinner party this evening. It will give me a chance to introduce the children to the society here. Most of the guests have never seen a human child before. In fact they fear them."

"It seems a strange thing to fear two young boys."

"Humans are not permitted in The Ending, and Mr. Whatley has put himself at great risk to fulfill our bargain. Allowing mortals into a place without Death has caused something of a sensation among the people here."

"And what sort of people are they, exactly?"

"Surely you must know by now. You've read some of the books. '*The remains of the day forged from shadows and clay, endless and moribund in twain. As the worlds flicker out and Death flits about, the Old Ones sip tea and champagne.*' "

"How dreadful."

"But beautiful in its way."

"Where do they come from?"

"I don't think they're from anywhere. They always were and always will be. '*The Ending, The Ending, full of nighttime portending, the place for the Things Above Death. In great houses they wait for the Season to abate, and for time to give up its last breath.*' "

I stood from the chair in front of the vanity mirror, and once again turned to face Lily.

"Such a long wait, I would imagine. It sounds very lonely," I said.

"I suppose that's why they've become so interested in the ways of mankind. To them, we're an amusing distraction, like animals in a cage. A pleasant diversion from their own complicated society."

"What will you do when they grow tired of this 'pleasant diversion'?"

"I expect humanity will be entirely extinguished before that could ever happen."

"And what will happen when the boys grow into men and stop visiting?"

We stood up and moved toward the door of the bedroom.

"I believe that we agreed upon two more visits after this one, did we not?" She opened the door and held it for me. "What will you do when they no longer need a governess?"

"Move on." With that, I turned in to the hallway.

We found that the boys had mostly dressed, despite the fact that James's head seemed to have been intentionally wedged into the sleeve of his jacket, and Paul was missing a rather sizable patch of hair. Together and wordlessly, Lily and I smoothed out their rumpled clothing, combed over the places where Paul's scalp was visible, and did our best to make the boys look presentable. When we were finished, we left for the drawing room. James skipped ahead of us while Paul shuffled morosely behind him, leaving Lily and me to walk side by side in silence.

The other dinner guests had already started to arrive and stood around the drawing room with drinks in hand, making small talk and gossiping whenever they were out of earshot to do so comfortably.

They were an eclectic group to say the least. There was a kindly-looking older couple doing their best to resemble humans, but their skin bulged uncomfortably in the wrong places, as if it had been put on very hastily or at least without much understanding of how it was supposed to fit. The couple excitedly greeted Lily, who introduced them to the children and me as Mr. and Mrs. Arthur Puddle.

"SO PLEASED TO MAKE YOUR ACQUAINTANCE!" said Mrs. Puddle as if she were speaking to a very slow child.

Lily cut in before I could reply. "There's no need to shout, Mrs. Puddle. Most humans have ears."

"Is that what you call them? How odd." She felt the sides of her head and found her own ears. They shifted uneasily, as if they had been pinned to her skull. James stifled a giggle just as Mr. Whatley joined us with a younger couple who seemed to more closely follow his philosophy of individuality.

The woman, if she could be called a woman, wore a sheath of

netting over the entire surface of her body instead of skin. Her innards pushed uncomfortably through the gaps in the fabric, red and glistening. Still, she was roughly shaped like a person, and she had features resembling eyes and lips that were fixed in a perpetual expression of haughty disdain. Mr. Whatley introduced her as Miss Yarborough, and she nodded to me without a word of greeting. The children gazed upon her with rapt fascination rather than disgust, for she was very much a living, breathing variation on some of the anatomical diagrams we had studied in class. I had to swat James's hand away before he could poke a finger into the wet flesh beneath her netting.

The gentleman, on the other hand, was most talkative. He had no body at all, as he was made of some thick, gaseous substance that coiled itself into a humanoid figure, but this did nothing to prohibit him from being the liveliest person in the room. He had no facial features, and as Mr. Whatley introduced him, he changed from the color of silver mist to a deep blue.

"Mrs. Markham, this is Mr. Snit," said Mr. Whatley.

The gentleman bowed deeply, so deeply in fact that it seemed he was mocking the very custom of bowing. He took my hand into his cool, misty tendrils and kissed it. "The pleasure is mine a thousand times over, my dear lady."

I blushed politely, and Miss Yarborough rolled her eyes. "Do sober up, Snitty, or you shan't make it through dinner."

Mr. Snit turned an indignant shade of red. "One must have a certain level of intoxication, my dear Miss Yarborough, to put up with you for an entire evening."

Lily pulled me away to the other side of the room for further introductions. There was a blond boy a few years younger than Olivia who was more beautiful than Miss Whatley could ever hope to be; his mother, a formidable but pleasant-looking woman; and a pair of tall, gangly creatures that resembled oversized centipedes, both of them with twelve different limbs along dappled undersides that curved into the air as they held themselves to conversation level, bulbous eyes blinking sideways.

"Mrs. Markham, I would like to introduce you to Mrs. Aldrich and her son, Dabney," said Lily, referring to the woman and her son.

Mrs. Aldrich nodded. "It's a pleasure to meet you, Mrs. Markham."

"Good evening," said the boy. When he spoke, everyone in the room seemed to stop to stare at him, watching his perfect lips shape themselves around the words. If he noticed the attention, he pretended not to.

"And this is the Professor and Mrs. Baxter."

"How do you do?" I greeted both of the centipede creatures, but as I blinked I noticed something odd about them. In the moment just before my eyes closed, and again just after they opened, the Baxters seemed to disappear. It was an odd sensation, and so I tried not to blink as I faced them.

"Hello," the Baxters said in unison, smiling together.

Fortunately I was rescued by the sudden incursion of Mr. Samson. He took my arm and steered me to the other side of the drawing room.

"Mrs. Markham! Pleasure to see you again, my dear." I could smell the bourbon on his breath.

"And you, Mr. Samson," I said primly, releasing myself from his grip.

"What do you think of the party?"

"An interesting collection of guests to say the least."

"I don't much care for them myself. Present company excluded, of course." He glared at the only guest I had not yet met, a gentleman with a squat, flat face, tendrils of graying hair obscuring the place where one might typically find a mouth and chin. His body was sheathed in plates of calcified, translucent skin, and in place of arms or legs he had boneless, trunk-like appendages that protruded through cracks in the dried-out husk of his flesh.

"It's impolite to stare," said Mr. Whatley, approaching us from behind.

Mr. Samson turned and poked his host in the chest. "Do you insult me, sir? By inviting that . . . creature?"

"Mr. Cornelius is a valued member of society, just as you are. As I have told you in the past, I play no favorites. Your disagreements are your own."

"You're playing a dangerous game, Whatley."

"They are the only kind worth playing. Wouldn't you agree, Mrs. Markham?" He gave me a knowing look and smiled with his lopsided smirk.

Mr. Samson huffed away, leaving me alone with the master of Darkling.

"A fair game is more interesting than a dangerous one," I replied, the edge in my voice unmasked.

To my surprise, Mr. Whatley nodded. "It can be difficult to distinguish between the two, especially when an opponent does not realize the advantages she possesses." To this I had no retort, and I glared at him more from confusion than from dislike. He nodded at me and announced to the group that dinner was to begin. We slowly wandered into the dining hall.

The room looked nothing like it had during our previous meals, as it was now exquisitely decorated for the occasion. Bolts of lightning had been captured and mounted on black metallic pedestals along the sides of the room. The walls were adorned with the glass paintings from Mr. Whatley's private collection, each depicting a different landscape: a bleak, cratered wasteland in one; a rocky seashore with a familiar-looking scarlet fortress in the distance of another; a massive, decaying metropolis in one of the grander pieces; and even a representation of the woods just beyond Everton. Upon closer inspection, I became aware that these were not merely pictures but actual windows into the places they showed. In the portrait of Everton, I could see the trees swaying and coils of fog drifting in the breeze.

Mr. Whatley sat at one end of the table and his daughter at the other. I found my name written on a dainty placard and took my seat between Paul and Mr. Puddle, who was next to his wife, while Mr. Cornelius sat beside the Baxters. Miss Yarborough was between Mr. Whatley and Mr. Samson, while Lily and James were between Mr. Snit and Mrs. Aldrich, whose son, Dabney, was next to Olivia and across from Paul. Once everyone was seated, the usual dinner conversation began as we waited for the first course.

"How do you find The Ending?" Mrs. Aldrich addressed me from across the table.

"I'm not sure that I have found it, as of yet," I responded coyly. "It is rather mysterious."

Mrs. Aldrich nodded in agreement. "We are a mysterious people, Mrs. Markham. All of us in our own little fiefdoms, our own great houses, separated by worlds upon worlds. But that is as it should be. Eternity is a very long time, and any society, no matter how enlightened it may be, is bound to tear itself apart just to prove that it can."

"Like the Romans." Paul jumped in and, to my surprise, smiled across the table at Dabney Aldrich.

The other boy spoke up, and once again, everyone stopped

what they were doing to listen to whatever it was he had to say.

"I'm afraid I must disagree with my mother, for if we truly lived in an enlightened society, a difference of opinion would not be enough to set the worlds onto a path of madness."

Miss Yarborough was about to respond when a servant wheeled a cart into the dining hall. On top of it sat a sauté pan and a small burner with a blue flame. Mr. Whatley rose from his chair and addressed his guests.

"The universe is a very large place, but not as vast as one might imagine. There are some commonalities that bind us all together, and here, even in The Ending, it is a custom to formally welcome newcomers with a gathering of friends. Thank you, everyone, for joining us this evening in welcoming our guests." He gestured to the Darrows, and there was polite applause as Mr. Whatley picked up a knife from the table. He held it out in front of him.

"It is our tradition that the host of any gathering make an offer of friendship, and the best thing that anyone can hope to give is a piece of themselves. With that being said—" Mr. Whatley's human hand unraveled into a conjoined grouping of tentacles. He sliced off one of the smaller limbs with the knife, and the hand re-formed no worse for wear. The foot-long piece of flesh fell into the sauté pan, and the servant quickly divided it into sixteen equal portions, tossing them in the air to brown them on all sides. When he was finished, he rolled the cart around the table and served each of the guests a cooked piece of Mr. Whatley.

Paul stared at his plate in horror, and then gave me a pleading look. Across the table Lily nodded at us to consume what we had been given, then scolded James for eating his before everyone else had been served. Paul and I looked at one another, picked up our forks, and placed our slices of tentacle into our mouths. It tasted as if a piece of squid had been stuffed with venison. The thought of where it came from was more revolting than the actual flavor, but it was certainly nothing that I was eager to try again. Paul choked it down and quickly guzzled copious amounts of ice water.

Eager to pick up their conversation where it had been left off, Miss Yarborough spoke up in a crisp, intelligent voice. "There is a difference between simple disagreement and outright rebellion. There are rules that make the universe what it is. Some of those can be broken, but to ignore others is to forget ourselves; we can only be the things that we are, and to pretend otherwise is an act of ignorance."

Mr. Samson jumped in. "A culture that never changes grows stagnant. If we cannot change, then we have nothing to lose and even less to learn, which is why humankind has overtaken our own."

"The essence of our culture is not something to be slouched off to appease some insufferable fad," answered the bearded creature Mr. Whatley had referred to as Mr. Cornelius. "And a dangerous one at that. With all due respect to our distinguished guests, humans do not belong in The Ending."

"A fad would imply a lack of social relevance," said Dabney. "Look around this table, and you will see the beginnings of a movement. We wear the skins of men to remind our brethren of how far we have fallen. If we refuse to evolve, then we might as well be human."

Miss Yarborough scoffed. "That is only a half-truth. You wear them to play at mortality, to pretend for a moment that your time is at an end. You wear them as a sign of solidarity, but it is only a badge of weakness."

"Hear, hear," said Mr. and Mrs. Baxter in complete synchronization.

Olivia sighed and shook her head. "Why must the way one dresses mean anything beyond simple aesthetic appeal? I for one am perfectly happy when I look as I truly am, but even more so when I am dressed as a human girl because it is something I choose to be. It makes me even more like myself."

"My darling daughter, if that is true then you have had more selves than all the guests seated at this table."

"Father is rather old-fashioned, I'm afraid."

Whatley nodded and continued. "A person may be fashionable, but one can only bend so far before one snaps and forgets oneself altogether."

Mr. Samson glared at him, but said nothing as servants returned carrying tureens of steaming soup.

I lifted the lid off of mine and found the bowl filled with a light blue sky. Dollops of cloud drifted across the surface of the broth, and as it cooled they turned to steam and wafted into the air. I dipped my spoon into the soup and brought it to my lips. It tasted of the cool wind that descends upon the land between winter and spring. It was very refreshing.

"At least you were good enough to invite Mrs. Darrow to stay on as my governess," said Olivia to her father. "I've been learning ever so much."

"A young woman must be prepared in this day and age to understand both sides of an argument. We live in dangerous times," said Mr. Whatley in his ironic way, his eyes flickering from me to Lily, and then down to his daughter. I was unsure if he had been talking about himself or about the brewing discontent within The Ending.

"Indeed." The Professor and Mrs. Baxter finished their bowls of soup at the exact same time and pushed them away. "We are quite afraid that civil war will soon be upon us."

"It will never come to that," said Miss Yarborough.

Dabney nodded in agreement. "Cooler heads will surely prevail."

Mr. Puddle leaned back in his chair. "Speck and Ashby are capable politicians. Surely some agreement can be reached."

I was transfixed by this entire exchange, but Mrs. Puddle shook her head with an exasperated sigh. "I do apologize, but I simply can't listen to any more talk of politics." With that, she pulled her ears off of her head and put them into her purse.

"Quite right," said a rose-colored Mr. Snit. "Why dwell on such depressing matters after a fourth glass of wine? Someone say something cheerful or I shall be forced to sing a filthy drinking song."

Miss Yarborough passed her hand through his body to grab hold of something solid at the center of his misty form. He squeaked and remained seated in his chair.

Mr. Samson ignored this and seemed to rise out of his state of agitation. "Young Mr. Aldrich is up for a very important apprenticeship," he said.

Dabney blushed, and Mrs. Aldrich smiled modestly. "One must not become overconfident, Mr. Samson," she said.

The chef entered the dining hall. He was an older, rotund gentleman with pasty skin and the curling mustache traditional for someone in his profession. The dinner guests applauded politely. The other servants raced around the room and gave each of the diners a small hollow pastry. The chef extracted a knife from his belt and held it in the air like it was part of some magician's trick.

Not again, I thought. But he took the knife and cut into his wrist. For any other occurrence of bodily mutilation at the dinner table I would have covered my eyes, but this was such a strange sight that it transcended revulsion. At first, nothing happened. There was no blood. He put the knife back into his belt, took out a medium-size mallet, and stood behind Mr. Whatley. He held his wrist over the plate, and after a moment, something bulged down his sleeve. There was something literally under his skin, crawling down his arm between layers of flesh and muscle, searching for the slit in his wrist. The incision bulged unpleasantly, and a small lizard slithered wetly out of his wound and into the hollow pastry. With his other hand the chef smacked the pastry smartly with the mallet, crushing both it and the lizard in a single blow. He moved to Miss Yarborough and did the same for her. When he got to Olivia, he had to put the mallet under his arm and hold the incision in his wrist closed, for there were more lizard creatures trying to escape than there were guests in the dining hall. James clapped excitedly and couldn't wait to taste his very own lizard, but Paul gagged and I stomped on his foot with the heel of my shoe.

"We must be polite, Paul," I said under my breath. The chef bowed out of the room when he was finished, and I nibbled at the edge of the pastry shell but was hesitant to dig into the meaty center of the thing. Paul drank more water and refused to touch his lizard pastry. He looked up eagerly to Dabney and asked, "What sort of apprenticeship?"

The other boy looked down and smiled humbly. "Mr. Samson is too kind. I will soon be competing for a position with Mr. Speck."

"It's one of the most prestigious apprenticeships in all the worlds," said Mrs. Aldrich with more than a little hint of pride.

"What does this Mr. Speck do, exactly?" I asked, for I could no longer suppress my natural curiosity.

Mr. Whatley, who had been sipping a glass of wine while the other guests finished their lizard pastries, set down his goblet. "Whatever needs to be done; Speck and Ashby are the leaders of our political parties."

The servants returned to clear away the plates and set out a small dish of green salad in front of each guest. After the last course I was relieved to eat something that had not previously been sentient. In no time at all the servants took away the salad plates and gave everyone an eggcup filled with what appeared to be a multicolored egg. I picked up my spoon and was about to dig into it, but then I saw the clouds hovering around the surface of the thing. Upon closer inspection I could see tiny continents and mountains, rivers and valleys. There was a whole world sitting in my eggcup.

Olivia whispered to me, "Don't worry, it's uninhabited."

"Thank heavens," I said. I scooped off the top of the tiny world with my spoon, revealing a warm red-orange center within, and ate it. It was crispy and smooth at the same time, with a hint of peppermint. At first it was cool on my tongue, but when I tasted the core of it I burned my mouth. Even before it slid down the entire length of my throat, I began to feel very full and could barely think of taking another bite. The other diners finished with their eggcups, and the servants cleared the table and brought out the final course. It was a small bowl filled with something dark but insubstantial. Olivia informed me that it was Sweetened Shadows, and after tasting it I had to agree that the name was appropriate. It had a hint of sweetness to it, but no distinct flavor. It was a pleasant way to end a very strange meal.

Mr. Whatley stood from the table, smiling congenially at his guests. "Shall we retire to the drawing room?"

The evening ended the way it began, with everyone engaged in polite conversation until Duncan entered carrying a tray of cordials. Mr. Whatley made another toast to good health, and slowly the other guests began to take their leave of the affair.

Mr. and Mrs. Puddle, who each shook my hand before their departure, were transfixed by the fact that my fingers could only bend in one direction and would not release me until Lily intervened and saw them out the door, leaving me to be approached by the bearded creature with the flat face.

"Mrs. Markham. We have yet to be formally introduced. I am called Cornelius." He bowed before me, which was for the best as I did not relish the thought of shaking one of his trunk-like limbs. "I hope we did not offend you with all the talk of politics." As he spoke, I could see appendages moving themselves to form words behind the curtain of his beard. The effect was deeply off-putting, but I kept my gaze focused on his dark onyx eyes.

"On the contrary, I found it most intriguing, though I confess I still do not understand the reason for the disagreement."

"As with most arguments, it is an old one hardly worth discussing." He ushered me to a far corner of the room where we could sit beside one another on a chaise longue beneath the window. "I do hope you'll forgive me for saying so, but I could not help overhearing your exchange with our host earlier this evening."

I stiffened. "That was a private conversation."

"Which is why I beg for your forgiveness. But you and I are of a similar mind. A game should only be played when both sides are evenly matched. Our host would do well to remember that."

"Then we are in agreement."

"I observed you listening intently to our dinner conversation. What did you make of our host?"

"His words appease one faction of The Ending, while his appearance pacifies another."

"Precisely. And yet, Mr. Whatley has a reputation for decisiveness. It is perplexing that he should be uncertain of where his loyalties lie, and a situation I am eager to end."

I peered at him carefully, absorbing his words and searching his black eyes for some hint of his character. "That is a most vexing problem, but why should you bring it to my attention?"

"There have never before been living humans in The Ending. For some, that alone could be viewed as an act of treason, but others are not so sure. I only wish to find some token of Mr. Whatley's allegiance to Ashby's cause, so that we might put away our suspicions."

"And what cause might that be?"

"To preserve our traditions, and, if I may be frank, some sense of stability. Speck and his compatriots are dabbling in things that could upset the balance of your world in addition to our own. You are here more than I; there are many rooms in the House of Darkling, and I am unable to explore them all. You can see my dilemma. It is for his own good, wouldn't you agree?"

"Why should I wish to do anything for the good of Mr. Whatley?"

"Because I can offer a token of protection against whatever game he has you playing." Mr. Cornelius reached into his beard and extracted a small iron key. He handed it to me before any of the other guests noticed. "Provide me with evidence of Whatley's allegiance, and I will protect you from him." He gestured to the key. "One turn in any lock will send for me."

I took the key and slid it into the folds of my dress. "How can I trust you?"

"I'm afraid, my dear, that you do not have much of a choice."

Mr. Cornelius and the Baxters left without saying good-bye to anyone, but none of the other guests seemed very offended. Mrs. Aldrich went to collect her son, who was seated next to Paul in a far corner of the room. They were deep in conversation and very cross when they had to part. More strange than anything during the evening was the abrupt disappearance of Paul's perpetual gloom. He began to smile and continued to do so even after Dabney left the house.

Miss Yarborough and Mr. Snit were the last to depart. The gentleman was so intoxicated by the end of the evening that he turned a nasty shade of green and had to be gathered into a milk jar to be carried out by his proud, haughty companion.

Lily and I said good night to the Whatleys and took the children to their room. As before, Lily took Laurel Parker Wolfe's book of fairy tales from the compartment beside the bed. The children wrapped themselves against her as she began to read.

The Seamless Children

Once upon a time, there was a village in the forest. The people were happy and prosperous for a long while until a sickness spread throughout the land and took the lives of many small children. The villagers were distraught, for the local doctor could not cure them, and with the coming of winter they would certainly not survive. It was quickly decided that the only thing to do would be to seek the help of the mysterious old wizard who lived in a cave deep in the wood.

The wizard, who was lonely and did not receive many visitors, was glad to help the villagers, but he cautioned them on the dangers of what they asked him to do. "The young ones will not survive the winter as they are. Bring them to me if you will, but I warn you that the task you present me with is a difficult one. I may not be able to undo it."

The villagers thanked the wizard for his warning but were so desperate to save their children that they bundled them in heavy fur blankets and carried them to the cave in the wood without a second thought. The wizard spread a large cloth sheet over the ground and asked that the children be laid in a circle on top of it. When this was done, he moved his hands through the air in an intricate pattern of unseen glyphs, all the while reciting some secret spell under his breath. The children grew smaller, down to the size of babes, and the wizard gathered the ends of the cloth sheet, shaping it into a sack. He twisted the ends together until they were closed, and kept turning them against the bulk of the shrunken children until their little faces pressed roughly against the fabric. The wizard continued the motion until the fabric came apart in many places, but the children were no longer inside. Instead, the pieces of cloth had been split and sewn together to form a family of rag dolls, one in the place of each child.

The villagers, who were not sure what to make of this change, had very little time to dwell on it, for as soon as the wizard finished he fell to his knees and died. The strain of the spell had been too great, and even as the doll children rose to their little cloth feet and stretched their little cloth arms, their parents backed out of the cave, unable to deal with what had been done to them and choosing instead to imagine that they had died along with the wizard.

It was a long, lonely winter for the dolls who had once been children. They buried the wizard as best they could, some of them ruining the threading of their delicate hands as they dug into the cold, hard earth. Most of them chose to live in the wizard's cave, but others tried to return home to the families that had abandoned them. These reunions never ended well, for even at their best, the parents still looked upon the dolls as little ghosts in cloth skin. The lucky ones were able to return to the cave, but more often than not they were burned and buried or torn apart in hopes of releasing whatever remnant of the child remained hidden within the body of the rag doll.

The single winter they had been made to survive came and went. Years passed, and the doll children slowly began to fall apart; threading unraveled, cloth skin split, and the stuffing that kept them whole fell out in clumps. It was decided among them that they could not go on for much longer. Some of them had heard during their unhappy trips to the village that there was a fairy in a nearby forest, and if the stories were true, she would be able to undo what the wizard had done.

Together the dolls traveled across the land, avoiding hawks and wolves by sleeping in hollowed-out logs, crossing large brooks so that their bodies became waterlogged, until finally they came to a small house made of colored glass at the edge of the forest. The company of dolls col-

lapsed before the door, summoning just enough strength to rap their cloth fists against the smooth entrance. The fairy found them in a sad state of disrepair and gathered them into her arms, setting them before a comfortable fireplace to rest and dry. When they were well enough to speak, she sat with them on the ground to listen to their plea.

"Good fairy," they said, "we who were once children wish to go back to what we were."

The fairy petted their soft cloth heads and nodded in understanding.

"Are you sure that is what you truly wish?" she asked them. "Instead, I could fix up your holes and strengthen your threading. You could go on forever, if you wish. The life of a child is hard and sometimes short."

But the doll children had come for one reason only and could not be dissuaded from their wish. The fairy placed them all into a large cauldron and cooked them for seven days and seven nights in boiling water until their cloth became skin and their stuffing turned to flesh, until their little bodies swelled and grew to their original sizes. They slept for the entire day when she was done. She found clothing for them, and a wagon with a horse, so that when they awoke they were ready to return to their families.

It was a bittersweet reunion. The families were very guilty about what they had done to their young ones, but the children who had once been dolls could not be bothered with anger or grief, for when the good fairy had returned them to their original forms, she had also brought back the incurable sickness that had driven their parents to seek the old wizard's help. They were put to bed, and surrounded by the families that had left them alone for so many years, they died as they should have done years before.

Lily closed the book and set it down in her lap. During the story James had squirmed away from her and moved to his own bed. Paul stayed by her side, his eyes closed and his arm around his mother.

"I don't think I like bedtime stories anymore," said James.

"I must admit that this one is a bit sad, but it has a very good moral."

"Accept your fate or suffer the consequences?" Paul yawned and stretched, releasing her from his embrace and settling into his own bed.

"No, not at all." Lily gaped for a moment, put off by his comment. "Enjoy the time you have with the ones you love. No matter what the situation."

James pulled his covers up to his chin as his mother tucked him in. "Do you think they were happy to die?" he asked her.

"Not to die, but to be with their families again, yes." She kissed him on the forehead and turned to do the same for Paul, but he was already under the blankets with his head on his pillow and his eyes closed.

"How could they be?" said the older boy. "They were abandoned for years and years. You can't forget something like that."

"But they did. When you only have so much time together, you must move on." Lily knelt beside him and kissed him on the cheek.

He squinted when she did so and turned away from her. "I'm tired."

Lily looked as if she'd been struck across the face. She left the room before I could and leaned against the wall outside. I closed the door and joined her in the hallway.

"Are you all right?"

"Yes, I'm fine. That story . . . I was trying to prepare them. You were right that these visits cannot go on for much longer. We have to move on. I have to let them go. Good night, Charlotte." She kissed me on the forehead the same as she had done to the boys and walked alone down the dark hallway to wherever it was that she went during our slumber. I did not have time to dwell on this.

I entered my room and found the curio set in the wall, opening the panel that held the tiny candle men. They were playing a game of keep-away with the smallest of their group, tossing his wax head back and forth between them when I cleared my throat in disapproval.

"Could you please take me to the dark room? You know the one I mean." They ended their game and hopped down to the floor, and together we paraded through the House of Darkling to the bas-relief sculpture of marble faces twisted in suffering. I pressed my finger into the eye socket of one of the characters, just as Duncan had done, and the wall behind the sculpture clicked open.

It was empty save for the frightening metal chair with its restraints and the wheeled table that stood beside it. I passed through the gauzy veiled partitions to the center of the chamber as the candle people waited for me outside, refusing to enter.

I knelt down and opened a compartment beneath the table, revealing a dozen rows of the smoky-colored phials, each of them featuring a white label with a concise description written in a refined, elegant hand. There were phials labeled STRAN-

GLED, INFIRMED, IMPALED, DROWNED, BURNED, SHOT, EATEN, FROZEN, and so on and so forth, each classified by some form of misfortune. I placed one marked DISMEMBERED into my pocket and paused at BURNED. I pulled out the stopper and sniffed at the contents. It smelled of charcoal. Not exactly appetizing, but to deliver Cornelius something useful, I had to know what I had found. I dipped a finger into the black fluid so that a small trace of it was left clinging to my skin, and placed it into my mouth, ingesting it as I had seen Mr. Samson do.

Suddenly I was not myself. The air was burning around me, enveloped by wreaths of flame and smoke. I was carrying something important bundled in cloth, running from room to room, my skin blistering and cracking, hair crisping against a blackened scalp. When I burst through the door into the cool night air, it pressed against the searing of my flesh, only intensifying the pain until I collapsed to the ground.

The parcel I clutched unraveled to reveal the scorched face of a woman with blond hair and a short, pointed nose, a face I beheld in the mirror whenever attempting to conjure the image of my late mother, a habit that always lent me strength, though at that moment the sight of it stripped away every shred of energy and composure I had left. I screamed, and as I screamed, the world slipped away into the blackness of oblivion, where I remained for what felt like an eternity, frozen in terror at the sight of my own body sprawled on the floor as I realized that the person running through the burning house had been Jonathan, and that, for a moment, I had felt what he had as he died.

Someone grabbed my shoulder. I spun around, nearly dropping the phial, only to find Duncan standing behind me, a finger pressed to the wry smile on his lips.

"Now you know."

For a moment I thought the mute had spoken, but then Mr. Samson appeared behind him, his eyes bloodshot, the lines in his face more visible than even at dinner.

"Death. All of them." I motioned to the smoke-colored phials with an exhausted wave of my hand.

"Many different kinds of death." Mr. Samson sat his large body on the metal chair and allowed Duncan to strap him in. "We dress as humans for many reasons, but for most of us, we simply wish for peace. Endless peace. This is as close as we are likely to ever get. Ashby, Cornelius, and the others . . . they fear us. Death has never been allowed into The Ending. If that were to change, then death for some would mean death for all." He pointed to one of the phials, and Duncan began to make his preparations.

"The death I saw. It was my husband's." I could scarcely get the words out.

"Is that so? A most peculiar coincidence. But then again, few things are coincidental with Mr. Whatley. He does enjoy his games. Despite what you think, or what he might wish you to think, he is a great man. He gives us peace, if only for a few moments."

I gestured to the phials, hands shaking. "Where does he find them?"

"He collects them. Observes them as they are happening, or so I'm told. Though I wouldn't put it past him to cause a few deaths in order to expand his collection."

My stomach lurched, and I had to concentrate very intently in order to stop myself from being sick. The man in black from my past had never been the specter of Death. It was Whatley who had plagued my life since I was a girl. But was he simply an observer of my misfortune, or had he taken my family from me to set in motion the series of events that would slowly steer me toward Everton, to Darkling, and into the diabolical game I now played with him? I had learned something important, for while I still did not fully comprehend the scope of his intentions, I now at least knew how to solve the puzzle of our game. The strongest connection between Darkling and Blackfield was not Susannah or Nanny Prum or even Lily Darrow. It was me.

"He must be stopped," I said through gritted teeth.

"On the contrary, Mrs. Markham. You have your own death. Leave us with ours."

Duncan held a darkened sugar cube before Mr. Samson's lips, and the gentleman bit down on it with a satisfied crunch. As his body began to convulse, I backed out of the room and retreated to what comfort could be provided by a strange bed in the strange house of the man in black.

CHAPTER 14
Lock and Key

The children and I ate breakfast alone, and when we were finished Duncan escorted us back through the orchard. We arrived at Everton, and I took the children up to the schoolroom to continue their lessons. It would be difficult to say which of us was more subdued. The boys answered questions without complaint and barely looked up when Ellen entered to inform me that Mr. Darrow required my presence in his study.

I meandered through the halls of Everton, and though I failed to find any trace of the boy with the keyhole eyes, I was unable to shake the feeling that I was being watched. The sensation only intensified when I entered Mr. Darrow's study. The master of Everton stood from his desk when I found him.

"Mrs. Markham."

"Mr. Darrow. I didn't see you at breakfast." I took my seat across from him, and something cool brushed against my leg. I looked down in time to catch sight of a length of chain disappearing around the side of the desk. I felt the color drain from my face, but Mr. Darrow appeared oblivious and remained where he was, leaning forward on the palms of his hands, apprehensive and clearly anxious. I resisted the urge to cry out or leap after the shackles, focusing myself entirely on his gaze.

"I've had a lot to think about," he said.

"As have I."

Mr. Darrow opened his mouth to speak, but no words came out as he looked into my eyes, searching for something to say. Behind him, the boy with the keyhole eyes crept noiselessly up the wall beside Lily's portrait, sniffing at it, his head twisted in an unnatural position so that his abominable face never left our direction, broken teeth poking out from between pale gray lips.

"What happened last night . . . I'm afraid I put you in a very bad position."

"You mustn't think that," I replied, nervous that my voice might betray the growing horror I felt at the sight of the creature perching itself in the corner of the ceiling. I tentatively placed my hand over Mr. Darrow's. He pulled away.

"But I do, and there's only one thing to be done about it." He sat down roughly in his chair and looked away from me. "I must send you away."

The anxiety I felt over Darkling and the terrible childlike creature faded beneath the weight of his words as they hung in the air between us, stinging. "You can't possibly mean that."

"I took advantage of your kindness and friendship, I see that now. It's for your own good."

"I don't wish to leave. Doesn't that amount to anything?" I felt it all slipping away—the storybook ending, my future with the children, Henry's happiness, Lily's redemption, my victory over Whatley—the pieces were sliding out of place.

"It can't. We have to think of the children. Your reputation."

"My reputation is perfectly intact."

"And I'd like to keep it that way. The servants will start to talk."

Then I began to understand. The anger I felt won out, and the mask made of rules and restraint that had been threatening to slip from my grasp finally did.

"I see. Of course, how silly of me, it's not *my* reputation that concerns you."

"That is not what I meant."

"Did you ever stop to think that perhaps it was I who took advantage of you?"

"No, never!"

"Well, perhaps you should have. Perhaps you are simply stronger than me, because I'll never be strong enough to deny the way I feel about you." He stared at me dumbly, mouth agape.

"Will you tell the children or should I?" I carried on. "I can't imagine what it will do to them to have another woman taken from their lives."

"I should be the one to tell them."

"Then I'll go and collect my things."

"Please don't be angry," he pleaded.

"I'm not angry, you fool. I'm heartbroken."

He moved his mouth in a mechanical sort of way, but no sound came out. I turned away from him and stormed out of his study, throwing the door shut with a satisfying crack that echoed down the hallway. I leaned against the wall to steady myself, fighting the urge to break down and cry.

Contrary to what I'd told Henry, I was angry. Not just with him, but at myself for becoming vulnerable to an illusion. I had overreached, placing my hopes into a fairy tale that was not real, that hardly ever happened. Men like Henry Darrow did not fall in love with their servants. They raped them and sent them away to raise their bastard children in poverty. I stopped myself. I was becoming dramatic. Mr. Darrow had taken no liberties with me save for our kiss in the kitchen, and again, I felt my loss. Men like Henry Darrow did not come along very often, and that made it all the worse.

I contemplated the different ways I could attempt to keep him until my mind drifted into dark places. *There is always blackmail.* I pushed the voice out of my head, but it returned again as quickly as it came. *Lily could help you. She wants you together. You have not lost.* At this I shuddered, for I did not wish to win or lose Henry Darrow. I wanted him to love me.

Tears welled in the corners of my eyes, blurring my vision to the point that I almost dismissed the shape of a head materializing through the closed oak door to Mr. Darrow's study. I lunged for it without thinking, grasping the boy with the keyhole eyes by the scruff of his neck and pulling him all the way out into the hall.

I looped his chains around my wrist and lifted him beneath the crook of my arm, trapping him as I ran down the corridor to my room. I passed by a single maid dusting the draperies, but I moved so quickly that she did not give me a second glance as the creature was roughly the same size as James. He squirmed beneath my grip while I struggled with the door, but I won out and slammed it closed, dropping onto my bed with the childlike thing in my lap.

"Now, what to do with you?" *Mysteries of The Ending* was locked away in a trunk at the foot of my bed, and even if I were able to get it open while keeping hold of the boy, I had no idea what his mistress might do if I showed up with him in hand. He writhed against me, and the chain jangled on the floor where the brass skeleton key connected to the last link caught on the fabric of my dress. I reached for it as he slipped away, grabbing hold of the key as the creature bolted toward the door. I yanked on the chain with all my might, and the boy jerked backward to the floor. I stepped over him to straddle his chest as I inserted the key into his right eye socket with the familiar click of metal against bone. He immediately went still and began to speak in a hushed, androgynous whisper.

"They meet in the night." I almost asked him to elaborate, but he continued without pausing for breath in a second, more familiar voice.

"For what purpose?"

"A sharing of affections. And it would appear that they drink tea."

"Most curious. Either way it shouldn't be much longer. You should prepare yourself."

"Am I still permitted to take the seamstress?"

"To what end?"

"I wear many skins for you, and I've always wanted to have someone to repair them."

"As you will, so long as you do as we discussed."

"Of course, Mr. Whatley."

With that, the boy with the keyhole eyes stopped speaking and began to melt into the floor. Refusing to lose him again, I looped the length of chain around my bedpost and watched as it was stretched taut, the other end of the shackles trailing away into the solid wood flooring as the boy struggled to free himself.

Despite all of my other failures, I took some solace in the fact that I had managed to detain him, and could make my way back to the dilapidated castle in order to return him to his master. Still, there was much left undone. Who would help the boys say good-bye to their mother? Who would protect them from the

House of Darkling? The answer was simple, really. If I was to be dismissed, then I would tell Mr. Darrow of his wife's bargain. If what Lily said were true, then the doorway between Everton and The Ending would be closed, and while the boys might hate me for it, I would at least get the satisfaction of knowing that they were safe from things I could neither fully explain nor understand.

The conversation I'd just overheard with the help of the boy with the keyhole eyes confirmed that Whatley's intentions were at least malicious toward Susannah. Considering how transparent he had been in his plotting, I found this hardly surprising. In fact, it was mildly comforting to know that I had at least discovered a part of his methodology. With a servant of Whatley's living at Everton, there was little choice but to send Susannah away to escape whatever designs had been fixed on her. If I was indeed the link between Darkling and Blackfield, then I hoped my departure and the removal of the door between the two worlds would be enough to divert Whatley's attention away from the remaining members of the Darrow family.

I felt sorry for Lily. She would never know what had happened, and I appeared unable to save her from whatever Mr. Whatley had in store. But I could not allow her relationship to continue without my supervision. It was too unpredictable.

I dug my valise out of the wardrobe and began to assemble my belongings. I couldn't bring myself to pack them away, so I laid everything into piles on the bed, carefully arranging and rearranging them until well after nightfall, when there was a knock at my door. I draped a blanket over the chain that disappeared into the floor and opened the door.

Ellen looked tired. "It's Mr. Darrow. He didn't come down for dinner, and when Roland went to bring him his plate, he was gone. We've searched the whole house, but he's nowhere to be found, and no one knows where he's run off to. What are we to do?"

I turned back to the spread of clothes I had assembled and braced myself from feeling too acutely the pain of my impending departure.

"Perhaps he's gone to the village?"

"Mr. Darrow never leaves the grounds of Everton if he doesn't have to, and never without telling anyone. It's not like him at all."

"Are the horses accounted for?"

"Yes. And the carriages and the bicycles. He couldn't have gone far, wherever he went, but with the weather getting on the way it is, he might catch his death." It was not so cold as to be freezing, but it was cool enough to signal the start of winter. Soon the lakes would turn to ice, and snow would begin to fall, and the house would prepare for the holidays. I had so wanted to spend Christmas at Everton. I snapped myself back to the matter at hand before I trailed off into self-pity.

Ellen and I went down to the kitchen and were joined by Roland, Fredricks, Mrs. Norman, and Mrs. Mulbus, the group of us deciding what to do and whether or not a search party should be sent out. Before we had made much progress in our pursuit of the master of the house, the doorbell rang and we found Mr. Scott on our doorstep with Mr. Darrow clinging to his side.

"Found him in the graveyard. Must have been there for hours."

Indeed, he looked very pale. I took him from the vicar and put his arm over my shoulder. He could walk, but only just. I helped carry him up to his bedroom, while Ellen kindled a fire in the hearth.

"What have you done to yourself?" I whispered as I tucked him into bed.

"She's gone" was all he said before slipping off to sleep. His forehead began to burn, and I summoned Dr. Barberry, who prescribed lots of fluids and plenty of rest.

Henry remained bedridden for a number of days, and I attended to his every need without regard to propriety. The children flitted in and out at will, monitored by Ellen and content with the fact that their father continued to be alive and well. The servants could talk all that they wanted, but I would tend to Henry until he was recovered and then I would leave.

A week after he became ill, I found his bed empty when I went to bring him his breakfast. I went downstairs, where he was in the dining room with the children. I tried to leave before he saw me, but I was too late. He invited me to eat with them. Color had returned to his cheeks, and even some of the dourness that had lingered in him for so long seemed to have abated.

"I take it you're feeling better, Mr. Darrow?"

"Yes, thanks to your diligence."

"In the future I hope that you will do everyone a courtesy and refrain from sitting out in the cold until you become ill."

"I was careless. About many things." He smiled at me weakly, not out of exhaustion or illness, but as a matter of apology.

"Do you think so?"

"More than that. I was wrong. I hope you'll ignore what I said."

"I could never do that. But we can speak later. The boys and I have a schedule to maintain."

"Of course. Some other time."

"Perhaps."

And with that, everything was back to the way it had always

been. I maintained my position and Henry kept his detachment, staring into the bottom of his teacup as I ushered the children up to the schoolroom. It was difficult to begin our lessons again after a weeklong absence, and progress was slow, but after four hours of reviewing everything from the fall of ancient Rome to the Pythagorean theorem, the boys were well primed and in need of a break. I didn't have to ask them what they wished to do. I could see the longing in their eyes radiating out of them.

It was the longest gap we'd had between our visits to Darkling, and no sooner had Duncan brought us to the steps of the house than Lily Darrow appeared at the door, red-faced and breathless as if she had run the length of the manor to meet us.

"You've come back!" Her eyes were wide and glistening, though whether it was from fear or joy I could not be certain. She hugged the children for a long while in a simple, moving gesture until James pulled away.

"Father was sick so Charlotte took care of him."

"I'm sorry to hear that. Thank you for looking after my husband." She did not look at me as she said the words. "Come. I'm afraid I'm in the middle of my lessons with Olivia, but you may join us." Lily took us to the ballroom, where Olivia was dancing languidly before Mrs. Aldrich and her son, Dabney. The woman stopped Olivia and placed her manicured hands beneath the girl's arms, moving them into a more rigid position above her head.

"The Dance of Infinite Sorrow requires the arms to be kept over the head at all times, as if you're holding the moon against the sky. Do you understand?"

Olivia bit the inside of her cheek and nodded politely but broke form when she saw that she had an audience. "Lily, you brought the children! How delightful!"

Paul became indignant at being referred to as a child. "I'm not a child! I'm thirteen." He said this a little more loudly than he needed to and quickly greeted his friend Dabney with a hearty handshake. The eerily handsome young man laughed and embraced Paul with a hug instead.

"Olivia is to have a coming-out ball," explained Lily. "And now I must insist that we continue with our lessons. Dabney?"

The boy left Paul's side and took Miss Whatley's hands into his own. They swept across the ballroom as Lily counted time, a graceful blur of golden hair and pale-skinned beauty. When Lily was satisfied with their progress, and only after Mrs. Aldrich approved, we sat for dinner.

Dabney's mother chatted with Miss Whatley at one end of the table while her son conversed quietly with Paul at the other, leaving Lily and me to catch up. James sat silently eating his meal, an uncharacteristic gloominess seemingly borrowed from his older brother, but other than that it was a perfectly delightful evening. I looked over to Paul halfway through the meal. He was smiling and laughing, as children should. He seemed completely transformed in the company of the older boy, and it dawned on me that perhaps there was some good in the House of Darkling after all.

The Aldriches left after the meal, and as always, Lily escorted us up to our rooms. But this time she kissed the boys good night without tucking them in, and the book of fairy tales was not taken out. No one mentioned this change, and so neither did I, but it was obvious that something had shifted, or was shifting, even in a place where such a thing was never supposed to happen.

I waited in the hallway for Lily as I always did, not expecting her to look so tired and worn down when she turned away from the door to face me.

"Is everything all right?" I asked. She seemed on the verge of tears.

"Life is never what one expects, and death is only worse."

"What's happened?"

"Nothing I can't manage." Her eyes darted around the hallway, and she led me into my room, closing the door behind us. "Please . . . when you leave tomorrow, don't come back."

"I don't understand. I promised you one last visit after this one. What's happened?"

"I wanted to say good-bye. Now it's done." She clutched the knob of the door, uncertain about something.

"But is it done for the children?" I asked.

"It must be. For their own good."

"What shall I tell them?"

"Something that will make it better."

"There's no such thing."

Lily nodded glumly and then left me alone to consider how I might tell the boys that their mother had left them again, only this time of her own free will. It consumed me, most of all because I did not understand why someone with such love and determination would give up everything she had fought so hard to earn. More important, I was not done with Darkling myself.

When I dressed for bed I removed the smoke-colored phial labeled DISMEMBERED and placed it beside the iron key given to me by Mr. Cornelius. I had still not sent him proof of Whatley's loyalty to Ashby's adversaries. Despite the murder of Nanny Prum and the continued harassment of Susannah, he was helping his people. What kind of murderer did such a thing? I wondered if I had something wrong, or if things would only get worse if I involved myself in a larger game than the one I was playing with Mr. Whatley.

I could not sleep, and so I returned to the library to collect my thoughts. I did not know what I was looking for, exactly. Perhaps I sought something to take my mind off the plight of the Darrows, or maybe it was something more substantial, to fix what could not be mended. I read through the various titles on the shelves until my eyes drifted up to the door on the fourth floor that led to Mr. Whatley's study. I walked up the spiral staircase with slow uncertainty, not sure what it was I intended to do, until I was in front of the door, about to try the handle, when it opened.

"Mrs. Markham." He wore a robe and nothing else, his muscled chest visible between the conveniently placed folds of the fabric.

"Mr. Whatley."

"Trouble sleeping?" He smirked at me with his usual indolent, boyish grin, so self-satisfied that it made me question my sanity for ever thinking that there could be something good and decent about him.

"Something like that."

"I wouldn't know. I don't sleep."

"How sad for you."

"Come in, if you'd like."

I considered his offer. I pictured him all in black, standing over the corpses of my mother, my father, Jonathan, and Nanny Prum. I had no evidence that he had actually killed them; just that he had somehow taken their memories of death, and that a piece from his collection had been used against Susannah and presumably Nanny Prum. But I still lacked the most important part of the puzzle: *why me?* I pushed past him without a word.

The room was much the same as it had been before. Mr. Whatley's chest glowed nearly as luminously as the alabaster statues that lined the walls of the first part of his collection. He continued on, past the glass portraits that led to real places, a room of trees that changed seasons every few seconds, fountains built out of water that flowed with streams of liquid marble, until we reached the end and turned in to a high alcove that resembled a cathedral, with vaulted ceilings and a bed at the far end that was like an altar. It was quite grandiose and ridiculous, but at the same time perfectly appropriate for someone of his character.

"Would you care to see my true collection?"

"That wasn't it?"

"Of course not. A true collector keeps the rarest items private." He walked to the wall behind the bed and found a hidden panel that opened a secret door. He slid inside, his features disappearing into shadow. I followed him, for I knew that he would not harm me. He would not end our game without a grander confrontation; of that much I was certain.

The secret room was a miniature version of the library, but instead of books it held a wide variety of people, each of them standing motionless on a labeled pedestal, their eyes closed as if they were sleeping, waiting to be stirred from a long, sad dream. There were men and women, old and young, beautiful and plain, of various colors and sizes, something different for every occasion. It did not take me long to find Lily, positioned at the center of the display like a living doll, her chin resting on her chest. At the sight of her my face grew flushed with anger.

This is where she sleeps. I had imagined her in another wing of the house, perhaps in a room adjacent to Olivia's or, as I already had a sense of Mr. Whatley's true character, one that was convenient to his own.

"What do you think?" Mr. Whatley's eyes, normally black and soulless, shimmered an inhuman silver-green in the dark of the room.

"It's disgusting." I spoke between clenched teeth.

"Perhaps a little. But all completely voluntary."

"That's even worse."

"They're all people of exceptional character. They did what they had to do in order to get what they wanted most."

"Which was what?"

"That depends. They all had different desires. What is it that you want most, Mrs. Markham?"

"To free her." I gestured to Lily. "And to beat you."

Mr. Whatley chuckled, the sound of it reverberating through the room. "You are hardly alone with the latter sentiment. Living humans in The Ending have begun to make Mr. Ashby's friends uncomfortable."

"I do not intend to stay after I've stopped you."

He raised an eyebrow, and the perpetual smirk stuck on his face twisted into one of greed. "Are you so certain of yourself?"

"You don't frighten me."

"Perhaps I should." He came closer to me, close enough to brush a strand of hair away from my face, which he did with his large hand. His touch was different from Henry's—rougher and empty of any emotion, but possessed with a power, like his voice and his eyes, that made me want to fall into him and pull away at the same time. I did not dare to move.

"Everything I've ever loved has been taken from me, piece by piece, year by year, to place me where I now stand. I have nothing left to fear."

"You think yourself very clever, yet I am older than you could imagine and that much more powerful. The only thing you have that I do not is a death, which some might consider a disadvantage. Do you think this will end well?"

"Not for you."

"I'm not afraid to lose so long as everyone else does. You'd do well to remember that, Mrs. Markham"

"But that's not how the story goes. Someone has to win."

"Indeed. But whose story is it? Yours or mine?"

"I suppose we'll have to wait and see." I turned away from him, confident that he would not do me any physical harm while my back was turned, and moved toward the door.

"Best of luck to you, Mrs. Markham. I can't wait to see what will happen next."

I walked the entire length of the long room feeling his gaze at my back, unwilling to turn around to see if he was following me. I reached the door to the library and closed it behind me. The place had lost all the comfort that it once offered. I returned to my room, but not before checking once on the boys to make sure they were still comfortably asleep in their beds, unthinking and unworried about what their mother might have done in order to see them again.

I lifted the smoke-colored phial and the iron key from where I had left them on my bed and stood before my bedroom door. I recalled the words of Mr. Cornelius.

One turn in any lock will send for me.

I inserted the key into the lock and turned. The door opened into a dank, chilly room with walls covered in a hard, emerald film. A shape appeared on the ceiling, and Mr. Cornelius scuttled down the wall to greet me, the feelers behind his beard formed into a smile.

"Mrs. Markham."

"There is a room in the House of Darkling where those who so desire might taste a human death. Is that the proof you require?" I handed him the phial labeled DISMEMBERED.

"It should do nicely." He tucked it into his beard and turned, pressing his flat face against the wall, pincers emerging from the graying tendrils of his facial hair to work into the glossy green surface, cutting and slicing at it until a chunk broke away into the stout trunk-like appendages he used as hands. He held it out to me. "A token of protection."

It was a clear disk of petrified green amber, with a single glyph scratched into it.

"What do I do with it?"

"Keep it close. Do be careful, Mrs. Markham. He won't like this, not one bit." He escorted me back to the door.

"Let it never be said that I'm an unworthy opponent."

We parted company, and when I attempted to retrieve the iron key from the lock of my door, I was not surprised to find it missing. Our bargain had been completed, and I was once again on my own. I crawled into bed clutching the green amber disk to my breast, and for the first time in all our visits to Darkling, I slept peacefully.

CHAPTER 15

The Christmas Guest

Winter finally descended upon Blackfield a few days later. The barren branches of the forest became gloved in white snow, stretched out beneath the pale gray sky and arranged around the glass shores of the lake in a frozen ballet bereft of movement or song, dormant until spring, when the ice would melt and stream off of them, their forms glistening from the extended concentration of holding a single pose all season long.

But the villagers themselves would not be forced into hibernation. Indeed, the winter months were some of the busiest of the year. After the bazaar there were dinner parties and special church services, winter markets and quilting circles, not to mention the grandest event of all: the Blackfield Christmas Ball.

It was not really a ball so much as it was a local dance festival, but since it was held in the home of Cornelia Reese it could not be called anything else, nor discussed without the highest reverence, at least not within the presence of Mrs. Reese. The Reeses lived in the largest house in the village, and although it was only slightly bigger than Everton, that was enough for Mrs. Reese to declare it the only proper place to hold such an event, for it could accommodate the entire population of Blackfield. There was nothing the woman liked more than to take pity upon the poor dregs of society, the common folk who were not so well off as she, so that they might know, for at least one evening, some happiness in their sad and dreary lives. Despite this fact, or perhaps because of it, the people of Blackfield had no problem converging upon the Reese estate, which was called Arkham Hall, and conversing very loudly among themselves about how dreary the interiors had become since the previous year, all the while piling copious amounts of food into their mouths and purses, completely willing to play along with Cornelia so long as they could take advantage of her generosity. After all, a party was a party.

That afternoon I cornered James after our lessons and threw him over my shoulder. He giggled and kicked his legs, always a willing participant in any sort of violence, but he did not pass up the opportunity to make a scene.

"Help! I'm being murdered!"

This was in very bad taste, considering what had happened to Nanny Prum. Fortunately Paul was old enough to be aware of such sensitivities and swatted his brother on the back of the head as we left the schoolroom. James, like many little boys of similar temperament, did not care for the idea of a bath. There were too many mud puddles to splash through, too many frogs to capture, too many trees to climb to bother with such provincial chores as bathing. However, once submerged in water, after the thrashing of arms and legs subsided, he was quite at home being naked and wet, imagining himself to be a fish and slipping through my hands as I struggled to soap him up.

When we finished I carried him back to his room, careful not to let him out of my sight before we left the house. Paul was nearly finished getting dressed, meticulously combing his dark hair. I was glad that Lily could not see him then. It wouldn't be long before he would be a young man, no longer requiring the services of a governess or a nanny. I placed James into his brother's care as I began my own preparations for the evening, and threatened him with Indian curses if he did anything to undo my work with his brother's appearance.

For myself I sat before the mirror and released my hair from the top of my head, smoothing it out with a brush and pinning it back into place with small jeweled pins that were once my mother's. That evening she did not appear in my reflection. I put aside my governess's uniform and stepped into an evening gown the color of deep midnight, the corset flecked with silver beads that gave the impression of stars in the night sky.

Just before dusk the children and I met Mr. Darrow in the foyer of Everton. His mood was unreadable, as he did not meet my gaze, but he had done a reasonable job of dressing himself for the occasion. His blond hair had been slicked back so that it did not hide his handsome blue eyes, and he wore a dark suit with a cream-colored vest and a deep blue tie that coincidentally matched the color of my gown. I doubted that he noticed, but I would not be the one to make mention of it. I was merely the governess.

Mrs. Mulbus and Jenny had already departed to prepare for the evening's festivities, and the other servants left the house in packs, wearing heavy coats over their finest dresses and suits. Even Mrs. Norman looked mildly less dreary than normal, wearing a feathered hat that made her resemble something like a peacock. She was escorted out of the house by old Fredricks, who secreted away a small silver flask in the folds of his jacket with the hand that was not holding Mrs. Norman's.

Roland brought a covered carriage around to the door and helped us inside. The boys immediately sat on the same side of the vehicle, forcing Mr. Darrow and me to sit uncomfortably beside one another. Fortunately the trip was a short one, and soon we were pulling into the modest driveway of Arkham Hall.

While the house might have been only slightly larger than Everton, it was better kept and much more ornate. Cornelia Reese still traveled to the city with some regularity to maintain her social calendar, and she always returned with a small caravan of antique dealers and artists to fortify the appearance of whatever room had lost her good favor.

Our carriage pulled around a marble fountain meant to emulate the antiquities of ancient Rome. It was a ghastly thing, with streams of water pouring out of eye sockets and battle wounds, but very appropriate for the home of Cornelia Reese. One of the footmen helped me out of the carriage, and with James's hand secured into my own, I entered the foyer of the house.

The festivities had already begun to pour out of the ballroom, with red-faced guests standing in the hallways, glasses of wine in hand, all of them talking much too loudly over one another. Backs were patted, hands were placed in front of peals of laughter as one party made a wry observation about another, and certain gentlemen made untoward advances that their wives would not soon forget. There were also plenty of children threading through the throngs of adults, and it took James very little time to find a playmate suitable to warrant his escape from my supervision. He ran off into the crowd, but not before turning back to deliver a devilish sort of grin. I knew then that it was going to be a trying evening.

The ballroom was tall and narrow, with a promenade along the second floor that allowed those not inclined to dance to observe and enjoy those who were. I looked out over the crowd, and a feeling of hopelessness descended upon me. The villagers seemed so happy to be together, and I dreaded the thought of something happening to disrupt that. If I could not stop Mr. Whatley, which of them might be next?

I found Mr. Scott; he had done his best to tame his hair for the occasion, but it still floated over his head with wispy abandon.

"I hope you've sorted out your problem with spirits?" he said with some difficulty over the volume of the music, for there was a small orchestra playing beneath us.

"I am sad to say that I have not."

"Ah, so James remains curious?"

"Belligerently so."

The vicar nodded knowingly.

"The boy reminds me of myself. I too have always been curious about such affairs, which prompted my entrance into the servitude of the Lord." He smiled, impressed by his own piety, but then faltered at his pride. He went on. "I have continued to think on the matter, and I've come to the conclusion that spirits must not have malicious intent."

"Do you think so?"

"They mustn't. They may act with some cruelty, but only to bring about some change in the world in the name of God."

"How can you be sure?"

"My dear, I cannot be sure of anything. I am a man of faith. But then this is all hypothetical, is it not?"

I thanked him for his advice and carefully maneuvered down to the first floor, where I spotted Susannah and Lionel dancing together. They were radiant, staring fixedly into each other's eyes despite the speed of the song, turning with one another around and around, all the while laughing with abandon until the music stopped and Susannah met my gaze. She appeared much healthier than the last time I had seen her. The wild look in her eyes was gone, and there was a comforting peace about her. Lionel went to fetch his wife a drink, and Susannah kissed my cheek in greeting. She could not seem to stop fingering the clear green disk of amber that hung at her throat.

"It suits your coloring," I said.

"It does, doesn't it?" She ran a hand through her wild red hair. "Wherever did you find it?"

"Ancient Indian talisman to ward off evil spirits," I lied.

"Whatever it is, it's working. Nothing has happened since you gave it to me." I began to wonder what was happening back in The Ending between Cornelius and Whatley, but then I shook myself. The evening was supposed to be a celebration, and Darkling would have no part in it. For the first time in weeks I felt a shred of relief and vindication. While I still had not solved the puzzle of Mr. Whatley's intentions, I had been able to circumvent at least one of them, though with my friend safe the rest of the village remained vulnerable. It was for this reason that I had kept the boy with the keyhole eyes chained to the bedpost in my room. The promise of further snippets of secret conversations was worth the rattling and scraping sounds that persisted throughout the later hours of the evening as he attempted and failed to free himself from my control. Luckily, he seemed disinterested in the boys, preferring instead to collect the secrets of adults.

Roland tapped Susannah on the shoulder and cleared his throat. "Excuse me, ma'am, but might I have this dance?" He had exchanged his dusty workman's clothes for a brown tweed suit, though his hair was still an unkempt tangle, ironic given his position as groundskeeper of Everton.

Susannah took his hand. "Roland, I would dance with you all night if you asked," she said to the man who had saved her life. They spun off onto the dance floor as her husband returned with their drinks, watching them with sullen jealousy. I tried to join him to keep him company but was cut off by the sudden appearance of Mr. Darrow.

"Mrs. Markham."

"Mr. Darrow."

That seemed to be the end of our conversation until the music began to play again and Mr. Darrow nervously offered me his hand. "Would you care to dance?"

"Are you sure that's wise? People will begin to talk."

"Let them."

"That is quite a change of heart."

"Life is too brief a thing to dwell on the opinions of others, especially when there is dancing to be done. Shall we?"

I took his hand and we joined the other villagers on the ballroom floor. The song was very fast, and we spent more time being thrown from one partner to the next than actually dancing with one another, and so it was a relief when the music slowed and each dancer was allowed to return to his or her original partner. Henry took my hands into his and looked at me, perhaps really seeing me for the first time since that evening in the kitchen, looking into me as we swirled and spun to the music, the hem of my dress floating as we turned, grazing his legs. We were not so very close together, but the interlacing of our hands channeled a friction through the empty space between us that dimmed the rest of the room, changing the music into something that could only be for us. I did not want it to end, and for a long while it seemed that it never would. We danced and danced until I could no longer feel my legs, just his touch against my own and the deep, primal thumping in my chest.

But it did end, and when it was over our hands stayed connected. We wove through the house, past a happily scandalized Cornelia Reese, who would have something dreadful to talk about with her friends and confidants for at least a whole month; past Mrs. Norman in her peacock hat, whose tight, severe lips broke into a faint smile of approval, until we were outside in the frosted gardens of Arkham Hall. Beneath the black and empty sky, behind a hedge dusted with ice, Henry pulled me against his chest and kissed me, passionately, deeply, with nothing like reserve or anxiety, our lips moving in tandem with one another, all fear falling away, unraveling as something new knit itself together, something good and pure and strong, full of promise and hope. I was losing myself in the moment until a stark and frenzied shriek broke through the chilled air.

It was a woman's scream, and I already knew who it must have been. I pulled away from Henry and ran through the gardens, following the echo of it, bounding off stone statues and empty bird fountains, a shadow of a sound frozen in the ice. I sprinted as fast as I could, the ends of my dress in my hands, the wind ripping against my skin as I darted around a lattice strung with withered vines, and found Susannah sprawled on the cold ground, her hands before her face as something unfurled above her, a shadow untwisting itself from the dark, separating itself, becoming tangible and textured, wet and glistening, the surface of it freezing from the cold and cracking as it slid a tendril around Susannah's neck and lifted her into the air, her feet scraping at the ground for some purchase but finding none.

The moment the creature touched her, the small, clear disk of amber that hung about her throat began to glow. A dull green light pulsed through the air, folding itself around Susannah, searing the flesh of the creature until it dropped her out of shock and anguish.

Immediately all the people I had ever lost swam before me, and the pain congealed into anger, into hate, and into action as I launched myself at the thing while it was caught off guard, kicking, biting, tearing at it with my fingernails, until it lashed me across the face with a dark, unknowable appendage. I fell to the ground, and the horror hovered over me, blocking out what little light there was from behind the luminous clouds, the smell of it overpowering, equal parts ammonia and brimstone. I did not fear death, for I knew that my loved ones were waiting for me, but as the creature crept toward me, a shot rang out and I felt a damp spray across my face. The thing winced and quivered, seeming to retreat into itself and pausing at the inevitable opening of doors and stirring of voices from the house, contracting into something man-shaped before fleeing ever more deeply into the frozen gardens.

I touched the side of my face, unsure if the wetness I felt was my own blood or the property of the thing that had attacked me. Susannah was sitting up, holding her knees in a fetal position, rocking back and forth. Henry was next to her, a smoking pistol in hand.

He helped me to my feet. "Are you all right?"

"Yes, I—I'm fine." *That was not the man in black,* I wanted to say, *that was something else altogether.* There were parts of Whatley's game that I still did not understand, and that worried me.

I did not let go of Henry's hand when I was standing again. I went over to my friend. Her eyes were unfocused and she was muttering to herself.

"You must keep them closed. Never open. When they're open it all comes out, all apart in the darkness . . ."

I knelt down beside her and kissed her on the forehead. "Who was it, Susannah? Who attacked you?"

"Wolf in sheep's clothing. Monster under the bed."

Henry shook his head and put his hand on my shoulder. "We'll get Dr. Barberry."

"Someone will have to find Lionel first."

"Of course."

The voices from the house were growing more distinct. I pointed to the pistol still tightly clutched in Henry's hand. "You had a gun."

"I still do."

"Why?"

"There's a madman on the loose."

"Do you really think it was a man?"

He looked at me strangely but had no time to dwell on it, for we were quickly surrounded by the other party guests, clasping at the throats of gowns and jackets, gasping at the macabre scene in the garden—the three of us standing over a frozen pool of black blood.

Lionel was summoned to take his wife back to their cottage, but not before the doctor looked her over with a dour expression. He mentioned to the barkeep that there were places for people who suffered extreme trauma, comfortable places where they could be made well again, but Lionel would have none of it.

Henry and I collected the children and rode home in silent reflection. When we arrived at Everton I ushered the children to their rooms, feeling Henry's gaze on me as we traveled up the stairs, unable to stop myself from looking back to meet his eyes.

The boy with the keyhole eyes was cowering in the corner

when I returned to my room, holding his knees against his chest as he pointed with a broken, blackened fingernail in the direction of my bed. Waiting on my pillow was a parchment envelope with a blue wax seal. I slit it open with a penknife and read:

You are cordially invited

To the coming-out ball of

Miss Olivia Whatley

Tomorrow evening, dusk

I reread the invitation a dozen times over and set it on my nightstand while I dressed for bed. Someone had placed the letter in my room, someone from the House of Darkling. This wasn't a simple admission of guilt; this was an outright declaration of war, though perhaps not enough to prove a connection between Whatley and Everton, effectively ending our game.

I wrestled with the implications of this well into the night, and when I finally found sleep I dreamt that I danced with Mr. Whatley on the brink of an abyss, turning and turning until neither of us could be certain which was about to slip off the edge.

CHAPTER 16

Mrs. Whatley

There was no way I could avoid bringing the children back to Darkling. If I went alone Mr. Whatley might realize that something was amiss. And what if the children came in search of me, alone in The Ending, vulnerable to whatever machinations the master of Darkling had set in motion? I could not allow it, as I believed Whatley to be responsible for everything that had happened in Blackfield in addition to the sad, doll-like imprisonment of Lily Darrow.

When we crossed the threshold from the forest into the House of Darkling, it was immediately apparent that something was different, for the fruit children in the trees had been unraveled from their leathery rinds, each of them holding tiny candles in their pygmy hands, the orchard transformed into a flickering sea of teardrop stars. Even Duncan was different, dressed in black coattails and bowing low in greeting before he escorted us to the great house, which glowed with a preternatural sheen from the inside out. It was actually welcoming.

We could hear the distant sounds of the party—laughter,

shouting, the clinking of glasses, an echo of music. Thanks to the arrival of the invitation I'd had enough forethought to dress the children for the evening's festivities, though neither one was happy to wear formal attire again so soon after the Christmas Ball. For myself, I had chosen a high-collared gown with an opal brooch at the throat.

When we arrived, the ballroom seemed to be in the middle of some sort of decorative metamorphosis, for the skin of the stone pillars that lined the massive room cracked and fell away, revealing tree trunks of nearly the same girth. The jewels set in the brushed metal of the walls dropped off, exploding on the ground with pops of colored light to the delight and annoyance of some of the party guests attempting to converse and enjoy their cocktails. Out of these fresh alcoves grew sinewy vines, creeping up the walls, which themselves became less opaque and more like mirrors, until the ballroom began to resemble a never-ending forest with flowers growing up through the grout between the black and white marble tiles of the floor.

"You shouldn't have come back." Lily appeared at my side and whispered into my ear, her voice earnest and desperate, but then the boys saw her and she was transformed into the mother they knew and loved, never sad or upset, always pristine and composed. She would have kissed them both if the lights hadn't gone out. A spotlight appeared at the front of the ballroom as Olivia Whatley entered wearing an ice blue evening gown, holding the arm of her father. There was a polite smattering of applause as they circled the room, and then he left her with Dabney in a wide, empty circle as the guests stepped backward to give her space. The handsome young man wore an expensively tailored plum-colored suit that contrasted strangely with the mysterious way he held himself: his arms out, head tilted skyward, almost in a trancelike state. Olivia stood before him, and he placed his hands around her neck.

It was then that I felt growing warmth in the pit of my stomach, traveling up my chest, into my throat, and I thought I was going to be sick until my lips parted and erupted into a sound that was like a song, or at least a part of one. I thought that I had gone insane, or that Mr. Whatley had done something to me in retaliation for my impertinent threat the last time we spoke, but then I looked around and realized that every other guest sang a different part of the same song, a five-hundred-part harmony blending together in the echoing cavern of the ballroom.

Dabney had disappeared from the room, and Olivia moved as we sang, swaying gently to the Dance of Infinite Sorrow. The five ice sculptures that stood over the tables of food at the back of the room creaked to life and stepped down from their perches to join her on the dance floor. She moved from one to another, slowly at first in a languid, dreamlike fashion, until one of them struck her across the face.

I felt my own cheek in horror, unable to forget the night before, but Olivia immediately fought back, pushing the dance partner who had struck her hard enough to tip him over, and he shattered into a million shards of ice over the ground. This seemed to upset the others, for they surrounded her, tearing at her dress so that it fell away from her body, leaving her naked and vulnerable. The sculptures clung to her, her nudity never completely visible, and as they did our chanting grew faster and the temperature of the room started to rise. The wooden pillars scattered throughout the room burst into flames; the ice dancers melted as Olivia's skin blistered over. It was an awful, terrible sight, and while I despised her father I wanted to help the poor girl, but Lily kept me firmly in place.

The pillars stopped burning and turned back to stone. Olivia, although severely burned, did not appear to be in any pain. She reached to the back of her head and peeled away large strips of her charred flesh, revealing the beautiful, healthy girl who had entered the room with her father mere moments before. The liquid remains of the ice sculptures collected themselves together of their own accord and slid toward her, up her legs and torso, freezing so that they took the shape of the same ice-colored ball gown that had been torn asunder.

We stopped singing as abruptly as we had started, and Olivia bowed deeply. Dabney appeared out of nowhere behind her, taking her hand. All I could think to do was applaud. I had no idea what had happened, or what it signified, but it had been most extraordinary. The other guests joined in while the chef from the dinner party many nights before pushed through the throngs of people with a wheeled cart and collected the scraps of viscera and skin left over from the finale of Miss Whatley's performance. He placed them into a crystal bowl, and Dabney performed a quick blessing over the mess while Olivia began to greet her guests. I decided then that I would not be tasting the hors d'oeuvres.

More traditional music began to play and the mingling turned into dancing. Olivia moved from one partner to the next, men and women alike, sometimes dancing with creatures that had no easily identifiable sex. Lily danced with James, free for a moment from any anxiety or fear, and I saw Paul accept an invitation from Dabney to join him in a rather slow waltz.

I was content to be by myself for a moment, and I spent the time observing the other guests. There were the Baxters, flickering in and out of sight as I stared at them; Mrs. Aldrich, at the center of a group of well-dressed women, doubtless bragging about her son; the Puddles, standing beside the large frame of Mr. Samson, already red-faced and laughing too loudly at one of Mr. Puddle's jokes; Mr. Snit, drifting from one cluster of people to the next, changing color as he did so and covertly absorbing the cocktails of whoever happened to be standing closest to him. Miss Yarborough stood at an opposite corner of the room in the same sheath of netting as the last time we crossed paths, her disdainful expression visible and well honed despite the skinless nature of her face. I spotted Mr. Cornelius standing off to the side of the room with a circle of strange-looking creatures, hunched over things with amphibious faces and spiny backs covered in quills of bone, all of them speaking to one another in strained whispers. He saw me as I approached and excused himself from his friends with some discomfort. The others peered at me with suspicion.

"Mr. Cornelius."

"Mrs. Markham. I had not expected to find you here this evening." His onyx eyes shifted from side to side.

"We were invited."

"I see."

"I must again thank you for your help. Your token of appreciation was most effective."

"I am glad to hear it."

I could see that my presence was making him visibly uncomfortable. His trunk-like appendages folded over one another, as if he were wringing them together.

I pressed on, undeterred. "I do wish that we could continue our arrangement. I fear that the game is not yet over, and I am nearly out of moves."

"On the contrary, Mrs. Markham. You have more control in this game than you know—" He pulled me close, the pincers behind his beard clicking together. "You should not stay long this evening." My lips parted to form the start of a question, but then Mr. Cornelius looked behind me and smiled. "Ah, Mr. Whatley."

The master of Darkling observed us through the crowd with his sideways smirk. Whatley greeted the other gentleman and took my hands into his large ones, leading me into throngs of dancers without asking for my permission.

"You look quite ravishing this evening, Mrs. Markham."

"And you appear as if you've just come in from a storm." His dark hair was a wild, windswept tangle, and his suit, fine as always, was unkempt and disheveled.

"I try to be consistent."

"Ah, the success of lowered expectations."

"The only expectations that matter are my own, and I always seem to meet them."

"How lucky for you."

"Luck has nothing to do with it. I play to win."

"And when you fail?"

"I'll let you know when that happens."

"It might be quite soon."

"Do you think so?"

The music reached a crescendo, and Whatley pulled me against his body. I blushed furiously. I tried to break away from him, but he held me firmly in place, refusing to let me go until he was good and ready. Finally he winked at me and retreated into the crowd. I looked around for Lily, but Whatley was already moving toward her. He said something in her ear, and she nodded unhappily while he waved at the musicians to stop playing. Mr. Whatley addressed the party guests.

"My friends, thank you for joining us on this most special occasion, as my daughter, Olivia, reaches maturity and sets off to make her mark upon the worlds. It is often difficult for a parent to let go of his children, but I am happy to say that I have found some solace, for soon I will be remarried. May I introduce you all to the future Mrs. Whatley." He took Lily's hand into his own as a smattering of applause moved through the crowd, accompanied by some uncomfortable murmuring, not the least of which was a short, angry squeak from James, who stood beside his brother and me, looking terribly confused. "But what about Father?" he stammered.

Mr. Whatley did his best to look sympathetic, but ended up only appearing to be condescending. "My dear boy, he is living and your mother is dead. There can be no hope for such a pairing."

But James would hear none of it. He ran out of the ballroom in tears.

"James!" Lily went after him, and suddenly I heard the familiar clicking of Mr. Cornelius's pincers close to my ear.

"Take them and do not return. Now. *Run*."

A chair crashed against the wall. A glass shattered to the tiled floor. Silence filled the room as the partygoers looked around in confusion.

And then someone screamed.

A woman pointed to the body of Dabney Aldrich, slumped on the floor, holding a gash that had appeared in his throat as he pinched the bloodless folds of skin together. The slimy interior of his true body, the one within the angelic human slip he wore, began to spill out down the front of his chest. One of the amphibian-faced creatures stood over him, spat out a hunk of Dabney's flesh, and roared.

The ballroom erupted into madness. Paul stared agape at his friend, unable to speak in the wake of such shock. He reached out to help pick him up off the floor, but I grabbed Paul's hand and ran, sprinting away from Whatley's guests as they ripped each other apart, bodies falling, never dead or dying, simply in pieces, the crowd pushing for the door all at once, blocking it until Mr. Cornelius tore them aside to make room for us.

"Remember what I've said." He nodded to me, and then launched himself into the brawl, his beard parting to reveal a hideous cluster of sharp, dangerous-looking appendages that sank themselves into the corpulent neck of Mr. Samson.

Paul and I spun through the house, from one room to the next, corridor after corridor, until we were in the entryway and outside, down the steps to the orchard, where we found Lily and James. The boy would have nothing to do with his mother, but we had no time to sort out any recent emotional baggage.

"I want to go home," he said. I grabbed his hand as I ran past.

Paul tightened his grip, breathless from our escape. "What about Mother?"

"Lily, you are coming with us," I called out behind me, but Mrs. Darrow shook her head in earnest.

"I can't. You know I can't." But then the chaos of the ballroom erupted into the orchard. A body was thrown from a second-story window, and the attacker leapt out after its victim, continuing to claw at it in midair before they had even hit the ground.

"Oh, I think you can." The four of us dashed between the trees.

Lily was on the verge of tears. "But I'm not ready," she said desperately.

James seemed to soften, seeing her in such a pathetic state, unable to defend himself against his mother's misery. We found the wall of coiling fog.

"Mr. Whatley is doomed, you cannot stay. But we can say good-bye, here and now," I said to her.

"I'm so frightened."

"The boys will be with you to the end. Isn't that what you always wanted?"

"What I wanted was more time. There are so many things I wanted to teach you," she said, taking the hands of her sons into her own. "Marry for love. See the world." We approached the veil of mist that separated the living from the dead. "Cherish every day with your children. Don't let your father become lonely. Treasure every single moment." Lily kissed both of her sons, the three of them in tears.

"We will, Mother," Paul replied, red-faced from the dual exhaustion of running and crying.

"I don't know what will become of me, but know that I love you both so very much," said Lily, her words breaking apart before they even left her lips. Still, she nodded to me, and together the four of us crossed over the threshold from Darkling into Everton.

But this time, there was a figure in the mist.

"I'm afraid I cannot allow any of you to leave." Mr. Samson was not himself. His human body had been completely torn apart save for his face, revealing a puckered mass of red flesh and many-jointed tendrils.

"We are returning home, sir," I said to him. "We are done with The Ending."

"But we are not done with you. We must have humans in The Ending. There must be *retribution* for what has transpired this evening." His body shuddered, and four boneless limbs slithered along the ground to grab hold of us. I kicked them away, and Lily launched herself at Mr. Samson. He flung her to the ground like a rag doll. I leapt behind him and jumped onto his back, pushing my fingers into what I hoped were his eyes, digging at them with all my might, but I could not keep my grip. He tossed me aside, my head bouncing against something solid. My vision filled with stars and I drifted out of consciousness, the names of the Darrows on my lips as the mist swirled above me until I heard someone calling my name, softly at first, then gathering substance like an echo in reverse.

"Charlotte?"

I opened my eyes. The sky blazed with the pink and purple bruising of twilight.

"Charlotte? What on earth are you wearing?" Henry leaned over me, and I realized that we must have looked very foolish wearing evening clothes in the middle of a winter afternoon. I was glad to have such a high-collared dress, and the opal brooch to hold it tightly closed against my throat. But then I remembered . . .

I sat up and whipped around. Paul and James were nowhere to be found, and behind the cage of roots, a path led into the heart of the forest. The mist was gone. I spun in place three times, my heart sinking.

"We came looking for you. You've been gone for hours," said Henry with growing concern. "We started to worry that—" He grabbed me by the arms. "Where are the children?"

"They were just with me!" I said in a voice hoarse with horror. I collapsed against him, unable to process what had happened, let alone speak it aloud. But still he asked me the question I dreaded:

"Charlotte, where are my children? What's happened?"

Words came out of my mouth, but I did not hear them. My voice cracked, and with it my entire world fell to pieces.

"They're gone."

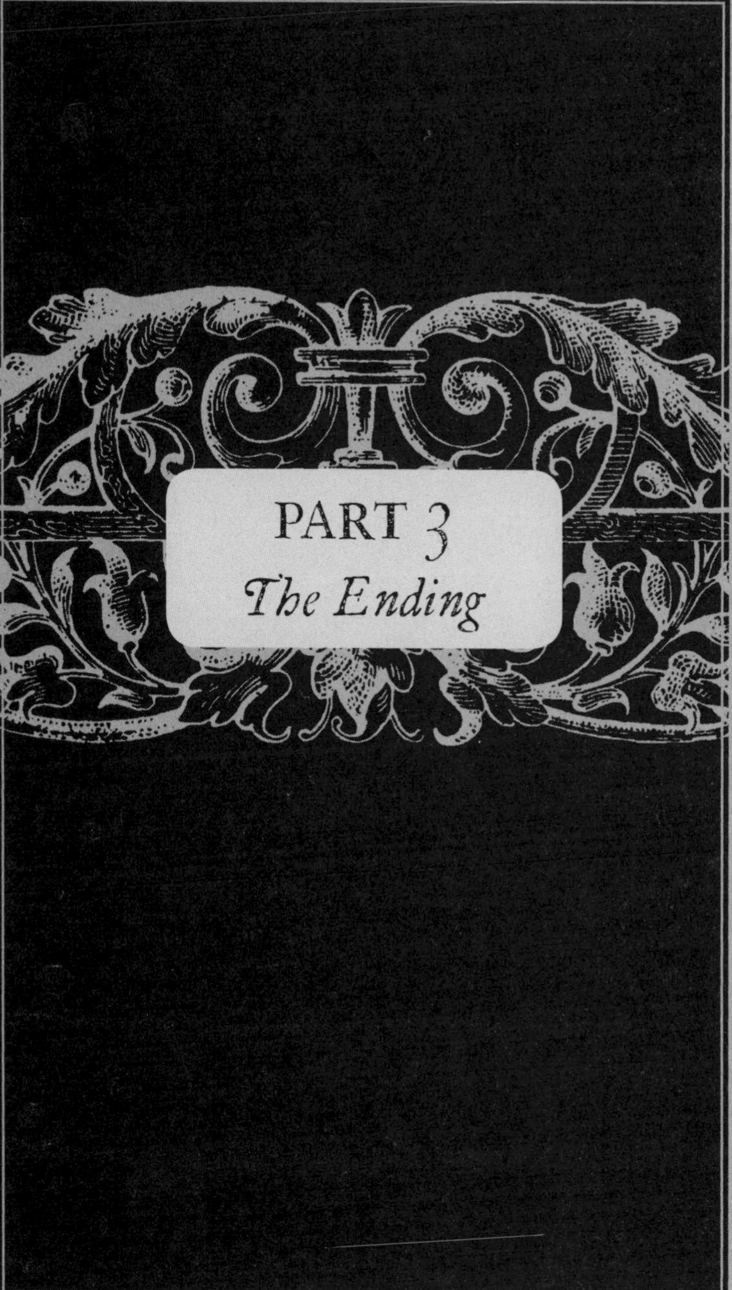
PART 3
The Ending

CHAPTER 17

An Interrupted Séance

"I believe you."

I had spent the better part of an hour seated on the frozen floor of the forest trying to explain to Mr. Darrow all that had happened during the past few weeks, and nothing surprised me more than those three simple words he uttered when I had reached the end of my tale.

"Completely? Without any question?"

"After what was done to Nanny Prum, and after seeing the thing that attacked Susannah Larken . . . yes, I believe you."

I threw my arms around him and rested my chin on his shoulder.

"We will find them."

I didn't know what to say. In a way I was grateful that the game of secrets had ended and that Mr. Darrow believed me, but in that moment I hated myself. In my vanity and arrogance I had used the children as pawns in a larger game between Mr. Whatley and myself, and that I had lost them was no one's fault but my own. It did not matter that my intentions were pure,

I had put them in danger and now they were gone, to be used as collateral in the civil war of The Ending. Or just as likely, to be stored away next to their mother in Mr. Whatley's secret chamber.

If Whatley survived. But I knew that was foolish. Creatures like Whatley always survived. It was the innocent who suffered.

Once I realized that we were all in danger, I should have severed our connection to Darkling and accepted the consequences. But I knew that wouldn't have been enough. There was still Susannah to consider, and Nanny Prum.

"We should get you back to the house," Mr. Darrow said to me. We stood together in the forest as the other men from the search party joined us. Roland looked on me with sympathy as I shivered in my evening gown against the cold midwinter's day. Mr. Darrow took off his jacket and placed it over my shoulders. I was too tired to argue. I wanted to throw off his kindness and race to find the children, but I had no idea where to begin. We walked out of the forest and into the sunlight. The warmth against my skin did nothing to alleviate the dread I felt growing in my chest, which swelled as my mind wandered to the night before, when Susannah was attacked by the mysterious, otherworldly assailant.

"Susannah, is she well?"

Mr. Darrow's eyes swept over me with pity, as if I could be foolish enough to believe that she had indeed recovered from nearly being killed by some nameless, shapeless monstrosity only days before Christmas.

"The last time I saw her I was with you. But it is difficult to forget her condition, since it is all the servants have been talking about. I understand that she continues to rave about impossible things, and that she screams whenever her husband leaves her side. Dr. Barberry attempted to take her away this morning, but Lionel would not hear of it. He is certain that she will recover on her own."

"And she will. I've never met anyone as strong as Susannah Larken."

Mr. Darrow said nothing more until we were halfway back to Everton. "We must talk to Lily."

"I have no idea how to contact her."

"She's dead," he replied as if he had lost her a second time. His voice cracked, and he cleared his throat. "There are ways, are there not?"

"What do you mean?"

"Mrs. Markham, after everything that's happened, I don't think it's out of the question for us to contact my wife through a medium." He said this in what I hoped was a tone a little more harsh than he intended, even though I knew I deserved it.

"You're perfectly right, Mr. Darrow." I was aware that we had not addressed each other by our first names in quite some time. "But where do we find one?"

Even as I said it, it sounded like the most ridiculous question in the world. We turned to one another at the same time and sprinted the rest of the way to Everton.

We found Mrs. Norman on the second floor of the house, busy reducing Jessica the chambermaid to tears.

"You call *this* dusted?"

The girl winced at the infliction of each word. "Sorry, Mrs. Norman, I thought—"

"No. You did not think. Not even to a degree that would be halfway acceptable."

Mr. Darrow intervened. "Erm, Mrs. Norman?"

The housekeeper turned to her employer, and her icy demeanor melted into something that was nearly pleasant.

"Yes, Mr. Darrow?" She spoke in a clipped, mannered rhythm that only highlighted the woman's predilection for structure and rules.

"Could I have a word for a moment?"

"Certainly." She backed away from the girl, who scampered off like a wounded animal.

"Mrs. Norman, it's no secret that you have a great interest in the supernatural."

"It is true, the Other World does hold a great deal of fascination for me, especially ever since dear Mr. Norman passed on." She crossed herself and kissed the cross that hung at her throat.

"Have you tried to contact him in spirit form?"

"A number of times, yes. And I was successful, once." She began to talk in an excited, confidential tone. She lowered her voice and looked around to make sure that we weren't being overheard. "He helped me find a shawl I had misplaced."

"Ah. Well. We would like to hold a séance. To contact Mrs. Darrow."

"A séance?" The housekeeper looked at me as if she had not noticed me standing there in such close proximity to Mr. Darrow. She rubbed her chin. "I've never performed one before; I typically use the cards, you see, but yes, I suppose it could be done. I would need time to consult my books—"

I interrupted her. "I'm afraid it's rather urgent."

"The dead can usually wait," said Mrs. Norman in a sharp tone that was much closer to her usual voice. But Mr. Darrow began to lose patience.

"I'm afraid that this time they can't." He spoke to her in the same tone he had used toward me, that of a master instructing a servant.

Mrs. Norman and I flinched at the same time, but she nodded in acquiescence.

"Let me collect my things upstairs, and I'll meet you in your study, Mr. Darrow." She lowered her voice to a whisper. "The servants are skittish when it comes to the supernatural." She went down to the servants' quarters while Mr. Darrow went to his study and I to my room, where the chains looped around the bedpost disappeared into the floorboards, the creature held by them off in some lower part of the house scrounging for private conversations.

I quickly changed out of the dress I'd worn to Darkling. I almost put on the black, somber governess's uniform that made me look and feel much older than I was, like an elderly spinster, the sort of woman I might still have become, alone and bitter, raising other people's children in a vicarious, unfulfilling life. But it seemed too much like a death shroud. I could not bear to imagine what was happening to the children. I found a casual blue cotton dress with white pinstripes and made my way to Mr. Darrow's study. Mrs. Norman had still not arrived, and the master of Everton stood gazing at his wife's portrait with not a small hint of dejection. He turned away from it when he noticed that I was standing in the doorway.

"We will find them, Henry," I said, regressing to our intimacy with more confidence than I felt. He smiled at me weakly and was about to reply when Mrs. Norman barreled into the room carrying a heavy-looking carpetbag in her arms. She dropped it onto Henry's desk with some relief and began unloading various pieces of occult paraphernalia.

"Mrs. Markham, set the candles in a circle around the desk. Mr. Darrow, pull those chairs here." She pointed to the sides of the desk and removed an old, heavy book with leather binding from the bottom of the bag, sending decks of tarot cards and phials of powders and liquids to the floor. She did not seem to notice the mess and opened the book.

"Sit and join hands." We formed an uncomfortable circle in the middle of Henry's study. "Relax, breathe in and out."

We did this for some time, until the room was heavy with silence and the smell of incense burning with the candles.

She continued. "Now, our beloved Lily Darrow, we ask that you commune with us and move among us." We sat in silence, waiting for something to happen. Mrs. Norman repeated the phrase a dozen times. Nothing happened. The room grew stuffy, and my fingers felt clammy in the hands of the others. I became very conscious of Henry's touch. I tightened my grip on his hand without thinking and was surprised when he returned the gesture. Then, the air in the room suddenly grew colder.

"If you are with us, please rap once," said Mrs. Norman in the dreamy sort of way one would expect a medium to sound, as if she had been practicing for this moment for some time. A knock sounded everywhere and nowhere, echoing and distant, perhaps upon some tabletop in another plane of existence.

"If we are communing with Lily Darrow, please rap once more." The ethereal rap sounded again. "I would like to invite the spirit of Lily Darrow to use my body as vessel to speak with us directly." The temperature continued to drop. The candles went out, and Mrs. Norman leaned forward in her chair until her head was hanging over the top of the desk. She snapped back up as the candles reignited themselves, but kept her eyes firmly closed. Henry and I looked at one another.

"Lily?"

Mrs. Norman spoke with her own voice, but it was higher and more melodic, with none of the cold authority that so characterized her.

"Henry?"

"Yes, love! I'm here with Charlotte."

"Oh, Charlotte!" Mrs. Norman let out a small sob. "I'm so sorry, I didn't want any of this to happen, you must believe me!"

I did not answer her directly. "Are the children all right?"

"Yes, but Mr. Samson refuses to let us leave, and he has forced Mr. Whatley to close the portal. The war has begun."

"But why are the children important?"

"He means to use them to destroy The Ending."

Henry looked at me in confusion, but I pressed on.

"There must be some way to bring them back?" I asked.

"I still know so little of The Ending, but there are different doorways, different methods of entry. The books in the library—"

"Oh!" I gasped, and my lips formed into a perfect circle of surprise. Lily/Mrs. Norman looked around the room blindly.

"Did something happen?" they asked.

"No, I just remembered, there are books from Darkling in my room!" I thought it best not to mention the eyeless, childlike thing chained to my bed.

"I'm afraid I'm terribly confused," said Henry. We both ignored him.

"Which ones did you take?" asked Lily through Mrs. Norman.

"I believe there's one called *Mysteries of The Ending.*"

The medium and the spirit within her became visibly troubled. "You can use the book, but you must be careful. You will have to travel a great distance through The Ending to reach

Darkling, but even then, what would you do when you got here?"

"Humans are a threat to The Ending, and I think I know why."

Before I could explain any further, there was a knock at the door and Roland entered the room carrying a clattering tray of tea and biscuits. Fredricks had taken ill when he returned from the ball, and the young gardener had been fulfilling his duties as he had been training to do. Lily stopped speaking through Mrs. Norman, the connection severed by the intrusion as the housekeeper recovered and became herself again.

Roland closed the door and set the tray onto the middle of the desk. "Tea, sir?"

Henry became very cross. "I am indisposed, Roland. Please take this away and make sure that we are not interrupted again."

But the young man ignored him. He placed a saucer and a cup before each of us and began to pour the tea, his hands shaking as he did so that the liquid spilled over the table.

"Roland!" Mrs. Norman lunged for her book, knocking over a candlestick onto a pile of Henry's papers, which ignited immediately into a small fire. The gardener suddenly grabbed her arm and lifted her into the air until her feet scraped at the carpeting. He threw her across the room so that she collapsed against a shelf of books.

Henry stood from his chair indignantly. "What is the meaning of this?"

Roland struck him across the face, sending him roughly to the ground. The room was burning now. I backed away, not from the flames but from the young man as he began to shake uncontrollably, his face contorting in pain, wrinkling in strange ways as if it were not a face at all. I realized that it wasn't when his throat bulged oddly, as if something were pushing its way out of his chest. I pulled Henry away from him and then ran to lift Mrs. Norman to her feet just as the boy hunched over the table and made a terrible retching sound. A tentacle slid out of his mouth, protruding from between his lips until the girth of the thing was so great it tested the very limits of his mouth. His throat continued to expand, and his cheeks split in a spatter of blood as the tentacle continued rolling out of his throat until it was two feet in length. It coiled into the air above the remains of his head and made a slashing motion at his throat. A nest of tendrils and feelers spilled out of the gash in his esophagus, over his chest, each one tearing at his flesh and undoing him, releasing him so that he expanded, a writhing mass of movement and gore, to his full stature, many feet taller than any human being could ever be. Roland opened like a flower, a blossom of black, wet, slithering appendages curling from the pulp of human mess, and was no more.

We did not stand around to wait for the end of his metamorphosis. The room was nearly engulfed in flames, and the three of us crept toward the door until Henry wrapped his fingers around the doorknob and pulled Mrs. Norman and me over the threshold into the hallway, slamming the door closed behind him. The creature shrieked from within the room, a fluttering, high-pitched buzzing sound that left me nauseated and oddly half asleep, as if it were all a dream that I could wake up from if only I concentrated a little harder. But then the door shook as the thing that had been Roland threw itself against it, tearing me from my reverie.

"We must get to my room," I said to Henry.

"Are you certain?"

"Trust me." I took his hand and we escaped down the hallway, but not before the door gave way and the creature slid out of the study, contracting to fit through the doorframe, a nightmare born into Everton, silhouetted by the blazing of the fire that had started to lick at the ceiling. The monstrosity filled the corridor, became a pulsating wall of tendon and viscera, churning and twisting toward us with a shapeless appendage that reached for my ankle but failed, moving on instead to Mrs. Norman, who was not as fast, and finding purchase around her leg. The housekeeper fell to the ground but grabbed hold of a cabinet against the wall, pulling it over and knocking a marble bust of some dead and forgotten member of the Darrow family to the floor, where it cracked into two sharp pieces. She seized a piece even as the creature slithered over her, hungry and unstoppable, and brought it sharply into the body of the thing.

The beast quivered, perhaps more in shock than in pain, for it did not release her from the struggle. Instead it parted Mrs. Norman's flesh as easily as it might have dipped into a pool of water. She briefly cried out in pain, but then the thing entered her mouth through the back of her head, severing the top of her skull and sending it to the floor.

Henry and I did not wait to see what would happen next. We took off through the house, warning away every servant we saw, telling them to run for their lives even as we went ever deeper, the creature still behind us and the fire ripping through the innards of the mansion, nearly stopping us at the stairwell as a wall curled away in a sheet of flames. But with the deadly alternative behind us, we pushed on, mostly unharmed save for a singed strand of my hair, the scent of which cut me more deeply than Roland ever could.

Jonathan.

History would not repeat itself. I refused to allow it, to allow anyone else to die. Everton might burn, but we would not be inside when it did.

We found my room at the end of the hallway and barricaded ourselves inside, the fire already smoking around us as I searched desperately for the books from Darkling. I had packed them away after Mr. Darrow sacked me, and I hadn't found the time to unpack since he'd changed his mind. I frantically dug through my valise, came up empty-handed, and then went through my steamer trunk, finally locating the volumes beneath a heavy thesaurus. They were tied shut with ribbon as a precaution against any further unwanted visits from the strange eyeless children, and try as I might, I could not get the small knot undone.

"I can't get it open." I handed the books to Henry, and as I went back to my trunk in search of a pair of scissors, the door to my room cracked completely in half and was thrown inward against him. The thing that had been Roland stood in the doorway. It hissed at us again, but before it could enter the room a length of blue chain looped around one of the ceiling beams exposed by the fire and was stretched taut. The ceiling collapsed in a hail of sparks and heavy timbers, piercing through the creature and pinning it to the floor, where it withered and blistered in the flames. The dirty little boy with the keyhole eyes appeared beside Henry and helped him to his feet.

"What is *that*?" Henry gestured to the strange little child.

"A friend, it would seem." I picked up the largest wooden splinter that I could find and turned to the creature trapped beneath the debris.

"You killed them both—Roland and Nanny Prum," I said to it. Something bubbled to the surface of the creature's viscous skin and broke open, revealing a small mouth with needle-sharp teeth.

"And Mrs. Norman," it said with sick pleasure. "But there never was a Roland. Only me."

"But why?"

"To set the game into motion." It squirmed in an effort to escape, but failed and resigned itself to its inevitable fate. "Nanny Prum had to die to place the children under your complete care. And you delivered them, just as he knew you would."

Henry turned to me for a moment as if to say something, but hesitated and began again with his attempt to untie the knot of ribbon around the books.

I went on with my interrogation. "Why did Whatley take the children?"

"Whatley?" The creature seemed confused by the question, but then its mouth, even without the benefit of any other facial expression, spread wide into a condescending smile. "How little you understand what you are meddling with. It was Samson who kidnapped the children. Whatley has only ever tried to protect them." The monster began to laugh at us, sounding somewhere between its human and inhuman vocal register.

I felt the swatch of wood in my hands and stabbed it into the beast's throat until I felt the wet crush of its flesh between the makeshift spear and the floor. The laughter went on uninterrupted.

Smoke was pouring into the room, and the heat was unbearable. I could scarcely catch my breath. I took the stack of books from Henry, procured the shears from the bottom of my trunk, and cut the ribbon that held them all closed.

"Are you ready?" I asked.

Henry looked at the creature still cackling to itself on the floor. "We have no choice, do we?"

I had nearly opened the book when I realized that all of my

belongings would burn in the fire even if I did not. I went to my nightstand and quickly collected my old wedding ring, my mother's lock of hair, and my father's pipe, which I kept in my memory box. They were the last relics of my family, the only pieces of my past. I would not leave them behind.

The boy with the keyhole eyes had fastened his chain around Roland's neck like a leash, and he held out his hand to me. I took it and went back to Henry, now choking, and together the three of us opened the front cover to *Mysteries of The Ending.*

CHAPTER 18

Charlotte Underground

At the entrance to the castle the book grew hot in my hands and turned to ash without igniting, the connection to Everton dying in the flames of the house. There was nothing to do but move forward. Henry watched as the ashes scattered to the wind. "Our home . . ."

I put my hand on his shoulder. "Houses can be rebuilt, better than they ever were before." He nodded glumly, and the grimy little boy showed us inside the crumbling stone fortress, dragging with him the bloodied, muttering remains of the creature who had been Roland the groundskeeper. The lady of the castle, still resplendent in her decaying elegance, greeted us from halfway up the collapsed staircase. The boy handed her the length of chain, and she patted him on the head as she brought her face close to the creature bound in shackles.

"Do you know who I am?" she asked.

"Yes, my lady." The thing could not meet her hard, steely gaze.

"And you agree to willingly serve me?"

"Yes, my lady," it said with a whimper.

"Then it is done." She handed his chains to her other children, and they took Roland away, deeper into the unseen parts of the castle. The little boy with the dirty fingernails stayed behind with his mistress. The woman beckoned for us to follow her into the room at the top of the stairs. Henry put his arm around me, shaking, though it was unclear which of us he meant to comfort.

The chamber was made of glass and windows, like a solarium, if such a place could exist in The Ending. The oppressive moon hung low in the sky, and we were so high up in the castle that the horizon was lost in a dark sea of stars. The woman seated herself in a high-backed silver throne and observed us without expression.

"You wish for safe passage into The Ending," she said.

This seemed to rouse Henry from his dejection. "My children are being held against their will."

"Of this I am aware. *Hostages*. Their continued presence in our world has set us on the brink of war. Would it not be careless of me to escalate the situation with two more humans?"

"On the contrary," I replied, "their rescue would only serve to mollify the tensions."

The woman was silent for a moment. She stroked the chains that circled her wrists. "You assume that you could get to Darkling untouched. Not even I could promise such a thing."

"That is a risk we are willing to take."

"There is also the matter of payment." She smiled, her teeth glittering like the metal of her fetters.

I stepped forward. "You trade in answers to unasked questions. Yet you haven't asked us what we will do once we get to Darkling. If you agree to send us on our way, I'll tell you."

The lady of the castle leaned back in her silver throne and motioned me forward with a slender index finger. I whispered my plan to her. At first she said nothing, and then a clicking sound escaped her throat, growing louder until it echoed off the glass walls of the solarium. She threw her head back and laughed: a dry, broken, thousand-year shriek of mirth that sent the dirty, eyeless boy scampering off into the dark corridors of the castle. I backed away from her, perplexed.

"You think I'm foolish?" I asked when she was done.

"I will allow you to pass. Is that not enough?" She lifted herself from her throne and took us onto an adjoining terrace that looked over a forest of black, jagged trees, a dirt path winding between them. A solitary crow stood on the ledge. The lady of the castle whispered softly to it, words that we could not hear, and the bird flew off into the night sky. The woman herself led us down stone steps etched into the side of a cliff, into the mouth of the wood.

"Follow the trail to the temple on the other side of the forest. Tell the cleric that the Blue Lady has sent you. You will travel along Mr. Samson's own rebel underground. Ironic, is it not?"

"Why would Samson's people help us?"

"He has kidnapped two children, a crime even in our land. His actions do not help the cause." The echo of the wind sounded around us without the benefit of a breeze, and the limbs of the trees creaked overhead. The only other sound was the clinking of the chains that trailed behind the Blue Lady, up the stairs, and around the throats of her grimy, blind children.

"Thank you for your help," I said.

"Do not thank me yet." She started to cackle again as she walked back up along the cliff, to the terrace of her castle. Henry stared anxiously into the woods and stepped in front of me before I could start along the path.

"What did you tell her?" he asked, looking into my eyes.

"The answer she wanted to hear." I moved around him and would say nothing more on the subject.

The trees were tall and lean, and as we went on the forest dwindled, plant life shifting in color from dark green to ash gray. The bark appeared to be chipped and dusty, ready to crumble at the slightest touch. Many trees had been pushed over and broken, the remaining stumps jutting sharply into the air. Then the forest stopped completely, and I stared out at a vast gray wasteland.

It was a dreary, oppressive place, an infinite desert pocked with craters, without stones on the ground or stars in the sky. There was only ash and the glow of the moon, rendered sallow and pale on the desolate landscape. We walked for what felt like miles until we stood on a ledge above an even greater expanse of gray nothingness. There was a building in the distance below.

We navigated down the slope of the rock with relative ease, and when we arrived at the bottom I finally heard it: a collective, raspy breathing coming from everywhere and nowhere. I felt surrounded, but then the little temple was still a mile off and there was no one around for as far as I could see. The path wove through the craters and the sound continued, rising and falling, a thousand different mouthfuls of air, as we walked to the lone building in the distance. I finally found the source of the sound just before we entered the temple.

It was coming from one of the pits, from a sad-eyed creature clawing at the sides of the cavity with a dozen bloodied appendages worn away from unsuccessful attempts at escape. I heard the gasping sound again, and the cavity in the earth closed in on the emaciated thing that still clung to the wall. Its eyes widened as it saw me, and remained open even as the pit closed around it.

Henry pulled me away, and we approached the entrance to

the temple. It was not a Christian building. The image of a serpent devouring itself was etched above the door. I knocked, and a small hunchbacked man answered.

"Are you the cleric?" I asked.

The man nodded.

"The Blue Lady sent us," said Henry.

The cleric observed us with watery eyes and moved away from the door. A narrow stairwell curled deep into the earth. We followed him down to the bottom, into an amphitheater with a glowing pool of water at the center instead of a stage. There were many tunnels leading off the room into other parts of the earth, more dark places with shadowy things that I had had quite enough of.

Our host stopped at the edge of the pool. "If you seek sanctuary, you must bathe in the pool."

"Must we?" I said under my breath. I considered myself a very open-minded person, but I was growing quite tired of the endless customs and traditions of the people of The Ending. Still, as there wasn't anyplace else for us to go, we had little choice but to comply. I unbuttoned my blue pin-striped dress as Henry took off the pieces of his suit. Truth be told, our clothes were becoming increasingly tattered, and it felt good to step out of them and even better to enter the gleaming pool of water.

We turned to one another after we were submerged, our nudity hidden by the opacity of the water. We kept our distance to maintain what little propriety remained to us, and we peered at each other across the pool.

"Are you all right?" I asked. I had never seen Henry look so haggard.

"You were very brave."

"I'm afraid bravery had very little to do with it. I'm rather fond of my life and quite willing to run in order to preserve it. If I had been brave I would have done something to save Mrs. Norman."

Once I said this, I realized it sounded like an attack on his masculinity and courage, which I didn't mean for it to be. I could not get the image of Mrs. Norman out of my head. She was the courageous one, with her final, rebellious act of violence. She had been a deeply unpleasant woman but did not deserve the fate she had been handed, which we had inadvertently dealt her. It had not been her fight or her mistake. It was mine, and I had failed her. I said as much out loud, but Henry shook his head.

"You couldn't have known."

"I could have. I should have. But"—I scooped a handful of clean water over my face to soothe my singed skin and lips—"there will be plenty of time for self-loathing after we've found the children."

When the hunchbacked cleric was satisfied with our informal baptism in the pool, he handed us robes and took us down a corridor lit by phosphorescent motes of dust that floated through the air, occasionally catching at my hair and skin, and causing me to glow the way that people do when light shines through their fingertips, pink and translucent. Henry brushed away one that had stuck to my forehead. The touch of his skin energized me despite my exhaustion.

"Thank you," I said.

"No trouble at all." Light cracked through his fatigue, perhaps the beginning of a smile before it faded again into weariness.

We were brought to a low, small room with no furniture save for a recess in the center that had been filled with furs and blankets. The luminous specks of dust had settled into the fibers of the sheets, and as we stepped into the alcove we quickly became covered in the stuff, our skin brought to life, our flesh an incandescent hearth at the center of the room. Our host left us, and we attempted to sleep, but I could not leave my hands alone, hypnotized by the trails of light they left behind. Henry was equally fascinated, and together we made as many shapes as we could think of, writing our names in the air, brushing ourselves off so that the flecks of dust became floating stars above our berth, until we settled in beside one another.

"Charlotte?"

"Yes, Henry?"

"What would you say to Jonathan, if you saw him again after all these years?"

I closed my eyes and summoned my husband's face, even as I could feel the warmth of Henry's body beside me. It surprised me to find that my feelings for both men were not mutually exclusive.

"I would tell him I loved him, that I will always love him. No matter what the future might hold."

Henry inhaled deeply, lost in thought for a long while. And then: "When Lily became ill, I stayed by her side day and night, wasting away as she did. I thought that if I could be there for her in every way possible, she might draw some small shred of strength from me. But she didn't. There was nothing to be done but watch her slip away. She died in my arms. I felt it happen, the breath leaving her body one last time. I kissed her then. Part of me hoped that I could draw her back from the Other Side, while she was still warm."

I took his hand into mine.

"I don't know if I can face her," he said.

"You can. You will."

"But what do I say?"

I did not know how to respond. We remained in the dark, our fingers entwined, and soon I drifted off into a dreamless, peaceful sleep.

In the morning, the hunchbacked cleric collected us and provided a change of clothing from the singed rags we had been wearing upon our arrival. We bathed quickly one last time in the pool, washing the glowing motes of dust from our skin and hair, before we dressed in what appeared to be servants' uniforms and were escorted back up the stairwell to the entrance of the underground temple.

Outside, I could still hear the gasping sounds from the pits in the ground. I turned to the cleric. "Those pits around the temple . . ."

"A political prison."

I stopped, disgusted.

"Is that what the rebellion is working against?" asked Henry.

"That is the rebellion at work. In times such as these the question of right and wrong becomes a complicated one." The cleric led us down the side of a hill behind the building, to an empty seashore of tepid waves, with a rickety boathouse perched at the end of a dock. He went inside and came out pulling a small rowboat through the water by a dirty cord.

"In you go," he said. Henry got into the boat first and then helped me off the dock. The hunchback cast us off and lumbered through the vessel, nearly capsizing it, to sit at the front. He looked back at Henry. "Oars," he said.

The former master of Everton took the oars and cut across the dark water, through a sea of green-black islands with rolling hills and barren trees that scratched into the air with clawed branches. I sat back and looked up at the stars in the velvet sky. Nothing moved among the trees and hills of the empty coastline, whose barrenness could not match the unease I felt watching Henry push us across the surface of the water, our destinies entwined as we moved blindly beyond the confines of our story, away from master of the house and governess, simply two people searching in the night for two lost children, and perhaps for themselves.

There was land on the horizon, black and cold in the moonlight with a thin spire of smoke climbing above its charcoal shores. The lamp of a crumbling lighthouse turned atop a precarious heap of rubble and cracked walls.

As we neared, the rocky coast gave way to a deserted shoreline of squalid cottages, a sad little town of molding walls and broken-toothed windows, huddled together against the lip of a demolished harbor. Nonetheless, it was not unoccupied. The smoke we had seen from the sea was coming from the chimney of a hut at the end of the lane, its windows glowing with the promise of fire.

The hull of the boat scraped against the shoreline, and Henry hopped into the water to drag the dinghy onto the beach. He extended his hand and helped me over the side. The hunchbacked cleric followed, leading us from the beach onto a path of ruined, uneven cobblestones. We walked silently down the narrow road to the house and knocked on the door.

A woman answered. She was shapely and round, with buttermilk skin and red ringlets of hair. The hunchback whispered something to her, and she opened her arms in greeting.

"Welcome. Please, come in." She led us to sit in front of the hearth.

The hut was small and decorated for Christmas. The frail tree in the corner of the room was gray, even by firelight, and clung to the sparse ornamentation perched on its branches. There were other guests seated next to us, old, broken, and decayed, staring deeply into the flames.

A cauldron hung above the embers, its bubbling contents hidden by brown, sticky foam. The woman brought us three coarse wooden bowls. She took a ladle from the wall and dipped it into the kettle. The head of the brew dissolved, and we could see something moving beneath the surface.

"No thank you, we've already eaten," I lied, starving, though the cleric heartily devoured his bowl of brown. The eyes of the other guests never left the flames. The woman sat at a table by the door to peel carrots. She placed one into a small cage that swung above her head, the animal inside gnawing at the stick as white, gelatinous foam dripped from its maw. It might have been a ferret, but the slaver had smeared its fur so that it was an indistinguishable mass of pelt and teeth. I slipped my hand through the crook of Henry's arm.

"There is trouble tonight," said the woman without looking up from her task.

"What do you mean?" asked Henry.

"The one who will take you is late. He is never late." She smiled as she fed the caged creature another sliver of carrot. We moved closer to the hearth, joining the others as they lost themselves in the fire. I imagined that the flames formed the walls of a house, and inside a small family of embers burned away their bright little lives to keep it intact.

Henry broke into my reverie. "I still haven't the faintest idea what we plan to do."

"You escape with the children, and I will sort out Mr. Whatley."

"Alone?"

"Hardly." I turned to him, widening my eyes in an effort to end the conversation. I was unsuccessful.

"Why must you be so cryptic?"

Annoyed, I put my lips to his ear and whispered sharply. "I have little experience traveling through rebel undergrounds, but I would imagine that they are not safe for private conversation." I motioned to the others seated beside us, all of them nearly catatonic save for one man who stood suddenly, kicking over his chair.

The woman with the red hair shouted at him. "Pipe down there."

But instead of reseating himself, the stranger leaned his head back, the surface of his skin gathering like beads of melted wax traveling up his face, a strand of it pulling away from his body, a thread of flesh rising into the air to attach itself to the ceiling.

Our hostess gasped a single word: "No . . ."

His body blasted apart with a wet tearing sound, sinewy tendrils erupting out of a husk of red meat to embed themselves in the walls and ceiling, scrambling around the room in search of prey. Where it touched the other guests, their flesh became its flesh, merged together and absorbed into an ever-expanding mass, none of the victims dead or dying, simply devoured whole.

As one of the tendrils made to slide around my leg, the hunchbacked cleric threw himself in its path, the thing entering his back and swelling around him. I did not have time to cry out, for Henry pulled me through the door, and together we ran into the night, looking back just long enough to see the hut crack and collapse, the plaster and rock consumed into the growing girth of the beast.

The town came to life, screaming. Doors opened all around

us, voices calling out for their loved ones as they ran into the streets; creatures and creatures in human skins, sobbing and shouting, pushed into each other. A young man ran past us carrying a glass bottle of jet-black liquid, a swatch of cloth sticking out of the opening. He lit it and chucked it at the monster in the demolished hut, but it fell short and landed at the base of the structure. At first I thought he had failed, but then the ground split open with a bone-chilling crack and began to fall away, creating an abyss where there had not been one mere seconds before. The creature scuttled for purchase at the edges of the chasm, but it had already grown too heavy for its own good and descended into the darkness below. The crowd of onlookers cheered momentarily, but then the rift continued to expand. Houses and whole streets succumbed to the schism, the edges of the earth flaking away into the void below.

Henry and I followed the crowd into a forest on the outskirts of town, winding between the trees until the chaos was behind us. When we were far enough from the townspeople that we would not draw unwanted attention, we collapsed against one another.

"Are you all right?" he asked.

"He saved me," I said incredulously.

"Who?"

"The cleric. Why would he do such a thing? He barely knew me."

Henry put my hand into his. "We should keep going."

"Where?"

He pointed behind me to a wide road. It had once been paved over, for the edges of the thoroughfare were crusted with pieces of crushed red brick, but the center of the highway had been worn to dirt from good use. It was the largest road that I had ever seen. It went on for as far as my eyes could see, and it was wide enough to accommodate twenty carriages riding beside one another.

Henry helped me to my feet, and we scampered down the side of a hill to reach the large expanse of road, but before we could leave the forest a person stepped into our path. He had a flat, open gash of a face, and a body that would have been snake-like had it not been for the heavy, muscular appendages that trailed along both sides of his torso. The person called out to us. "Hello, my friends!"

We stared at the man wordlessly.

"My companion and I are faced with a bit of an imposition. We're travelers like yourselves, you see." Another person appeared behind him. He was taller than any man, with arms and legs like very strong sticks, and half a mouth, with no bottom jaw but many long, sharp teeth. "We've lost the third member of our party."

"I wish we could help you, but we must be on our way," I replied.

"But you can help us," said the man who was almost, but not quite, like a snake. "Our friend was with you, the large gentleman in the hut. You were ever so quick to part with him." The two highwaymen leered at one another. I tried to run, but the stick man grabbed ahold of me and threw me to the ground, my head throbbing in pain though I refused to let him see it by meeting his gaze.

"Eager to leave us as well?" said the snake. "We should be insulted. It's a good thing Mr. Ashby is asking for you alive."

"A good thing indeed." The stick man's breath was dry and sour.

"But still . . . he would be ever so cross with us if we grabbed the wrong person. Best make sure you're human, after all. Blood will tell, as they say." He removed a long, thin knife from his jacket and cut away my cloak. He was about to do the same to the rest of my clothes when Henry leapt onto his back and began to strangle him with his arms. The snake man shrieked and dropped his knife to the ground, while the other swatted Henry through the air and into the forest.

The highwaymen congratulated themselves and hovered over me, unaware of a shadow moving behind them, black and dangerous, shifting along the ground, alive. As it passed over the stick man, his limbs shattered into thousands of bloodless little pieces and the back of his head was knocked through his mouth.

The snake man shrieked at the sight of his fallen companion, and he took off down the road. But the moon was high, and the shadow stretched after him as well. It embraced him so tightly that he stopped moving and fell to the earth, his skin peeled away in one swift motion. His flesh followed with a moist rip. But as this was The Ending, neither of the highwaymen could die even if he so desired. The stick man quivered in a fetal position on the ground and attempted to slurp the contents of his head back into his mouth. His partner, all bloody pulp and bone, pulled himself up the road, gathering his flesh and skin.

The shadow subsided as it lifted Henry from the floor of the forest and set him into a wagon near the side of the great road. As it approached me, it took the shape of a middle-aged man, impish and dark-featured, with a slender finger pressed against his sly lips.

"Duncan!"

Whatley's manservant brought me to my feet and climbed into the driver's seat. He did not wait for me to join him before whipping the side of the animal that pulled the wagon. The squat, headless thing with hundreds of fleshy flaps of skin squirmed forward like so many caterpillars, but it proved very fast as it took off. I quickly retrieved the knife that had been dropped by one of the highwaymen and barely had enough time to jump into the back of the vehicle as it started forward. I tucked the weapon into the folds of my dress.

"Why did you come for us?" I hardly expected an answer, but Duncan reached into his coat pocket and extracted a parchment envelope with a blue wax seal. I tore it open and read the two words written in Lily Darrow's handwriting: *Trust him.* I handed it to Henry.

"He did save our lives," he said. That was hardly sufficient, but given what few options we had, I reluctantly turned to face the back end of the wagon. We twisted down through the dark hills of The Ending, the wagon lumbering along the hard, beaten earth between patches of broken brick.

We passed by great houses and manors with candlelit windows and oddly shaped figures scuttling about behind them. I wondered if the boys would remain unchanged after having lived among such strangeness. There were other orchards, and a lone clock tower on a small island at the center of a lake. Henry and I soon settled into the quiet rhythms of the wagon. We took turns sleeping while the other remained alert, but no one passed us by. We were completely alone.

The hills grew taller as we continued, and the road sloped upward along the side of a mountain. There was movement in the valley below. Shapes in the darkness bounded after one another, their ridged backs glistening with sweat in the moonlight. Barbed tentacles lashed cruelly at tender undersides, and talons tore through flesh and fat and bone. Blood was thick on the ground, black as midnight.

Duncan did not bother looking down at the carnage below, and the creatures seemed to be paying us little if any attention, for we went down the other side of the mountain without trouble.

I realized Henry and I had started holding hands, but I could not recall when it happened, or why. I felt so many things all at once—fear, anger, exhilaration, doubt—each of them vying for my attention, surging through my body in alternating waves of anxiety and relief, to the point that I shut them all out and focused instead on the fact that I was glad to have Henry by my side at that moment. With my other hand I felt for the last relics of my former life, which I had rescued from the burning cinder of Everton.

Jonathan. I fell asleep despite my anxieties. My body demanded rest, and I dreamt that I went to a traveling carnival with my family.

We drifted from tent to tent, from the jugglers to the fortuneteller and finally to the magic man. He stood on his collapsible stage, a man in black making doves appear from his throat and fire dance at his fingertips. He called my mother from the audience and placed a sheet over her body. With a clap of his hands she disappeared. Then he took Jonathan, who vanished in a flash of light. My father was the last person chosen from the audience. The magic man placed him in a chair and levitated him into the air and out of sight. I clapped and clapped when the show was over. I waited at the entrance for my family to return, but then the gypsies packed up their tents and drove away in their caravans, leaving me alone on an empty hill.

"Charlotte." My eyes fluttered open. Henry's face hovered above me. I sat up and realized that I recognized the landscape. There was the orchard and beyond it, the House of Darkling alight with activity. There were other carriages on the road now, all of them in a long caravan to the front entrance by the Star Fountain. Duncan avoided this, steering us through the tall black iron gates, past human-shaped guards who waved us through without a second glance, and around the back to a servants' entrance, where arm in arm, Henry and I entered into the House of Darkling.

CHAPTER 19

The Man in Black

The lower floors of the manor were characterized by crooked hallways and room upon room of sweating, anxious servants, all of them frantic to respond to the panels of angry, chiming bells that heralded the needs of the hundreds of guests upstairs. Duncan did not allow us to linger, urging us onward until we were expelled from the inner workings of the house into the wing where the children and I had slept during our visits. To my surprise, he opened the door to my own quarters and pushed us inside.

A woman stood in the center of the room, her back to the entrance. She was dressed in a white gown that flowed from an ivory bodice of lace down the curves of her body into a pool of silk on the floor. A veil hid her face, but Henry knew her all the same.

"Lily . . ." he said breathlessly.

"Henry?" She sounded weary and sad, but her voice left her entirely when her eyes turned to meet her husband's. He took a single step forward, then another, and another, as if approaching a dream, careful to hold it for as long as possible before it slipped away. When he reached her he pushed back the veil to stroke the side of her face. She trembled, closing her fingers around his wrist. They stayed in the same pose, a silent conversation playing out in their mutual gaze, which remained uninterrupted by any further physicality. They simply looked into one another.

I could not help but feel a slight twinge of jealousy at the sight of them together, even as I reminded myself that they were still husband and wife. A shadow passed over Lily's face, and she became very melancholy.

"I'm afraid you might be too late." She motioned to her wedding gown.

Henry seemed to see it for the first time and backed away in confusion. "You can't be. You mustn't."

She ignored him. "I sent Duncan to fetch you after we last spoke, so that you could see the children safely home. They do not belong here."

"Neither do you. Come with us," I said.

"We tried that once before, don't you remember? They'll never release me. I'm the only one in The Ending who has ever died. They worship me, and Whatley *will* marry me."

"You deserve peace, my love," Henry interjected.

"This is exactly what I deserve," she said bitterly. "I am glad you came, Henry. I had so wanted to see you one last time."

"I don't understand. Why didn't you summon me here with the boys? Your death broke something inside of me, Lily. I would have been here in an instant."

"That's exactly why I tried to keep you away. I went so far as to tell the children there was a spell keeping this place connected to Blackfield, and if they spoke to you of their time here, it would be forever broken. I was afraid, Henry. To say good-bye to the children was my duty as their mother. Their hearts will mend. I couldn't bear to see yours break all over again."

I felt a pang of foolishness at my own gullibility, but it was washed away by all the other emotions that swept over me during this exchange.

Lily must have seen this, for she closed her eyes and summoned the strength to turn her husband away. "They'll be coming for me soon. I think you had better leave."

"We can help, Lily," I said.

"How? What could you possibly do?" When I did not respond, she turned away from us once more. "Take the children back." Her voice cracked as she spoke, and she nodded to Duncan. He went to the wardrobe and extracted two black cloaks, draping them over us. The hoods hung low before our faces, like shrouds.

Lily handed me a silver skeleton key without looking in my direction. "You may find passage back to Everton in Mr. Whatley's study. But for myself there is no other choice."

"That is where you're wrong." I tucked the key away into the folds of my dress. "There is an alternative to The Ending."

"Death offers his gift but once, if at all. Now, please leave me. The ceremony will begin soon and you had better find the children."

We pleaded with her, but she ignored us and continued to prepare for her wedding. I pulled Henry grudgingly out of the room, but as we left he spoke to her one last time.

"I love you."

She observed us in the reflection of her vanity mirror but remained silent as she watched us leave. I thought I noticed tears in her eyes, but Duncan was already weaving us through the house, carefully out of sight of the other guests, who lingered on the periphery of Darkling, voices raised, cutlery scraping together, heels clacking against tile; ghosts who lived just beyond the edge of sight.

When Duncan entered the dark room, I stopped and touched his arm. "We need to find the children," I whispered. He observed me drily, the smile on his face slipping for a moment as he pushed his finger into the eye socket of one of the marble faces, opening the door to the circular chamber enveloped in concentric rings of silk veils. A boy sat on the metal chair, his feet dangling just above the floor.

"There you are," he said. "I was worried you weren't"—his face fell as we pushed back our hoods, the words dying on his lips—"coming."

"What on earth are you doing here?" I asked him. James hopped down from the chair and approached us with caution and very adult suspicion. He was dressed in a black suit with a gray vest, a red cummerbund circling his waist. Yet even disregarding the finely tailored clothing, he held himself differently than the last time I'd seen him. He did not look any older despite the years that had doubtlessly passed for him since our separation, but nevertheless there was something changed in him.

"You came back," he said to me.

"I never meant to leave."

"But you did." He hugged his father in a mechanical gesture without any emotion.

Henry did not seem to notice. "My boy," he said. He smoothed out the curls of his son's blond hair with unguarded sentimentality, but James pulled away, his face contorted in confusion.

"I'm not a child." He shuffled back to the metal chair in the center of the room, where he removed a smoke-colored phial from his pocket. It was labeled INFIRMED.

"James, put that down!"

"Do you even know what it is?" Though he appeared to be only five, he spoke with all the stoic assurance of an adolescent.

"Someone's death."

"Not just anyone's." He held it to the dim light, picking at the stopper in a distracted way. "I remember the night she died." He looked to his father. "You don't think that I do, but you're wrong. You left me alone with her to talk to the doctor, and she started to make a sound. There were noises coming out of her; she was gasping, and her eyes were wet, like she was drowning from the inside out. I think she was crying.

"I tried to give her a hug, but she jerked away from me, like I had hurt her. So I just stood by her side. I heard the doctor say that she was blind by then, but I felt like she could see me because she grabbed my hand. She pulled me close and tried to whisper something, but she couldn't speak right. The words were all broken. But then she said it again and again, and I realized that what she said was 'I want to die.'

"One night I asked her about it, if she remembered me there and if I helped make it easier. I wanted her to know that I cried when she was gone, but it only upset her and she ran from the room before she could answer. I haven't asked her since."

"And that's her death?" I gestured to the phial still in his hands.

"I think so. I found it hidden in her room. I was waiting to open it, and tonight seemed appropriate. Duncan was going to help me." He held it out to his father. "Would you like to try it instead?"

Henry went very pale, and a bead of sweat dripped from his brow. Yet he did not reach out to accept the phial. "No, thank you, James. I think we both experienced enough of your mother's death firsthand."

The boy nodded and handed the glass container to Duncan, who secreted it away in the folds of his jacket.

"Are you taking us home?" James's green eyes found my own, and I could barely hold back tears of guilt.

"Yes, of course we are. I'm so sorry, James. It's my fault you were trapped here alone."

From the expression on his face I was certain that he felt pity for me. "We weren't alone. Mother was here, and Mr. Whatley." I noticed he hadn't corrected me, but then he had no reason to. It *was* my fault that the door between Everton and Darkling had been closed, but that he had confirmed it made the changes wrought in him since the last time we had been together all the more clear. He had grown up.

"Did Mr. Whatley hurt you?" I asked, looking over his face for any signs of abuse.

"No, not at all. He protects us."

"From what?"

"His friends."

I found myself in the strange position of feeling gratitude to the master of Darkling. Fortunately Duncan chose that moment to usher us all out of the chamber and back into the claustrophobic darkness of the other room. We pulled our hoods over our faces and followed him in silence, James taking his father's hand as we began to encounter the other wedding guests, mysterious figures garbed in cloaks identical to ours, human-shaped creatures much like Whatley, Samson, and all the rest of their circle.

Duncan escorted us into the medieval banquet hall that Lily had shown us on one of our prior visits, but instead of containing the mysterious ever-changing door that had tormented Susannah, it was now filled with row upon row of hospital beds, all of them occupied by poor creatures in varying states of decline.

The patient nearest to us might have once resembled an oversized earthworm, but it had been torn into pieces, its stumps bound in white gauze and placed along the length of the bed, struggling to squirm together in sequential rhythm despite the fact that they were no longer part of the same whole. Another victim was riddled with perforations in its head and torso, and thick metal spokes had been placed into the gaps of its flesh to brace the body against complete collapse. There were no doctors or nurses to tend to the wounded, only a dark-haired boy who stood at the other end of the room, struggling to help place what was left of Dabney Aldrich into a human-shaped suit.

Paul wiped a streak of sweat from his brow and scowled at his little brother. "I told you not to visit me here, James."

"Come along, Paul," I said.

He gaped at us, not understanding until we came close enough for him to see beneath the shrouds of our cloaks. He gently laid Dabney back onto the bed. The other boy's face was just as angelic and beautiful as it had been before, but beneath his neck his human body was matted with the pieces of his actual one, bound together in bandages in a hopeless effort to give him something of a human shape.

Paul ushered us to a far corner of the room, away from his patients. "You've been gone for so long. I didn't think we'd ever leave," he stammered, rubbing the back of his head with his hands as if he were trying to decide something.

"What on earth are you doing here?" asked his father.

"The night of the engagement marked the start of the war. Someone had to tend to the victims, the ones damaged beyond repair. Their families either are in worse shape or have disowned them." He gestured to Dabney, and I recalled the haughty dignity of Mrs. Aldrich. I could not imagine her having the compassion or the patience for long-term care. "I've stayed by their sides and helped as best I could."

"That's very brave of you," I said to him.

"No, they're the brave ones. They endure without the hope and mercy of death. I only manage to find strength in their resolve." His eyes shifted to me for a moment, wordlessly referencing our conversation by his mother's gravestone all those months before.

Dabney stirred on his bed. "Paul." His voice was a weak shadow of what it used to be. Still, the elder Darrow boy lifted him upright and helped dress the remains of his body for the wedding as we looked on in discomfort. When he was done, Paul placed his friend in a wheelchair. The other boy reached out and took his hand. "Are you leaving us?" he asked.

"I'm taking you to the wedding, just as you wanted, my friend."

Dabney smiled and stared off into space as Paul wheeled him out of the makeshift infirmary.

"Is Mother coming with us?" Paul whispered. Henry and I exchanged glances. "We can't leave her here."

"And we won't. Leave everything to me," I said with a note of finality. I replaced the hood of my cloak as Duncan led us to the dining hall, where the guests had been informed that the wedding was about to begin.

A thousand wedding guests in hooded shrouds began to file into the ballroom, lavishly decorated for the event. Silver cages filled with firebirds hung from the ceiling. Sad, languid music was being orchestrated on a twenty-foot-long harp that took a dozen people to play it, some of them standing on ladders.

The Darrows and I sat down with Dabney while Duncan bowed to us and retreated to the far end of the hall. Across the aisle Olivia chattered flirtatiously with some of the younger guests, throwing her head back gently in a demure scoff, pleasantly scandalized by some rude observation. Her eyes flittered over us but did not stop. She gazed at her father with an expression carefully guarded by a well-practiced blank smile that did not show in her eyes as he took his place at the front of the aisle, smirking victoriously.

The music died out and the room became hushed in silence. The harp players began to strum their instrument until the notes resembled a wedding march. Lily Darrow stood at the entrance to the ballroom, dressed in her elaborate white wedding gown. She strode down the aisle. When she reached the section we were sitting in, she turned to us with a weak smile.

"Don't do it, Mother," James whispered to her loudly enough for everyone to hear. Lily looked from the children to Henry. Mr. Whatley grew increasingly impatient at the end of the aisle. She turned back to the task at hand, and Mr. Whatley glowered at the boys triumphantly. I removed the small, thin knife that I had taken from the highwayman and hidden in the folds of my dress.

"Do you trust me?" I asked Henry.

"Of course."

"Then stay by my side and help me with the children."

"What are you—?"

I took a deep breath and, hands shaking with conviction, plunged the knife into my chest. It did not feel as I thought it would. I had imagined more pain, more terror, but it was all very numb. The world slowed down, and I collapsed into Henry's arms in slow motion. Lily turned to see what had happened, her veil fluttering before her eyes, one step behind the progress of time. She ran back down the aisle to my side. I pushed the hood of the cloak away from my face, and the crowd stood up to observe the chaos, blurry figures at the edge of my vision that I felt I recognized, but could not quite make out.

They were elated.

I heard Mr. Whatley above the crowd, demanding to know what had happened, for he could not see over the throngs of wedding guests despite his unnatural height. Henry cradled me in his arms, unsure what to do and trying to calm the children, who were beside themselves in shock and horror.

"It's all right," I choked, trying to comfort them even as my teeth became slick with blood. "Look!"

A storm had gathered outside, the moon obscured by a writhing tempest of black clouds that spilled down from the sky and into the horizon, churning over the bleak pine-colored hills of The Ending in a frigid, swirling vortex that pressed against the windows until they shattered inward. The firebirds extinguished themselves, and the lights in the room went out. A doorway made of night opened to meet us where we stood, and from within it there appeared the shape of a man clad all in black.

I had summoned Death to The Ending.

Some of the wedding guests began to cry with tears of joy, while others knelt in reverence.

"Really, there's no need for that," said the man as he stepped forward. Mr. Samson appeared beside him.

"We bid you welcome to The Ending, my lord."

"While that's very kind of you, I am no one's lord, and I'm afraid I have more pressing matters to attend to." He observed me on the floor with Lily, a pool of blood spreading before us, staining the hem of her white dress. The man bent over me and looked at my injury. He gestured to the knife. "Shall we remove this?"

I nodded to Lily, and she pulled the knife from my torso. I winced, gasping for air, the pain of it nearly causing me to black out, but I gritted my teeth together and bore through it.

"There, all better," he said drily. If I hadn't been in so much pain I would have laughed aloud. "Now, to the matter at hand. One of you has been dead for some time, and the other is dying in a place where death has never before occurred. What am I to do with the two of you?"

I sat up, and a gout of blood spilled down the front of my chest. "If I may, sir, there is only one reasonable course of action."

"And what is that, Mrs. Markham?" asked the man. At the utterance of my name, the crowd fell away, and Mr. Whatley finally saw me with his fiancée. His eyes went very wide, and for what I assumed was the first time in a very long time, he was speechless.

"A soul must be taken," I continued. "Lily passed on, but not completely, and I cannot die in a place where death does not exist. Reason would follow that you should take her into the light, and let me keep my life."

"A reasonable point, but wrong all the same. Death did not exist here, until now. Hello." He turned and waved to the crowd of onlookers with good cheer. "But this is still The Ending. I am, if anything, a man of the people, and the people of The Ending are different. New rules are needed."

"Please, sir, take us with you," Samson blubbered at his side.

"Yes, some of you would like that very much, but others would prefer to persist, even though they might say otherwise. I can sense it throughout this room. Normally it doesn't matter, I would take each and every one of you all the same, but you don't *die*. If I left, you would simply keep ticking away until the end of time. That is where you're different, and that's why I will give you the chance to decide. Come or stay, live or die." He spun around again to face Lily and me. "The same goes for each of you. Which will it be?"

Lily Darrow looked at her children, and at her husband. Tears began to stream down her cheeks. "I think I've kept this gentleman waiting long enough."

"This is outrageous!" bellowed Whatley, taking several steps forward until the man in black raised his hand with unveiled antipathy toward the master of Darkling.

"Do not interrupt us again, sir, or I shall be encouraged to take you instead. Do I make myself clear?"

Mr. Whatley fumed and glared, but remained silent.

James clung to his mother's side, the adolescent confidence he had earned temporarily forgotten in the wake of his mother's decision. "No, Mother, you can't!" he cried.

"I must accept my own death if any of you is to ever live your own lives. I'm sorry if I've been selfish, but I love you so much I couldn't bear leaving you behind." She hugged the boys. Henry caressed the side of his wife's face.

"I'm sorry, Henry."

"Never be sorry."

"Do you still love me?"

"Until the end of time."

He kissed her softly on the cheek. I felt my heart pounding

in my chest, but then it could have been due to the loss of blood. As they parted, she wiped her eyes. "Charlotte, you will see to it that they get home to Everton?"

"Yes, of course." The pain was settling into my body now, not softened but endured.

"Thank you . . . for everything," she said as she took her place beside the gentleman who was Death.

"I'll return in a moment," said the man. "I imagine that you wish to be next?" He gestured to Mr. Samson, who nodded excitedly, nearly beside himself with joy.

Suddenly Paul stepped forward, pushing Dabney's wheelchair in front of him. "If you please, sir. The injured should be taken first." Paul placed a hand on Dabney's ruined shoulders, and the other boy nestled his head against Paul's arm with unspoken intimacy.

The man in black nodded in agreement. "An admirable observation." He spun around and gestured to the broader crowd. "Would all interested parties please line up? I do love a good queue."

Paul wheeled Dabney toward the door made of night and knelt beside him. I could not hear what they said, but by the end of it they were both crying, and Dabney watched Paul return to us as his mother accepted the hand of Death.

"Are you ready?" he asked Lily.

"No, but I imagine few people ever are," she replied.

Together they passed through the door made of night and were engulfed by it, their forms obscured and faded in a dim burst of light even as the door persisted.

Mr. Whatley shrieked and collapsed to the floor in visible pain. Olivia ran to his side and took his arm to help him to his feet as the crowd began to murmur with excitement, some of the guests lining up beside Dabney and Mr. Samson, hand in hand, to follow the man in black into the afterlife.

I could see Mr. Whatley staggering up, somehow diminished in Lily's absence. He met my gaze and cackled with manic abandon, his body shaking with the timbre of his voice. "You warned me, but I didn't believe you. You threatened, and I ignored you. You've stolen my wife from me, Mrs. Markham!"

"Father, please!" Olivia had not released his arm. She held on to him very tightly, her fingers digging sharply into the fabric of his suit jacket.

"Boys, it's time to go. Help me up." I put my arms around Henry's shoulders and fastened a piece of cloth around my side to lessen the bleeding.

"You're simply leaving, just like that?" spat Mr. Whatley at his guests as they stood waiting for Death to return. "What do you think Ashby and Cornelius will do when they find out what's happened?"

"I don't suppose I'll be inclined to care by that point," said Mr. Samson. "There needn't be a war at all. We could simply die."

Whatley tried to escape from Olivia's grasp, but she held herself tight against him until he reached down with both hands and released her fingers from his arm, then pushed through the crowd as Henry, the children, and I left the ballroom, a thin trail of blood marking our path.

"Markham!" he bellowed after us.

James looked up in fear. "Where are we going?"

"Quickly, to the library!" I said. We turned down a corridor, but I stopped in shock. Before us was one of the blurry figures that had been standing over me in the ballroom, made all the more clear as I continued to hemorrhage. It was my mother, wrapped in bedclothes, with dried, bloodied mucus crusted beneath her chin.

"Mother?"

"It's time to rest, my darling." She smiled and held her arms apart to embrace me. But I don't believe that anyone else saw her, for Henry half carried me away as the boys led us into the library.

"Stay with us, Charlotte!" he cried. We threw ourselves into the room and bolted the door shut. I wanted to go back to my mother, but I was becoming more and more confused. I tried to focus on the task at hand—I had to save the Darrows. I had to save myself.

"The end is nigh, my peppercorn." I saw my father in the green leather armchair that had been Lily's favorite. He had his pipe in his hand and a halo of smoke encircling his head. I wanted to run to him, to drop into his lap, to cry into his shoulder, to have him kiss away the pain in my chest, but instead Henry drove us onward.

"Up the stairs, into the study!" I could barely speak, focusing all my energy on each step as I leaned against Paul and Henry. The pain in my side throbbed with each beat of my heart. I wondered briefly what would happen when I had no more blood to spill.

As we rounded the third floor of the library, Mr. Whatley banged roughly on the door, then ripped it off its hinges.

"More games? How delightful! Shall I come after you then?" His body shuddered and strained against his suit, shredding it and the façade of human skin beneath it as his voluminous tendrils and appendages released themselves from the confines of human clothing. He stretched and threw himself against the wall, using his many limbs to climb each bookshelf as if it were a step.

I urged the Darrows to quicken their pace. "Hurry, we're almost there!"

As we reached the door to Whatley's study, I extracted the silver skeleton key Lily had given to us and inserted it into the keyhole. It clicked as I turned it, and the door opened just as Whatley reached the footbridge. The Darrows and I entered the room and slammed the door shut before Mr. Whatley could reach us.

The room was the same as ever, quiet and gloomy, like a mausoleum. We lurched past Mr. Whatley's emotions and to his collection of faintly glowing glass paintings. I directed the boys to the glass prominently displaying the smoking remains of Everton and kissed them both on the cheek.

"Be strong for me," I said to them. James touched the glass with his hand and passed through the other side as if he'd fallen over a short wall. Paul followed after him.

"After you," said Henry.

"I can't."

"Of course you can."

"Someone has to stay behind to destroy the painting."

Henry's eyes went wide, and he ran his hands through his blond hair. "I can't allow it, Charlotte. I've already lost Lily."

"Your children need you, Henry."

"And I need you!"

"But you can't have me." I moved my hand away from my chest. The bleeding had stopped, and I no longer felt as weak as I had before.

"I can't do this again, Charlotte."

"You can and you will."

"We can have a life together!"

"If there's a way for me to come back, I will," I promised.

Whatley broke through the door. "Markham!"

"Good-bye, Henry." I pushed him hard, and he fell backward through the painting. I could see the children pick him up on the other side as he stood, bewildered and heartbroken, crying. I tore the thing from the wall and smashed it into hundreds of glittering pieces, severing the connection between Everton and The Ending.

"I could always create another painting to Blackfield, you know." Mr. Whatley observed me from the other side of the room. He had reverted to his human form, but his clothing hung in tatters over his muscular body.

"But you won't."

"Why's that?"

"Because I'm the one that you want."

"You've done well." His hair was as wild and untamed as ever, but in his eyes I could see that there was something subdued in him as he walked toward me.

"Stay where you are."

He stopped. "And what will you do if I refuse?"

"You've seen what I can do," I spat.

"You changed the outcome of the story."

"It's not finished yet."

"True, but there are pieces missing. Or have you put them together? Even as a little girl, you were very clever."

"You know nothing about me."

"That's where you're wrong. I know everything about you.

I've watched you for years. You've sensed it, I know you have." I thought back to the figure who stood over the bodies of everyone I had ever lost.

"The man in black . . ."

"It became dangerous for me to travel between the worlds myself, and so eventually I had to begin sending Roland. But the deaths of humans were my favorite things to collect. Mortals cling to their endings without even realizing it. They are simple to see, and even easier to predict. Your mother was one of many, but you were the first who tried to attack me, and after I met you I realized that I could not see your death. You are an enigma, Mrs. Markham."

"Do not attempt to justify your failure."

"This is not a justification, it's an explanation. I feel that I owe one to you."

"Do you admit to killing them then?"

"Your mother, no. It was a twist of fate that we should meet, but once I had found you I couldn't let you be. I will take responsibility for the deaths of the others. I needed you in the right place for a new game . . . my final game. You and I are more similar than you know. How many of our actions are the results of the things people expect of us rather than the things we want?"

"Murderer!" I tore another picture away from the wall and threw it against the floor as hard as I could. It cracked in half, and Mr. Whatley doubled over in pain.

"I'm practical," he continued after he had composed himself. "You had to engage with me over the fate of Lily Darrow so that, when you defeated me, no one would doubt that I got what I deserved."

I was about to destroy another of the paintings but froze when he said this. "Why should you want to lose?"

"There's a war coming. It's already started, but the two sides are filled with fanatics. One side wants to live forever and subjugate all the worlds, while the other wants to bring about the end of all things. I tried to placate them for as long as I could, but I refuse to commit myself to causes that have no center. I mean to provide a third alternative to Ashby and Speck, but I could never do so publicly. When they both began to suspect my intentions, something had to be done to remove me from the board. It's much easier to start an underground movement when everyone assumes that you're as good as dead."

"My father and husband, Nanny Prum and Mrs. Norman . . . Did you kill Lily as well?"

"I might have helped her illness along, yes."

"Over politics?"

"This is not simply politics. The existence of the universe hangs in the balance. If either party should win this war, it would mean the end of your world in addition to ours. What are a few people when the alternative is so grave?"

"And now you expect me to simply help you disappear."

"You have no choice."

"There is always a choice!"

"There is now. So much of your life was decided for you, but the game is ending; you will be free after this one last thing."

"And if I refuse?"

"Then they will come for me, lock me away, and everything that's happened will have been for nothing."

I screamed in anger and ran into the gallery, using my emotions and the accompanying burst of adrenaline to tear the paintings away from the walls one by one with bloody hands, dropping them to the floor so they shattered against him, cutting into him as he withered and shrank with each act of destruction. I tightened my fingers into fists and realized that they felt different than they had before my brush with Death. They were cold, harder somehow. The pain that had racked my body continued to abate as I settled into this new state of living death.

Whatley cowered on the floor, clutching his face in pain. The human features it had once contained were starting to fade. His hand uncoiled into a grouping of tentacles.

"Yes, just like that." He cackled through his agony. "What is a collector without his collection?"

I was torn. I wanted to inflict on him as much anguish as possible, but at the same time that was exactly what he was begging of me. "Every day, every feeling, each bit of joy or sadness or fear I've ever felt, none of them are anything compared to the hatred I hold for you, that I will wield against you. You may not choose to die today, but someday I will come for you, and I will make you suffer as you made us suffer."

"Give me the time to overthrow Ashby and Speck, and I will willingly put myself before you."

"The Darrows are never to be bothered again."

"You have my word."

"Is that worth anything?"

"I wouldn't know. I've never given it before." He smiled at me with his crooked smirk.

I could not bear to look at him. I destroyed more of his collection, raining down fragments of colored glass and shards of alabaster until the floor was covered in the stuff and a cloud of destruction hung in the air. Mr. Whatley disappeared piece by piece until he was a shrunken stump of a thing cowering on the floor.

I wondered what to do about the remainder of his collection. There were still the lifeless, doll-like figures trapped in the compartment behind his bedroom. I lurched down to the private alcove where he slept and found the panel he had pressed to open the secret room. All of them were where they had been before, save for Lily. I picked up the one closest to the floor, a young man with ivy instead of hair, and set him on his feet. He immediately came to life and looked at me with confusion. "Where is Mr. Whatley?"

"He's indisposed. You're free," I told him.

The boy became suddenly anxious but then saw my wound and proceeded to help me extricate his brothers and sisters from their perches against the wall. The more dolls we freed, the quicker the process became, until all of them were milling about in Mr. Whatley's room trying to understand what had happened to them and what they would do next. I slipped out in the confusion, averting my eyes from the pathetic state Mr. Whatley found himself in, a wriggling thing on the floor amid shards of alabaster and glass. He looked up at me, his black, reptilian eyes suddenly desperate.

"I am sorry for what I've wrought upon you," he said in a small voice. "People like us, we are stronger. We must do the things that others cannot."

"No matter the cost?"

"In spite of it."

"Good-bye, Mr. Whatley."

"You can't leave me here. There is work to be done! Markham!"

I left him alone in his study with the former pieces of his collection and made my way slowly and steadily through the house.

The wedding guests that had not been taken by Death were still milling about in the ballroom. They had apparently decided to hold the reception regardless of the presence of the bride or the groom. Dabney's wheelchair lay empty in the corner. The pain in my chest began to throb again, and I steadied myself against a wall, nearly toppling over when someone put an arm beneath me and carefully lifted me into the air.

I blacked out from exhaustion, and when I came to I found myself stretched on a metal chair, back in the room with the turning veils. Duncan stood nearby, fussing with a tray of tools on the wheeled table. I cried out in anguish, my wound still smarting. He turned to me, and rather than putting a finger to his lips, he opened his mouth and spoke.

"You're awake." His voice was soft and musical.

"You can talk?"

"A recent development. The servants of Darkling grow into the needs of the house. With Whatley in decline, someone must speak for the estate. My brother was much the same, or so I'm told. I think you knew him."

"Roland."

"I believe he caused you great sorrow, though he was only following Mr. Whatley's instructions. I cannot make right what has already passed, but I can at least give you something for the pain."

"That would be worth more than you know."

He nodded and held a smoking cup to my lips. "Drink this. It will help." It tasted of citrus, and as it passed through my body, it brought with it a cool, soothing sensation.

"I need one more thing. I won't be but a moment." He left me in the room, the veils spinning gently across the walls, hypnotic and serene. I had nearly slipped off to sleep when I felt the presence of someone else in the room. I sat up as best I could, and a man stepped forward.

"Charlotte?" His voice was familiar, but the room was so dimly lit I could not make him out until his face was close to my own.

"Jonathan?" His body was still blackened from the fire.

"I'm afraid you've seen better days, my love."

I touched his cheek and felt his blistered skin. "How are you here? You're dead."

"What do you think you are?" he asked.

"Nothing can die in The Ending unless it wants to."

"You can't live as you are."

"I miss you."

"Don't change the subject."

"Do you want me to be dead?"

"I want you to be comfortable."

"Who are you talking to?" Duncan had returned, a small velvet jewelry box in his hand.

"My husband is here," I said, looking from one to the other.

"I've been under the impression that he was deceased." Duncan did not or could not see Jonathan, who shrugged his shoulders.

"That doesn't seem to be stopping him."

"You do not look well." Duncan peered at the gash in my chest and placed his hand over it. "We must tend to your wound immediately."

"Where will that leave me?"

"What do you mean?" he asked.

"Will I be alive or dead?"

"I do not know. I suppose that it cannot be good for you as long as you can see your late husband."

Jonathan brought his ears close to my lips. "You must let him, Charlotte. It's not your time. Not yet."

"I miss you so much."

"I'm always with you. Can't you feel me?"

"It's not the same."

"We will meet again, at the end."

"You'll be waiting for me?"

"Forever and always."

"This will feel peculiar," said Duncan, interrupting my goodbye. He opened the jewelry box and extracted a small hooked needle attached to a golden spool of thread. He placed the needle into my wound and backed away, the thing moving of its own accord, tugging at the severed strands of muscle and artery in my torso, stopping the tepid flow of blood and leaving me with a mildly sore sensation where there had once been excruciating pain. When it was done he plucked the needle from my skin and set it back on the table.

"How do you feel?"

"Like the living dead."

"At least you are living."

I looked around the room. Jonathan was gone, but I felt the loss of him less than I would have in a dream, for he had truly been with me and I had chosen to make him go away. The pain of it was softer because of this.

"That was quite a wedding," said Duncan. "Or at least it would have been."

"I'm afraid that Mr. Whatley may be indisposed for some time."

"It wouldn't be wise for you to stay here," he said.

"Yes, I know."

"Where will you go?"

"Back to Everton, of course."

"But how? It seems as though you've destroyed every way back, and Mr. Whatley is in no position to help you."

"Perhaps someone in the underground will know the way."

"You should be careful. You've brought Death to The Ending. Ashby will come for you." Duncan pulled a fresh cloak and a plain dress similar to the kind I had seen worn by the servants of Darkling from beneath the table. He helped me change into them.

"What will happen here?" I asked.

"Mr. Whatley will gather his strength for the time being. After that, I do not know. Are you able to walk?" He helped me out of the chair. It was much easier to stand than before. He led me out of the chamber to the back of the house, where the orchard stood waiting, now empty of the carriages and wedding guests.

"I wish you the best of luck, Mrs. Markham."

"And I you, Duncan."

We shook hands, and I stepped out into the night air. My body must have been nearly drained of blood, and I had no responsibilities, no companions, and no idea of where to begin my journey home. Yet something else was wrong, something that sat heavily against my breast.

I reached into the dress and extracted my father's pipe, my mother's lock of hair, and Jonathan's wedding ring. I had brought them all this way with me from Everton to The Ending, but I could not recall why I needed them. I knew who they were, what they smelled like, how their laughter sounded, how they smiled. I saw them every night in my dreams, reliving old memories and making new ones that could never have happened. I had seen them, and I would see them again someday. I knelt down to the ground and pushed aside a handful of soil, burying the three articles I had saved from the fire. When I was done, the weight I had felt was lifted.

With the moon hanging low in the sky, I followed the winding path away from the House of Darkling to the large gate at the edge of the property. There was a man waiting for me, a man dressed all in black.

"Lovely to see you again, Mrs. Markham." The gentleman who was Death tipped his black bowler hat to me.

A man waits for you. He watches you.

"You've come back," I said.

"I've never been to The Ending. Much to do and see, I'd imagine. And people in need of my services."

"Some of them might not be so glad to see you."

"Few are. And where will you go?"

"Home."

"What kind of gentleman would I be if I did not offer to escort a lady home on a dark moonlit night? Perhaps we should walk together. We both seem to make friends wherever we go," he said with a measure of playful sarcasm, extending me the crook of his arm.

I accepted it. "Am I dead?" I asked him.

"I'm not quite sure. This is new for me as well. A road untraveled. Shall we make it up as we go along?" He pushed the gate open.

I thought of Henry and the children, and oddly enough, of Mr. Whatley. The game had ended, and my life was now my own. There were no more rules to adhere to, no shadowy figures taking the lives of my loved ones; the things that defined me had been stripped away, leaving behind not the person I was but the one I could become.

I took a deep breath and crossed the threshold into The Ending arm in arm with Death, the one constant of my past and my future; for whatever came next, all roads would only, could only lead back to him.

Acknowledgments

I find myself growing sentimental as I prepare to send *Charlotte* out into the world, and this morning I went back to read through a bit of the first completed draft of the novel, dated February 9, 2009. To say that it was a different book is an understatement, and I am indebted to a number of people for helping me discover the right voice (both mine and Charlotte's) over the course of the past three years.

Danielle Taylor was the first person to ever read the manuscript, and gave me the confidence that I had some idea of what I was getting myself into, along with Laura Stephenson, Sara Stephenson, William Couch, Katherine McKee, and my stepmother and father, who all provided me with invaluable feedback and asked the right questions.

Rakesh Satyal, my proverbial fairy godfather, brought the book to HarperCollins. Without him this novel would not exist in its current form.

The fearless editing duo of Maya Ziv and Chelsey Emmelhainz coaxed *Charlotte* out of her shell, and helped me see the light so many times.

Amanda Goldman and Reece Runnells brought my website to life so flawlessly that they made everything look easy.

And finally, there is my agent, Sandy Lu, who said "yes" and loves this novel just as much as I do. Her enthusiasm and guidance have been more important to me than anything throughout this entire process. I am lucky and grateful to have her by my side.

I will happily ply any of the above individuals with free alcohol whenever they so desire.

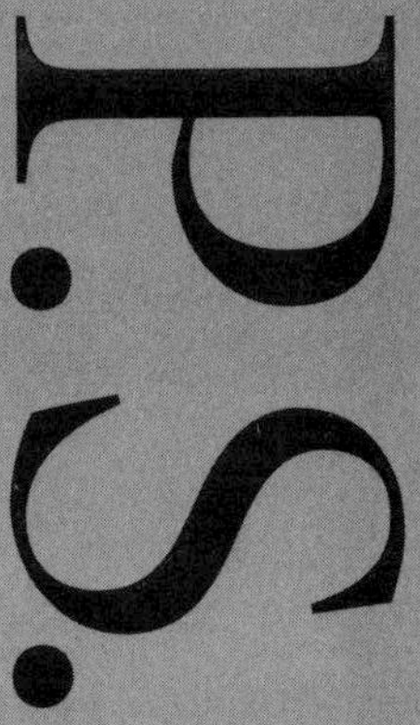

About the author

About the book

Read on

Insights,
Interviews
& More . . .

About the author

Meet Michael Boccacino

Christian Coulson

BORN IN UPSTATE NEW YORK and raised in central Florida, Michael blames his love of books on his father, who began reading him the *Lord of the Rings* trilogy when he was six, but stopped when he found out his son had snuck a VHS copy of the animated adaptation because he couldn't wait to see how it ended. Eventually Michael learned enough patience to earn his BA in Creative Writing from the University of Central Florida and his MBA from Rollins College. In addition to writing, Michael likes to travel to far-off places and pretend that he's Indiana Jones, or experiment in the kitchen and convince others that he might not do so terribly on *Iron Chef*. He was quite possibly British in a past life, but he lives in and loves New York City. ❧

Behind the Book

Charlotte Markham began life, quite literally, as a dream. The setup itself was fairly simple: an English governess stood on the side of a dirt road with her two young charges as they consulted a homemade map. They were debating whether or not to enter a forest up ahead and I knew, as dreamers often do, that something terrible awaited them in the woods. I remember being fascinated by where they were going, and the next morning I wrote the first draft of what would become Chapter 4. I filed the scene away, but it didn't really crystallize until my mother died of cancer at the age of forty-four.

I was the only member of my family not at her side when she passed away, mainly for the reasons given by Paul over the course of my novel. Her body was cremated before I could get back home, and so one day she was alive, and the next she was simply gone. I'm not sure I ever completely came to terms with her death, and a lack of closure can play tricks on the mind.

I dreamt of her nearly every night for the next few years, and though we both acknowledged in those dreams that she was supposed to be dead, we continued to have some semblance of a relationship. Sometimes she told me she had eluded Death, that her illness was a mistake, a simple misunderstanding. Or we would fight about old arguments with such ferocity that I would wake up shaking. Occasionally we just sat in a room and talked about our problems. Reconnecting with her in this way fascinated me, and I realized that the children from my previous dream were looking for a way to reunite with the mother they had lost.

Though it seems hard to believe now, it took me a few drafts to realize that I was writing about myself every time I mentioned the Darrows. I knew that I was writing in response to my mother's death, but the deeper I got into my revisions, the more I came to understand that I didn't know *why* I was writing. I was searching for something: a reason why I continued to haunt myself with with my mother's memory.

Two months before her death, she wrote letters to each member of our family to say the things she couldn't verbalize without bursting into tears. I read my letter exactly once in the weeks leading up to her death, when she was too sick to see or speak and the disease peeled away the last pieces that made up the woman we loved. I didn't think about her writings again until this past December, as I struggled to complete my final revisions to the novel.

I was having trouble finding the emotional center of the story, and as I sat in my dad's house during the Christmas holiday, staring at the manuscript on my laptop, I asked him about the letters. He looked far away for a moment, but nodded and said he would figure out where he had put them. A few days went by, and I asked him again. He promised that he would get around to it before I left to go back to New York. He just ▸

had to dig them out of his closet, where they sat in a lockbox, untouched and unread since before their author had died. The day I left, he woke me up and handed me a small, nondescript black notebook.

After years of dreaming up imaginary conversations, I held her words in my hands. To say that I was excited sounds morbid, but it would also be an understatement. I'd read my letter once, years before, but I was so distraught at the time that I could hardly remember what she'd written to me. It could have been anything and everything: my relationship with my mother, boiled down, isolated, extracted, and scrawled in her own hand over the course of less than three hundred words; a reason for the dreams; an explanation for the book. I read what she had written:

> To my son Michael,
>
> I just want to let you know how much I love you and how proud I am of you. You are my little boy, the apple of my eye, always smiling. I remember you teething and drooling on my shoulder. I just loved it until you bit me hard . . .
>
> You are such a creative person. All the leads in plays, etc. Your writing, even though you haven't let me read anything. Your teachers always said how creative you are.
>
> I think you will go very far. You are handsome (beautiful), talented, smart, and very motivated. You are such a joy and the best little boy. You loved to cuddle up with me to watch TV. You loved to read with your

dad at night. When you went to college it was the hardest. I couldn't even say your name without crying. Now you are 22 and I know you won't be living at home again and that's ok. I still get sad when you leave.

Dad and I wish we could of helped you more with school. That upsets me. But we didn't have the money; we just didn't plan well. I'm sorry. But having you work and go to school has made you independent and that's a good thing. That's what my parents did for me. I think you are a very well adjusted person.

I love you with all my heart and always will. Think of me with happy thoughts. Be happy in your life. Think of all the fun things we have done with our family. You are my Bud. You are my son and I love you.

—Mom

I surprised myself by smiling instead of crying. It was her voice, real in a way my dreams had never been able to capture, and yet in her last memories I am forever twenty-two, still angry about not getting to go to the expensive private university that would have crushed me beneath a ridiculous amount of debt. People often say that loved ones stay with you after they die, but in a way, reading my mother's letter made me realize that while the departed might stay with you, there's no way for you to stay with them.

A month later I saw my dad again at a cousin's wedding. We were having some wine, and I thanked him for finding the letters. I knew it was painful for him, ▸

Behind the Book ***(continued)***

just as he knew it was important for me to find some way to reconnect with her. He sighed and became visibly uncomfortable before admitting that there was something he had kept from me and my sisters. My mother had a tape recorder with her in the weeks before she died. The doctors thought it would be good for her to record her thoughts. No one else knew about it and he was never able to bring himself to listen to it. It might have been blank, or she might have talked for hours. He was sorry he had never told me, and I put my arm around his shoulder. We said nothing more about the tapes.

Two weeks later, a package arrived at my apartment containing a silver handheld tape recorder. I wrenched it out of the box, popped in some batteries, and placed it gingerly on the table in my living room. I sat cross-legged on my couch and pressed the play button.

"Hi family. It's on Thursday around eleven, and I want to tell you about my day . . . I'm much better," her voice cracked, and the next few words were unintelligible as she fought back tears. She sounded groggy, and her voice was higher than I remembered. She talked about the people who had visited her, what she had to eat that day, and where she was going, before she settled on addressing each member of our family individually, as she had done in her letters.

"Michael, you do well at anything you touch. You're a very brilliant boy. You're a procrastinator, which you shouldn't be, but you're really a very talented boy; man, I should say. Keep it up and not be such a procrastinator, Bud. You need to get things done and not wait. Like with summer school now, you're struggling, 'cause I'm sick and you have to go to school and work. It's tough for you and I know that. I'm sorry we couldn't help you with school, but . . . that's how it goes sometimes. And we apologize for that. We weren't financially able to. But, anyway. You'll do well in your business degree. I hope you get accepted to Columbia, that'd be awesome."

I'd forgotten that I was even going to apply to Columbia; another reminder that this was an echo, both of her and the person I was. She went on.

"My lunch just came in, so I'm going to take a few bites, and I'll be back. I love you Michael, Stephanie, Lauren, and my honey. Hopefully I'll be coming home tomorrow, and I think I'll feel a lot better being home. Bye."

Silence. I let the tape play on, trying to will her voice back into existence, but that was where it ended. She spoke for just over eight minutes. I listened to it again, and again. These were the sad, frightened recollections of a person faced with her own mortality; she didn't offer any revelations about herself. I know no more about my mother today than I did the day she died, and perhaps I never will. But that, I came to realize, is beside the point.

I didn't so much write the novel *to* ▸

Behind the Book ***(continued)***

her, but in response to what happened to her and our family. Now that it's finished, the book will never change, just as the voice on the tape will always apologize for the things that upset her in the weeks leading up to her death. Like the letter and her recording, *Charlotte Markham* is a portrait of a moment in time; the ghost of an emotion to match the one she leaves in my dreams. The two have each other now, and nothing can ever take that away. Not even death.

—Michael Boccacino
March 14, 2012

Have You Read?

THE FOLLOWING BOOKS were helpful and/or inspirational in the writing of this book.

For Gothic angst: *Jane Eyre*, by Charlotte Brontë, and *Wuthering Heights*, by Emily Brontë

For other problematic governesses: *The Turn of the Screw*, by Henry James

For an examination of mortality: *Never Let Me Go*, by Kazuo Ishiguro

For repressed, unrequited love: *The Remains of the Day*, by Kazuo Ishiguro

For mommy issues and creepiness: *Coraline*, by Neil Gaiman

For one of the best Victorian/fantasy mash-ups ever written: *Jonathan Strange and Mr Norrell*, by Susanna Clarke

For the Old Ones: *Black Seas of Infinity*, by H. P. Lovecraft, selected by Andrew Wheeler

For the best in new "weird fiction": *Perdido Street Station*, by China Miéville

For luck: The Harry Potter series, by J. K. Rowling

Don't miss the next book by your favorite author. Sign up now for AuthorTracker by visiting www.AuthorTracker.com.